KILL FISH JONES

Caro King was born in London and raised in Surrey. She now lives in Croydon with her partner, Kevin. She studied art and has had a variety of jobs since then, including working at the Office of the Official Receiver and as a greengrocer's assistant. Her first novel, *Seven Sorcerers*, was shortlisted for the Waterstone's Children's Book Prize.

Praise for previous titles

'Rich with extraordinary incident and a whole new perspective on bogeymen . . . a vivid evocation of a place peopled with strange beings and immersed in magic. Who could ask for more?' *Daily Telegraph*

'Truly moving and involving' *Sunday Times*

'Gripping. Intricate, melancholy, occasionally gruesome, but quickened with deft touches of humour' *FT*

'Witty and clever' *Family Interest Magazine*

'The narrative is well written, flows well and will capture the reader's attention, and as one of the bogeymen says: "It's been fun, what wiv everyfin'. Even the scary bits, an' there've been plenty enuff o' those"' *School Librarian*

KILL FISH JONES

CARO KING

Quercus

First published in Great Britain in 2011 by Quercus

21 Bloomsbury Square
London
WC1A 2NS

Copyright © Caro King, 2011

A CIP catalogue reference for this book is available
from the British Library

ISBN 978 0 85738 146 0

10 9 8 7 6 5 4 3 2 1

Typeset by Nigel Hazle
Printed and bound in Great Britain by Clays Ltd, St Ives plc

For my Mother, with love and happy memories.

And to Kevin, as always.

Book One

THE CURSE OF LAMPWICK THE ROBBER

1

LITANY

Perched on his usual gravestone, Grimshaw turned his corner-to-corner black eyes upwards and scanned the dull grey sky. It was empty. Empty was good, because anything at all in the sky, here in the Limbo world, usually meant trouble.

He heaved a sigh and swung his tail slowly to the left and then to the right. It was something to do. He scratched his ears with a clawed paw.

Close by, Lampwick was snoring again. Grimshaw glared at him. He didn't know how the human managed to snore when he was not technically asleep. Nothing that existed in Limbo was allowed to sleep, not the half-alive creatures like the demon Grimshaw, or the half-dead ones like the human Lampwick. Even the Sisters didn't sleep, and Grimshaw was pretty certain the Horsemen didn't either. Not that anyone who met *them* ever stopped screaming long enough to ask.

Still, propped against the tombstone that marked the spot where his mortal remains were buried, Lampwick snored away, his robe spread about him in a pool of tattered fabric. Bored with the sight, Grimshaw switched his gaze to the scenery. There wasn't a lot.

Limbo, or Grey Space as it was often called by its inhabitants, was a poor imitation of Real Space, which was where all the properly alive things were. This meant that the hills and valleys and roads and buildings that made up Real Space were all there in Limbo, just horribly grey-looking. The major difference between the two, the one that really grabbed your attention, was that Limbo didn't do the properly alive part of things. So, although the basic landscape was all in place, there were no trees, grass, flowers, birds or animals on it to look at. Nor was there any weather, because although it wasn't alive as such, weather was far too energetic for Limbo. The end result was like the stripped-bare foundations of the real world done in various shades of grey.

In the graveyard, apart from the one referring to Lampwick, the tombstones were blank, because the names of the properly dead had no place in Limbo. Lampwick wasn't properly dead. He was the Architect of a deathbed curse upon his fellow men and so his spirit wasn't allowed to move on to Whatever Comes Next until the curse was completed. Lampwick's dying words had also created Grimshaw, because all curses need a demon to carry them out.

Grimshaw snuffed the air. It smelt of old socks. It was not warm exactly, nor was it cold. It didn't waft about in breezes or draughts, either. It just sat there. Next he stared moodily at the church, looming up over

4

the graveyard in which Lampwick was buried. The building looked slab-like, a big chunk of grey stone with no trace of the elegance that in Real Space would make it a beautiful piece of architecture. Grey Space didn't do elegance.

He sighed again and flipped his ears. Then he looked at the device strapped to his wrist. This was his chronometer, one of the two possessions that all curse demons were born with. It had two dials around an inner face, all etched with numbers and symbols. It had five hands and, on the outer edge, a small red button. At the moment, the chronometer was telling Grimshaw that the time was somewhere about the middle of eternity and the place was the Limbo version of St Michael's Church in the small town of Chillingdean. Both of these were things that Grimshaw knew already. He wondered how long it had been since the last update.

Because Real Space was constantly changing, as everything that lived in it got on with its life, every so often Limbo had to rearrange itself to reflect those changes. It did this every third hour throughout the day and it always felt to Grimshaw as if the world had blinked.

Unfortunately, the updates were mostly boring. Apart from the appearance of a new tombstone or the odd hail of falling plane parts, very little altered in Grimshaw's world. The problem was that Lampwick, like all the half-dead, was tied to his mortal remains. He could move up to twelve feet away from his Limbo coffin, but that was all. And Grimshaw was tied to Lampwick's command, which meant that (unless Lampwick allowed him to go) he had to stay in the graveyard with his Architect. Not that anywhere else in Limbo was more interesting, but it could be nice to be bored somewhere different for a change.

The second possession that all curse demons were born with was a Litany of Sufferers – a list of all those people who were subject to the curse. Lampwick's curse involved horrible things happening to *anyone who bothered him*. This meant all the people who had been bothering him at the time of his death, and went on to include anybody who might be foolish enough to bother him *after* his death as well. As a result, the curse wouldn't be completed until Lampwick's mortal remains – still decaying quietly away in Real Space – were so much dust and couldn't be bothered in any way ever again. Just to make the point, on Lampwick's tombstone, underneath his name, were the ominous words 'Leave Him In Peace'.

When Grimshaw had been created, long ago in the days of Queen Victoria, he had had work to do in Real Space, wiping out his Litany of Sufferers. The list had been a long one, covering Lampwick's landlady, the doctor who had tried to help him on his deathbed and the policemen who had tried to arrest him, as well as any unfortunate nosy parkers who might have been hanging around to find out what all the fuss was about.

But that list of names had been long since finished,

and for many decades Grimshaw had been confined to Limbo. Most curse demons, including Grimshaw, looked forward to the possibility that one day their curse might be invoked again and they would have more Sufferers to deal with.

Lampwick gave a particularly hard snore, making Grimshaw jump. The demon stared hard at the cadaverous face of his Architect, trying to see if the man's eyes were open a slit, watching. Grimshaw stuck his fingers in his mouth, pulling down the corners to show his yellowed teeth. Then he wrinkled his nose, scrunched up his all-black eyes, waggled his ears and stuck his tongue out.

The half-dead man opened his eyes and glared. 'A little respect, if you please,' he said sniffily. 'Remember, I am your creator!'

Grimshaw snarled under his breath and shook his ears. 'You might have made a slightly better job of it!'

He took a deep breath and clenched his paws tight, trying to calm down. He hated the fact that when he got angry or irritated he began to twitch. Sometimes it was just his arms and legs, but sometimes his whole body would jump like a firecracker. Already he could feel the tension building up in his limbs.

'Don't blame me for your shortcomings,' snorted Lampwick.

'And you needn't snore so loud,' snapped Grimshaw, 'I know you're not asleep.' He twitched violently, nearly falling off the tombstone.

Lampwick settled back with a smug smile tugging at his thin mouth. Grimshaw gritted his stubby teeth, angry with himself for letting his irritation show. Now Lampwick would snore all the louder. Dangling behind the tombstone, Grimshaw's tail tied itself into complicated knots of frustration. He sighed as Lampwick began to snore again. It sounded like a buzz saw with a megaphone. Sneakily, Grimshaw peered down at the ground, looking for a small stone to throw into Lampwick's open mouth. Preferably a nice muddy one.

The world blinked.

Lampwick sat up and gave a startled yell. His scrawny shape writhed in agony, crumpled up and vanished with a sound like a cork coming out of a bottle. Grimshaw gasped and stared wildly around the graveyard. Apart from the disappearance of his Architect, everything looked exactly the same.

'I conjure thee, APPEAR!' yelled Lampwick's disembodied voice, echoing doomily in Grimshaw's head.

Hurriedly, Grimshaw spun the dials of his chronometer, setting all five hands to zero.

'I conjure thee, GET A FLAMING MOVE ON!'

'All right! All right!' Grimshaw hit the send button, the red one on the side of the chronometer. When a curse demon set his chronometer to zero, it acted as a direct route back to his Architect. So a second after he zapped out of existence in the graveyard, Grimshaw zapped back into existence in the middle of the stone floor of a crypt filled with tidily arranged coffins. He gazed around in confusion.

Lampwick was on his feet, waving his arms excitedly.

'Look at this! Look! Don't you know what this means? Oh come ON! Dunderhead! Idiot! THINK!'

Grimshaw twitched his ears, then checked his chronometer.

'We're still in Chillingdean,' he said, 'but it's a different church! St Peter and St Paul – right over the other side of town!'

'Never mind which church,' cried Lampwick. 'The point is, we were in a graveyard, now we've been re-arranged to a crypt. In Real Space, *someone must have dug me up and moved me.*'

Avatar and Architect stared at one another.

'Look and see!' whispered Lampwick, his voice trembling with anticipation.

Nervously, Grimshaw reached into the pocket of his trousers and pulled out a notebook with an old-looking document tucked into the cover. His paws shook as he removed the yellowed paper and unfolded it, laying it on the ground between them.

On top of the document, written in something suspiciously blood-like, were the words:

Litany: Sufferers for the Curse of Lampwick the Robber

Beneath that it was blank . . . except . . .

'Ahhhh!' Lampwick sighed as words began to appear, their shape rising through the paper in coils and loops. They were names, and there were four of them.

'Four!'

'And they'll all have loved ones. A wife or husband. Children.' Grimshaw was bubbling with suppressed excitement.

'Mothers, fathers, brothers, sisters.' Lampwick waved his arms excitedly, lurching about the crypt. 'So much to be taken away! And homes too, don't forget. And jobs. Lives. They will all have lives.'

'But not for much longer,' said Grimshaw. His tail swayed to and fro eagerly. 'Not for much longer!'

'Hah!' said Lampwick gleefully, almost dancing with joy. 'Serves them right for tampering with my mortal remains, eh! That qualifies as bothering me all right!'

Grimshaw's cat-like face stretched into a happy, horrible grin. Once again, he had work to do.

2

BRIGHT YELLOW EXCAVATOR

The burly man in the hard yellow hat and the overalls glared at the red-faced man in front of him.

'Look, Wayne,' he snapped, 'what with the exploding dog and the falling tree, I can do without you carping on about soft furnishings, got it?' He wasn't shouting yet, but he sounded like a man who might start at any moment. His face was tight and his eyes glittered.

Wayne swallowed hard and stood his ground. 'It's just . . . There are curtains . . . and I was thinking . . .'

'Oh, thinking, were you?' sneered the burly man whose name happened to be Jon Figg. 'Don't make a habit of it!' He passed a hand wearily over his face, then went on irritably, 'How do I know why there are curtains? Maybe the last owners couldn't be bothered to take them down. Who cares? Just GET ON WITH THE JOB!'

Wayne opened and closed his mouth. Then he gave up and climbed aboard the bright yellow excavator.

Comfortably settled on top of the nearby postbox, Grimshaw watched with satisfaction. He was sitting in plain view because there was no need to hide. Apart from those exceptional occasions when fate allowed a child to be born gifted with extra-special vision, humans couldn't see half-alive creatures like Grimshaw, unless the half-alive wanted them to.

Everything was going to plan. It was a month since Lampwick had been dug up and Grimshaw had been given the new Litany of Sufferers. In that time he had made good progress. Already, two of the four names on his Litany were finished.

He flicked open his notebook, looking for the page where 'Sufferer 3: Jonathan Figg' was neatly written in cramped printing. Because Mr Figg was the man who helped the man who moved Lampwick's coffin, Grimshaw had added the words 'The Man Who Helped' underneath the name. Grimshaw liked to be organised and proper.

Also under Mr Figg's name was a list of the things that Grimshaw had to take away from him to make him suffer. These were: dog, car, house, job and wife. When all of these were gone and the Sufferer was in despair, then Grimshaw would take away the only thing left: the Sufferer's life. Currently, Grimshaw was working on the fourth item – Jonathan Figg's job. Retrieving the pencil stub jammed behind one pointed ear, Grimshaw licked the end, then wrote, 'Frayed Nerves and Inconstant Temper leading to Poor Judgement'.

By now, Wayne had started the excavator rolling forward, grinding up the neat garden path and crushing the flower beds. An empty milk bottle wobbled, then fell and cracked, rolling down the doorstep and under a bush. The excavator went on right up to the front door. By now, a crowd had begun to gather, prevented from coming too close by the barriers put up for their safety, but getting a good view anyway.

The excavator stopped rolling forward. There was a lot of grinding as its long metal arm slowly unfurled and reached out. The huge claw-like part at the end paused for a moment, then lunged forward, smashing into the wall and pulling it down. Under the onslaught of the heavy machinery, the side of the house crumbled as easily as if it were cake, not solid bricks and mortar. The excavator went back for another bite. Bricks and tiles tumbled. Windows shattered, the harsh sound tearing into the summer day. The crowd gasped.

Moving the arm of the excavator to reach more of the house, Wayne went in for another go. And another. A central portion of wall came down and the front of the house suddenly crumbled, sliding into a sea of rubble. The air was filled with the sound of thunder. And dust. An awful lot of dust.

When the dust settled and everyone could stop coughing and open their eyes again, what they saw looked like one of those doll's houses where the front swings off to show the rooms inside neatly laid out in cross section. Upstairs revealed a newly decorated bedroom – the bed still unmade – and a blue-tiled, bathroom. On the ground floor was a hall, with wellington boots in a cubbyhole under the stairs and a door (still standing) through to the living room. There would be other rooms at the back, but the excavator hadn't got there yet.

One or two of the crowd, the more thoughtful ones, began to look worried, but nobody did anything about anything, which was fine with Grimshaw. He knew that humans mostly thought that other humans knew what they were doing and so didn't interfere, even when it was glaringly obvious that something was wrong.

Jon Figg was looking at his watch again. In the excavator's cab, Wayne had forgotten his worries and was beginning to enjoy himself.

So was Grimshaw. He flipped to the next page of his notebook, which had the heading 'Sufferer 4: Susan Jones, The Woman Who Knocked'. He smiled happily to himself. The whole event had a lovely symmetry and, frankly, Grimshaw was proud of it. He turned his all-black eyes towards the end of the road, because any minute now Mrs Jones and her weird son, Fish, were due to come home. If it qualified as home any more, which was doubtful.

Just about the time the roof fell in on the sofa, crushing it into a ruin of chocolate-brown cloth and stuffing, they arrived.

The crowd fell silent. All eyes were on Susan Jones and the boy with white-blond hair and hazel eyes.

Fish Jones had been having a really great morning, right up until he turned the corner of the road to see ruins where he had expected to see their home.

It was only three hours since he and his mother had left the house, and then it was still standing and looked very solid and not at all likely to fall down. In that three hours, they had gone into town, where Fish had spent the morning at the swimming baths with his friend Jed, while Susan had gone shopping for the new jacket she needed. Afterwards, they had visited the Star Bar, where Jed had talked happily about waterslides and jumping in the deep end, and Susan had told them all about the people she had seen in the shops. Fish, who much preferred listening to talking, ate his ice cream and watched their faces, and laughed so hard at one of Jed's stupid jokes that a spoonful went down the wrong way and they had to bang him on the back until he stopped coughing.

When the boys had finished their ice creams and Susan had drunk her coffee and eaten her doughnut, they headed back home, dropping off Jed on the way. Fish was looking forward to lunch followed by an afternoon in the park with Alice, who had promised to teach him to roller-skate. Or at least to roller-skate and still be upright at the end of it!

So when they saw the bright yellow excavator grinding forward over the wreckage of their home, it came as a horrible shock.

Fish's first thought was that they had accidentally

walked down the wrong street. Then he saw the sofa, lying mangled and broken in the middle of the rubble, and his heart turned over in his chest. He'd spent many rainy afternoons reading on that sofa and would know it anywhere.

Although he was horrified, shocked and not a little bewildered, Fish's first thought was for his mother. He looked up at her. She had turned pale and her eyes were oddly bright and shiny as she struggled to take in what she was seeing. She put one hand up to her forehead, pushing back her wavy brown hair that refused to be neat.

'Wha . . . ?' she said.

Thinking that she might be about to faint, Fish took her arm supportively and looked around for help. He immediately spotted Ray Harris, who lived over the road, and waved at him. Mr Harris was already hurrying forward with a chair, which he put neatly behind Susan just as she sat down from shock, saving her from some nasty bruises.

Patting Susan reassuringly on the arm, Ray looked at Fish, sighed and shook his head sadly. Fish nodded, to show he understood that Ray would have stopped this if he had been able to.

'I don't know, Su,' Ray was saying now, an embarrassed look on his kindly face. 'I got home from the golf course and they were already . . . well . . . at it, if you see what I mean.'

Fish certainly did see what he meant. The evidence

was all over the place in the form of bricks, dust and the mangled remains of their belongings.

A burly man in overalls picked his way over the devastation towards them. Susan got to her feet, looking upset but composed. Irresistibly drawn to the wreckage of their life, Fish edged away towards the rubble.

'Is there a problem?' Jon Figg asked Susan. He still sounded irritable, but underneath the irritation there was an anxious note.

'I'm afraid there is,' Fish heard Susan reply. Her face was ashen, but her voice steady. For a moment, a puzzled expression crossed her face, as if the man in front of her looked familiar, but the thought was soon pushed aside by the awfulness of what was happening.

'A very large problem,' she said. 'You've got the wrong address.'

Jon Figg paled. He cleared his throat nervously. He was having the same feeling of faint recognition too, as if he knew Susan from somewhere but couldn't quite place her. He shook the feeling aside.

'Hey, Wayne!'

Wayne, who had climbed out of the excavator, headed over to join them. When he reached Fish, he sent the boy a sharp glance and paused.

'Oy, kid,' he said, 'get outta there. It's not safe.'

Fish stopped in his tracks and sent Wayne a look. It was one of his special looks, the sort that made people immediately want to switch their attention somewhere less complicated. He didn't use it often, not even when

17

he was late with his homework, but he used it now because he was, quite suddenly, very angry that the person who had knocked his home down should now be telling him to keep out of it. Fish didn't often get angry, he didn't see the point in it, but right now it was the only feeling that fit.

Wayne's blue eyes met Fish's hazel ones for a single second, before he gave in and looked away. Blinking, Wayne cleared his throat and amended his words to, 'Be careful, right?' before hurrying over to join the throng gathering around Susan and Jon Figg.

Fish took a deep breath, then returned to exploring the ruins, looking for anything salvageable. It was very clear by now that his whole life, or at least his life as he knew it, had just been brutally ripped away. For a moment, he felt angry again, but he let it pass and dropped to one knee to rummage in the debris at his feet.

'What's the address on the worksheet?' Jon Figg was demanding, over on the edge of the demolition site.

Wayne hurried to a van parked nearby, dug out a clipboard and squinted at the typed notes pinned to it.

'Trod on my reading specs this morning,' he grumbled. 'Blowed if I know how they got on the stairs like that. Right . . . Number . . . twenny-seven . . . Nightingale . . . Road.'

Eyes swivelled to the road sign. All except for Fish's. He pulled something out of the rubble, inspected it and threw it away.

Jon Figg grinned. It was the grin of a man who was trying not to look doom in the face. 'Right . . . er . . .'

'Row,' said Ray. 'This is Nightingale Row. Ar, oh, doubleyew.'

Beads of sweat broke out along Jon Figg's forehead. He tried to say something, but it came out as a meaningless croak.

'So, what you're saying is we demolished number twenty-seven, Nightingale *Row*, when we should have demolished number twenty-seven, Nightingale *Road*, right?' Wayne was asking carefully.

'Right.'

'And there's, like, people living here?' Wayne wore the expression of a scorned man proved right. Which he was.

'Not any more there aren't,' snapped Mr Harris. 'Didn't you check the address? How on earth did this happen?'

'I know.'

Many pairs of curious eyes turned to look at Jon Figg. A few yards away, Fish looked up from his search to listen. Seeing the movement, Wayne sent him a nervous glance.

Jon Figg had gone the colour of unbaked pastry. He rubbed an arm across his clammy forehead, pushing back his hat and leaving a grimy smudge.

'It's like this.' His eyes went glazed. 'I was late this morning, see, on account of the dog exploding and the tree falling on the roof and crushing the car and all that.

So what with the worry, because my Emily was in the car and got her head bashed, see, I guess I wasn't paying attention when I read the address and I got it wrong. Wayne couldn't see it properly anyway, so he wasn't able to spot the mistake. When we arrived he did point out that there were curtains up . . .'

Wayne nodded righteously.

'. . . but I was just too wrapped up in my own worries to listen.'

Fish studied him. Jon Figg looked like a man whose world was falling apart, which Fish thought was pretty grim since all he had done was misread an address. But then, demolishing people's homes while they were still living in them was pretty grim too.

His gaze left the sagging form of Jon Figg to sweep over the curious faces of the watching crowd and then beyond them to the long curve of the street. In that glance he saw cars and houses and trees and the postman and a small grey cat. He saw a bicycle with a bent wheel propped against a wall, a scrap of paper dropped on the pavement, and a fallen dustbin.

And he also saw a demon on the postbox.

3

NOT ORDINARY

A shiver of fear ran down Fish's spine and he hastily switched his gaze back to the circle of people around his mother – his direct gaze, at any rate – but out of the corner of his eye he watched the demon cautiously. The creature was sitting in full view, confident that ordinary humankind couldn't see it.

Fish didn't know why he was different. He had always been that way and had come to the conclusion that he was just one of those unfortunate people that fate had allowed to be born with extra-special vision. There didn't seem to be any reason for it that he could figure out. At least, he hadn't found one so far. Apart from Alice and Jed, the two friends he trusted absolutely, Fish had never told anyone about his extra-special vision, not even his mother. He knew how hard it would be for her to believe. She would worry, and take him to the doctor, and it wouldn't be good.

Now, so it wouldn't guess that he could see it, Fish tried to act as if the creature wasn't there. He hoped it would go away soon, but he had a nasty feeling that it wouldn't, that it was somehow connected to the destruction of their home.

From this distance he couldn't make out the details, but the demon reminded him of a bony cat, only nearly the same size as Fish. It had a horrible skinned look about it, sort of red and glistening. It moved, raising its head to examine the group of humans in front of it. In case it spotted him looking, Fish switched his attention back to the rubble around him. After a moment, he risked one more quick glance at the demon. Strangely, the creature seemed to be writing in a notebook.

Unaware of Fish's scrutiny, Grimshaw had flicked back a page and was adding 'Wretched with Humiliation' to the notes underneath Jon Figg's name. He then put a tick through the word 'Job'. As he turned back to Susan Jones, Grimshaw felt that glow of pride again. Symmetry, that was definitely the word. Under her name he put a bold tick through the word 'Home'. There were no comments yet. He was hoping for something like, 'Screaming and Crying followed by Collapse and Ambulance', so he sat with his pencil poised and his tail curling and uncurling as he noted their every expression.

Susan Jones took a quivering breath, drew herself up and looked Jon Figg in the eye.

'I'm sorry about your terrible day,' she said with the faintest quiver in her voice, 'but the fact is you've just made a horrible mistake.'

Grimshaw flicked his ears, surprise registering on his

ugly features. He stared from Mrs Jones to his notebook, and then back again. None of the usual comments would do. Finally, after an inner struggle, he wrote: 'Dignified in the Face of Disaster'. Reading it over, he nodded, satisfied. It was fitting and it made a nice change too. Lampwick wouldn't like it, but Grimshaw felt that it was important to be honest about these things.

By now Jon was the colour of old dishcloths. He nodded speechlessly.

'We will, of course, be in touch with your company about this,' Susan went on. 'In the meantime I don't suppose I can go . . . the word "in" doesn't seem quite right, but . . .' her voice tailed off then picked up again. 'I mean, there must be things in the . . . remains of the house that we could save?'

Fish stood up from the rubble and looked at her. She caught his eye and sighed as he gave a brief shake of his head.

Jon was in agony. 'Erm . . . see . . .'

'I suppose it's too dangerous for us to go in there. Even if there was anything to save.'

Jon nodded dumbly, though she had really been speaking to Fish.

'I thought so. Then we'll just have to make do with what we've got.'

The crowd murmured. Some of them were already slipping away, their eyes suddenly guilty. With great concentration, Grimshaw wrote, 'Of NOBLE Bearing'.

He put noble in capitals because he liked capitals and felt they gave things a certain style.

'Where will you go?' asked Ray.

Susan squared her shoulders. 'We will go to my sister's,' she said. 'We will go and live with Marsha.'

Impressed, Grimshaw added, 'And BRAVE', then underlined it. He wasn't used to his Sufferers behaving so well. Not to mention that he had already encountered Marsha and thought the Joneses were in for a rough time. Well, up until he killed them, anyway.

By now the crowd had disappeared, apart from one or two hardened disaster-lovers who didn't care how much they were intruding on other people's lives, so long as there was a good tragedy to look at. Jon was having a long conversation with his HQ on his mobile phone, and Ray was pressing Susan to at least have a sit-down before she set off for her sister's.

Susan shook her head. 'Thank you, Ray, but we should go straight to Marsha.'

While they talked, Fish took a last look round. This time, something caught his eye, something in the wreckage that he hadn't noticed before, although how he had missed it he didn't know. It was sticking out of the rubble, and right under his nose too.

He leaned down to pick it up. It was his favourite book, the one about a girl who had her whole life stolen away, and apart from a little dust and a bent cover it was all right. He stuffed it into his back pocket. Then he stood in the ruins of his home and, with a hollow feeling inside his chest, said a silent goodbye to his past. A whole chapter of his life had just been closed without warning. Which meant that a new chapter was about to begin. He was afraid it might not be a comfortable one.

That done, he hurried back to his mother.

'Then let me drive you, mmm?' Ray was saying. 'You won't want to worry about the journey after a shock like this.'

Susan hesitated, but Fish got in front of her and nodded firmly, looking Ray in the eye. It was just what they needed. Rubble blocked the garage and driveway, Susan was obviously still light-headed with shock, and the trip to Marsha's by public transport meant going on the train. From Fish's point of view this was a bad thing because he would have to face the whispers that loved the dark and tended to hang out in attics, cellars, telephone lines and railway tunnels. Whispers were the echoes of things that people buried deep inside, the darknesses from the corners of their mind that they would die rather than say, or even think, out loud. And since they had no place in their owner's heads, they had to go somewhere. These whispers were not something Fish wanted to deal with today.

Susan picked up the message. 'Thank you, Ray,' she said gratefully, her voice cracking.

Fish pressed his mother's hand and she squeezed back, giving him a small but reassuring smile. He could see past it to her eyes, which were the dark grey they always went when she was unhappy, so he looked into them firmly. Her smile widened and, more importantly, her eyes lightened.

'You're right,' she said. 'We'll be fine!'

By now, Ray had run the car out of the garage and was waiting for them. Susan climbed into the front and Fish into the back. It felt strange, as if they were starting off on a long journey and had forgotten their luggage. As they drove away, Fish turned so that he could see out of the back window. He knew that anyone who saw him would think that he was taking a last look at his old home, but he wasn't. He was looking at the postbox.

The demon that had been sitting on top of it was gone.

4

A SHEEP FROM ABOVE

Susan's finger had hardly left the doorbell of her sister's large and very expensive house when the door was jerked open and Marsha appeared. She was dressed in black from head to foot.

'Oh! Susan! I'm so glad you came! It's been the most terrible day!'

Susan blinked, taken by surprise. 'Um . . . yes, it has rather.'

Fish shivered, though it wasn't cold. There was something wrong with his aunt. She looked . . . shiny. Really shiny. Not just glowing with inner feelings or anything, but actually radiating light. His heart chilled as he wondered what this meant. From the things he could see that ordinary humans couldn't, he understood that children, the newly in love, and the truly innocent always wore a golden light around them, but the shine that came from Marsha was paler, more silvery. He had seen people with it before, but they were just people on the street or in shops, no one he knew well enough to find out why they were shining.

'Welcome, dear sister,' sighed Marsha. She hugged Susan as soon as they were through the door, though Fish thought that old-fashioned, romantic novelists would describe it more like, 'She clasped Susan to her bosom,' or some such. Marsha read a lot of romantic novels. In fact most of the time she thought she lived in one.

When she let Susan go, Marsha turned to Fish. She hesitated a moment then pursed up her mouth and kissed him delicately from as far away as she could manage. Fish didn't blame her. Once, when he was very small, he had bitten her when she tried to cuddle him, because he didn't like the stifling sweetness of her perfume. She had kept her distance ever since. Now, he smiled at her. Marsha gave him a confused look.

'Darling child,' she murmured.

'How did you know?' asked Susan, taking off her coat and dropping it over the banister.

'I was about to ask the same thing! Some kind of sibling telepathy, I suppose! How wonderful! But then we were always so close.'

'We haven't spoken for over a month, we only see each other at Christmas and birthdays . . .'

'Oh, don't be so tiresome, dear. Sibling telepathy goes so much deeper than mere visits!'

Gently, Fish pushed Susan ahead of him in the direction of the lounge. Waiting for an invitation from Marsha was like waiting for mountains to crumble.

Marsha's lounge was beautiful. It was also pale cream and gave Fish the heebie-jeebies, because every smudge showed up like a beacon of muck. The clouds had darkened on their way here and it had rained briefly but heavily. Fish hoped he hadn't stepped in any puddles walking to the door.

'Mind the carpet, dears,' said Marsha, as if they could avoid treading on it.

'So, what exactly is the matter?' demanded Susan. Fish edged her towards the sofa. She sat down and he settled next to her, relieved. Once she was sitting down, her voice dropped again to more like its normal softness.

'Tell me, Marsha, has something bad happened to you?'

Marsha's face trembled as she struggled to speak. Fish watched her, fear growing in his middle. He was about to find out what it meant when people shone like that and he knew it wouldn't be good. He leaned forward, his eyes on her face, waiting.

His aunt passed a hand over her forehead. 'Only the worst thing! My darling Reginald is dead!'

As she said the words, Marsha's pale blue eyes dimmed and a look of shock and loss swept over her face. The shine around her grew stronger as she spoke and, suddenly, Fish understood. All those people he had seen who glistened with silver light had lost someone they loved.

Then, delicate tears filled her eyes and she dabbed at

them with a lace handkerchief, just at the corners and doing no good at all. The tears tracked gracefully down her plump cheeks.

Susan was staring at her, aghast. 'Reg is dead! Oh, Marsha.' Her own blue eyes filled with tears too, real proper ones that made her lids go pink and her nose run.

Fish drew in a slow breath, full of fear and grief. Reginald Power had been one of the few people that he felt completely at ease with, who could sit in companionable silence without expecting any conversation. But now was not the time to break down. He had a bad feeling that there was something else going on here, something hidden behind the visible tragedy. He found himself glancing anxiously about the room and realised that he was looking for the demon. Although there was no obvious reason to think it had anything to do with Reg's death as well as the demolition of their home, Fish thought there must be a connection. He shivered, remembering other terrible things that had happened recently to people they knew. Things like the death of the vicar.

'It was this morning,' Marsha went on. She blinked at them and looked away. 'Out of the blue. It's terrible how a single second can alter the course of your life forever!'

'But what . . .'

'I was going to telephone you at once, dear, but I was so distraught! I couldn't stop crying! And then when I was able to speak, I rang and rang and there was no reply . . .' She gave Susan a reproachful look.

'I'm sorry, but we were out and the house was being knocked down anyway . . .' Susan dried her eyes on a tissue and gave Marsha a warm if watery smile.

'So I just waited here alone, little knowing that you would sense my pain and come to me!' Marsha clasped her hands together ecstatically.

Susan winced. 'Look Marsha, I want to help you and I'm glad we came, but it wasn't because I had a premonition or anything. We're here because the house was demolished by mistake and we've nowhere to live.'

Marsha looked at her blankly.

'We have to stay with you,' said Susan firmly.

'Oh my dear! That is so noble of you! I could certainly do with the company if you're prepared to put up with a poor, weeping widow.'

Susan took a deep breath. 'Well, that's settled then,' she said soothingly. 'Now, how about a drink? I don't suppose you've had anything all day. I'm sure Fish will make us some tea.' She smiled over at her son.

Fish was already on his feet and out of the door. It only took a minute to boil the kettle, get the milk from the fridge and set out the cups, and then he was back in the living room with the tray in time to hear his mother say, 'But, Marsha, you still haven't told us how Reg . . . what happened to Reg.'

'It was the most awful shock! One moment he was healthy and happy and going down the road to get a newspaper. Next he was dead! Just like that!'

Setting the tray down next to his mother, Fish studied Marsha carefully, his hazel eyes taking note. Once again she blinked and turned her head away as she spoke. It dawned on him that she didn't want to tell them how her husband had died.

'Why is that boy staring at me?' said Marsha suddenly. Her voice took on a slight whine, but underneath it was sharp.

'Fish, you know it upsets people,' said Susan without looking up from pouring the tea.

Fish sighed and concentrated on adding the milk – straight from the bottle instead of using the jug – which earned him a pursed-up-mouth look from his aunt.

'That child needs help,' said Marsha. It was a funny thing, but people often talked about Fish as if he wasn't there. He didn't mind as he preferred it when they didn't notice him much.

'He's fine,' snapped Susan.

'He's too small for his age. And does he *ever* talk?'

'Only when he needs to.'

'If you ask me, it's not normal. And why do you call him Fish anyway?'

'Look, he's bright and healthy and if he chooses not to say anything unless he thinks it's important, I for one am not worrying, OK?' said Susan, worriedly.

'All right, dear!' Marsha shrugged.

'He gets on fine at school and has a couple of nice friends . . .'

Fish nodded. It was true. He had Jed, who loved bright colours and refused to be parted from his favourite red jacket, and Alice, who wanted to be a news reporter. They talked to and around him and didn't expect it to be any other way. The fact that Jed wasn't very bright and Alice's mother often forgot to wash Alice's clothes was neither here nor there. They both helped Jed with his lessons and Alice usually remembered to wash herself, so she didn't smell too bad. Anyway, when she forgot, Fish let her know because he didn't like the dirt demons that hung tangled in her hair or perched on her shoulders, glaring at him with eyes the colour of sludge. And because Alice knew about the things that Fish could see, she always went straight home and had a shower. Usually looking a little sick.

Marsha sniffed disbelievingly, but she didn't say any more.

'Now,' went on Susan, 'since we can't even save any of our things, we need some clothes and toothbrushes and so on . . .'

'Why ever didn't you pack a suitcase, dear?'

Although he didn't use them often, today was clearly an exception, so Fish gave his aunt one of his special looks. He was astonished that she could be so dense, even allowing for the death of her husband. The glare got through because Marsha twitched and sent him a nervous glance.

Susan winced. 'I told you. Our house was demolished . . .'

And for the first time that day Marsha looked out of her own world long enough to hear what Susan was saying. Instantly there was a flash of the old Marsha, the Marsha underneath all the flounce, who knew how to care about her little sister.

'Oh lord, Su! How on earth . . . ?'

'They got the wrong address, would you believe?' For a moment Susan's voice quivered.

'Sue them,' said Marsha firmly. 'I've got a good solicitor. And you can stay here as long as you need to.' She sent Fish a resigned look. He smiled at her, hoping it came over as reassuring. It must have worked, because she gave him a tiny smile back.

'Thank you, Marsha. We've had a bad time between us, haven't we?' Susan smiled ruefully. 'But what you must have gone through is terrible.' She put a hand out to touch Fish gently on the arm and he knew that she was glad she had only lost her home and not someone she cared about. 'But you never said what happened?'

This time Marsha didn't blink and look away. She fell silent and looked down at her teacup, her face growing slowly redder.

'A sheep fell on him,' she said at last.

'Sorry?'

'A sheep. It fell on him.' She struggled with herself for a moment, then burst out, 'It's just so . . . so . . . RIDICULOUS!' Now that the truth was out, Marsha hurried on, words tripping over themselves to get out of her mouth.

'He went for the newspaper like he always does of a morning, and halfway down the avenue they're building a block of luxury apartments and there's scaffolding everywhere. And Reg must have cut across the building site. And it turns out someone left the gate open to Lockes Field and there was this one sheep got out, and somehow it got on to the platform thing and was hauled up the scaffolding! And it panicked, you know, and tried to get down again and . . . fell.'

There was silence. Marsha had gone from red to pale and was sitting very straight in her chair with her plump, ringed hands clasped in her lap.

'I'm . . . so . . . sorry.'

'It fell from several floors up. Reg was killed at once. And so was the sheep of course.'

'Of course,' murmured Susan faintly. There was another silence.

Fish went and sat next to his aunt, put his hand in hers and squeezed it. By now her shine was much brighter.

'Thank you, dear,' she said, and burst into tears.

�֎

That evening, when Fish was alone in his bedroom – Marsha had several spare ones – he took a careful look around for the demon, but pretending not to in case it realised what he was doing.

So, as he tracked down an old pair of Reg's pyjamas,

35

he looked in the wardrobe and searched through every cupboard. When he closed the window, he checked behind the curtains. Finally, he dropped his watch on the floor and bent down to pick it up, glancing under the bed in the kind of way that might be accidental, just to see if it was hiding there.

It wasn't, which was a relief.

At last, Fish was ready for bed. He climbed in, nervously turned out the light and lay staring up through the gloom at the ceiling. It wasn't totally dark in the bedroom because he always kept the curtains open to let in some light and keep out the whispers. Tonight, though, he was more worried about something else.

Although the demon wasn't around right now, he was sure that he hadn't seen the last of it. He wondered if it had been there when the lost sheep had stumbled off the edge of the scaffolding and ended the life of his uncle. And if the creature brought bad things with it, then where was it now and was some other poor person suffering while it looked on and took notes?

5

THE MAN WHO HELPED

'A sheep!' Lampwick said indignantly. 'A *sheep!*'

It was early the next morning and Grimshaw had just finished giving his report. Lampwick always required a blow-by-blow account of every event, right down to the expression on their faces and with exact sound effects.

'Take it or leave it, it's what you got,' Grimshaw muttered irritably, flicking his tail.

Lampwick sniffed. 'Can't you take lessons from that friend of yours, Tin or whatever his name is?'

'Tun,' muttered Grimshaw. 'It's Tun. And I *know* you always get it wrong on purpose.'

'I mean,' went on Lampwick, brushing the comment aside with a wave of his hand, 'isn't he the one who took Sufferers' lives by ripping their still-beating hearts from their bodies? You wouldn't find a demon like *him* killing anybody with a *farm animal!*'

Grimshaw had to agree. It was legendary among curse demons that Tun's last-ever victim had been found huddled against a wall with a look of such terror on his face that *no one dared to look at him* for fear his tortured gaze would haunt their dreams forever.

'And then there's that one with the head like a dog, who visits such ghastly tortures on his victims . . .'

'. . . jackal, and his name is Hanhut . . .' muttered Grimshaw.

'. . . that their insides end up being their outsides!' Lampwick chuckled, shaking his head.

'It's different for them,' snarled Grimshaw, clenching his paws.

Lampwick turned away from him and lurched stiffly up the crypt, hands clasped behind his back, tattered robes flapping around him. What with having been dead for so long, most of the feeling had gone in his legs.

'They are *first-rate demons*,' went on Grimshaw, hoping that Lampwick would fall over. It always made him laugh to watch his Architect floundering about on the floor like an overturned beetle. 'Hanhut was created by a powerful Egyptian queen with a *whole dynasty* at her command, and Tun's Architect is an actual, *real* magician, who also happens to be of ancient and noble blood. Me, I'm a *third-rate demon* created by a *pretend* magician with about as much nobility as a turnip!'

He glared at Lampwick, who had reached the far wall of the crypt. 'And in case you hadn't noticed after over a century of half-life, there are *Rules*, and third-rate demons aren't allowed to *show* themselves to Sufferers, let alone visit Death upon them *personally*.'

The Rules applied to all types of Avatar – that is to

say creatures of spirit rather than flesh – whether they were demon or angel. Even the high-up ones like the Pomp. But it seemed to Grimshaw that the most unfair Rules of all were the ones that applied to third-rate curse demons.

'Third-rate demons like *me*,' he went on sulkily, 'created by third-rate humans like *you*, have to make use of *anything handy* to bring about Deaths by accident. For example a SHEEP!'

'You're twitching again,' said Lampwick, wrinkling his nose disdainfully. 'Do try to behave properly. It's very distracting having you bouncing about like a jumping bean when I'm trying to have my afternoon walk.'

Grimshaw screamed at him. 'Don't you understand what I'm saying?' he howled. 'It's ALL YOUR FAULT that I'm like this.' Another twitch shook him and he stopped and shut his eyes, then drew in a long, deep breath.

'Well, anyway,' he said firmly, glancing at his chronometer, 'time's running on. I can't sit here talking to you all day, I've got work to do.'

'You'll sit there as long as I tell you to,' sneered Lampwick. 'I want you to go through it all again right from the . . .'

Grimshaw just about managed to suppress a scream. 'Let me go now,' he said through gritted teeth, 'and I'll soon have something *new* to tell you.'

Demon and Architect stared at one another for a moment.

'Go on then,' said Lampwick gleefully, 'get on with it. And make sure there is plenty of blood.'

❦

About the time Grimshaw was making promises to Lampwick, Fish got downstairs to find his mother making breakfast.

'I was going to scramble some eggs,' she said, 'but the gas isn't working, so it's just tea and toast, I'm afraid.'

Marsha, already at the table, gave him a warm, if wan, smile.

'That was my Reg's favourite,' she said affectionately, nodding at the T-shirt Fish was wearing, even though it swamped him. It had a line drawing of a fish on the front and the word 'fish' written underneath, which was why he had chosen it. 'I'm glad you've got it now.'

Before Fish could smile a thank-you, the doorbell rang.

Everyone froze. After the traumatic events of yesterday, the doorbell ringing at half past eight in the morning didn't feel like good news.

Susan let out a slow breath. Marsha had gone pale.

'It's too soon for someone from the gas company,' said Susan, doubtfully. 'I only just rang them.'

Fish got to his feet and hurried out of the kitchen and up the hall, leaving his mother and his aunt staring after him anxiously.

The front door opened on a well-built man in jeans and a crumpled shirt. He looked as if he had been up all night, and he also looked familiar, but the first thing that Fish noticed about him was that he glowed all over with a silvery shine. Fish's heart went cold. This man too had lost someone dear to him. Bad things were stacking up all around them and it didn't bode well.

The man smiled at him gravely. 'Fish Jones?' he said.

Fish nodded.

'If your mother is here I need to speak to her. It's important.'

The man's blue eyes met Fish's hazel ones and a look passed between them. It was a look that sent Fish's heart plunging to his boots. Whatever it was that the man had to say, it wasn't just important, it was life or death. And in that moment, Fish recognised the man as Jon Figg.

He put out a hand. Startled, Jon Figg took it. Fish clasped it for a moment, his face grave.

Jon Figg swallowed hard. 'Thank you,' he said, understanding the look in Fish's eyes, 'but how did you know? About Emily dying last night . . .' He stopped, emotion twisting across his face.

Fish stood back to let Jon into the house, the man's huge bulk filling the hall. With Fish in the lead they went back to the kitchen, where the only sound was the ping of the toaster as it popped up four golden slices.

'I know you!' cried Susan at once. Her voice had taken on an odd edge. 'Of course, it's Mr Figg! I didn't recognise you without the yellow hat and overalls.'

He stepped forward and offered her his hand. 'I am

41

deeply sorry, ma'am, for all that happened yesterday. I had my troubles, it's true, but I should have paid full attention to my work or stayed at home. I am responsible for your current situation and I want to help you if I can.'

Susan smiled and put her hand in his. They shook solemnly.

'Apology accepted, and don't worry, my sister is looking after us. Won't you sit down, Mr Figg . . .'

'Call me Jon, please.'

'. . . Jon, and have some breakfast?'

'I'd like that, for I have some other things to tell you as well, and a cup of tea would be most welcome.'

He settled at the table in between Fish and Marsha, and Susan poured tea for all of them. She set the toast on to a plate in the middle of the table, then put some more bread in to do. Jon took a long gulp of his tea. He drank it like a man in the desert would drink water, and when he had finished he drew a long breath.

'Thing is, Mrs Jones . . .'

'Susan, please!'

'. . . Susan, we've met before. I mean before I knocked down your house, though you might not remember. When I saw you yesterday, I thought there was something about your face that I recognised and suddenly, last night, the penny dropped.'

Fish had turned to look at Jon as he spoke, which meant that his range of vision moved to take in the corner of the kitchen and the space next to the sink. His heart turned over as he realised that the demon was there, sitting on the floor, with its notebook in front of it and its pencil clutched in its paw. It was watching them carefully, so Fish turned his head away, hoping it hadn't noticed him looking startled or horrified.

Susan was nodding. 'I felt the same!'

'It was a few weeks ago,' Jon explained, 'when I helped out a friend of mine. He had a large job on and needed some extra hands. He's in the grave-digging business . . .'

'Marble Hill!'

'That's it. Marble Hill Cemetery. At least it used to be. But the Church of St Michael's was sold off and the company that bought it want to turn the whole place into a residential home for old folk. They bought the graveyard too, and that's where my mate comes in.'

'That's right. They dug up the coffins and reburied them in the cemetery at St Peter's.'

'Not all of them are buried yet, but I'll get to the reasons for that in a moment. For now, the last few coffins are being kept in the crypt at the Church of St Peter and St Paul, where they were taken when they were first exhumed.'

'Good Lord!' muttered Marsha. 'How do you come into this, Su?'

'You know I do voluntary work for St Peter's sometimes? Well, the vicar asked me if I would help . . . um . . . organise the coffins.'

'And *that's* where we met before. I was with my mate Steve, carrying the coffins to the crypt, and you were keeping a record of the details and telling us where to lay the next one and so on. Made us a lovely cup of tea too. You only spoke to Steve, but I was the one standing right behind him.'

Susan nodded again. 'Yes! I do remember now. You were the man who helped.'

Fish risked a glance at the creature in the corner. It was watching Susan and Jon with great attention. Because it was so close now, Fish couldn't help a shiver as he noticed its eyes, which were inky black from corner to corner. It was dressed in patched trousers with a hole cut out for its tail and had a complicated watch strapped to one skinny wrist. Fish also noticed that what he had taken for a hump was actually a filthy old backpack, made of worn leather with tarnished buckles and a couple of sturdy pockets on the front. Suddenly, the creature looked up, as if it sensed Fish's gaze. Quickly, Fish turned his attention back to the conversation.

Jon's voice had become sad as he went on. 'Thing is, Steve is dead now, which is part of the reason why those last few coffins haven't been buried again – they haven't found anyone else to finish the work yet. He drowned in the lake after his house burnt down, his wife fell off a roof on to the railings, his son had a horrible accident with a fire hose, and his daughter got crushed in some revolving doors.'

Marsha and Susan were staring at Jon in horror. Fish felt an icy trickle run down his spine. Things were getting worse and worse. The web of death and disaster stretched further than he had realised. All over again, he found himself remembering the vicar's horrible death.

'And then, just after Steve's death in fact, my dog exploded, the roof of my house was crushed in by a falling tree and Emily got bashed on the head and went to hospital. The bash on the head didn't kill her straight away, but last night . . . She never regained consciousness, not even once.'

Jon bowed his head, the tears running down his cheeks. He didn't try to stop them or to wipe them away. Susan put out a hand and touched his arm.

Fish sent a look of undiluted fury at the creature, sure that it was somehow responsible for all this horror. It was scribbling in its notebook and didn't notice the look, which was good because if it had it would have known at once that Fish could see it.

Jon got a hold of himself and straightened up. He raised his head. Fish thought he looked afraid.

'And how is the vicar?' Jon asked. It seemed like an innocent enough question, but Fish knew at once that it wasn't.

Susan looked puzzled, then sad, then terrified. 'He died just the other day. He was up in the bell tower and . . . Of course, some people said it might be suicide because of his house collapsing due to subsidence, his wife falling off that mountain in Switzerland and his . . . his mother being run over by a lawn mower, but I *knew* him and he *wouldn't*.'

The icy trickle had spread, seeping through Fish to his core. Suddenly the catalogue of pain was full of hidden meaning. The terrible things that had happened to the vicar were linked in some way to the terrible things that had happened to his own family, to Jon Figg and to Jon's friend Steve. Was the demon causing it all somehow? And if so, why?

He felt his mother's eyes on his face, looking at him searchingly, so he met her gaze and put his hand in hers. He ignored the demon, which was watching them all intently, as if waiting for something.

With a sigh, Jon nodded. 'Yes, I thought that might be another reason why the reburial of the coffins from St Michael's hasn't gone ahead.'

Marsha was staring at them with wide eyes full of shock. It was as if fear had infected them all, spreading from one to another like a plague.

'And then . . .' Marsha gasped, her brain putting all the pieces together and coming to one inescapable conclusion, '. . . and then Susan's house got knocked down and my Reg died.'

Four pairs of eyes locked across the table, and Fish's heart turned over.

'It's . . .'

In the corner, Grimshaw waited for someone to say it. Sooner or later someone always said it. And then they would try to run. Sooner or later, they always tried to run.

'It's as if . . .'

He fixed his eyes on Marsha, willing her to finish the sentence. She did.

'It's as if we're all under some horrible curse!'

6

HEREIN LIES THE BODY OF LAMPWICK THE ROBBER, DARE NOT TO DISTURB

'What you have to ask yourselves,' said Jon, 'is why?'

Fish had made them some more tea, pouring it strong and hot and adding plenty of sugar. He was still cold right to his core and knew that the others would be feeling the same. Hot, sweet tea was just what they needed to help thaw their hearts and give them back some strength. The toast was still on the plate. The second batch had been done long ago, but was cooling, unnoticed, in the toaster.

'I think now is the time to tell you about the exhumation of Lampwick the Robber,' said Jon. 'It was on the last night of the job, just before all this awfulness began. We only had a few graves left to do, but there was this particular one that spooked the hell out of me. Something about the feel of it, an air of wakefulness, like the deceased wasn't properly gone. I think, subconsciously, we'd been avoiding it, but it was the only one left so at last we had no choice but to dig the coffin up.'

Jon hesitated, as if he didn't really want to say any more. Fish shuddered, and out of the corner of his eye he saw Marsha and Susan do the same.

'Go on,' said Marsha, her voice full of fear.

❧

It was one of those lovely mornings, Jon began, *before the sun is up, when the horizon is just showing a promise of dawn. For some reason, probably to stop people coming to gawp, exhumations are always done after dark and so I was glad to see that morning was on its way because it meant the job was almost over. Someone had to move the bodies from the old graveyard to the new one, and Steve was the kind of bloke who did his work with respect. Even so, I didn't much care for the thought that we were disturbing the dead.*

This last grave, the one we had been avoiding, was an old one – the deceased had been buried way back in Victorian times. The headstone was covered in lichen, and bushes had grown over it, making it difficult to get at. I couldn't read the inscription at first, just the name. Lampwick. I tried to clean it up, scrape off some of the lichen and that. When I'd done, I could see the words. 'Leave Him In Peace'. It seemed like a funny thing to write on a headstone, more like a threat or a warning.

I won't bore you with the digging. Enough to say that we got down to wood at last. And then, as if it hadn't been bad enough already, things got really creepy.

It was early morning, like I said, and the sun was just coming up over the horizon as we reached the coffin. The birds were singing their hearts out the way they do, to welcome in the new day. As soon as our spades scraped the coffin lid, they stopped.

Silence.

Not a tweet.

Now, Steve isn't the imaginative sort. You don't go in for grave-digging as a career if you've got a lot of imagination. But even he stopped what he was doing and looked at me.

It only lasted a moment. Then the birds got going again and everything seemed normal. Except for the coffin. Instead of a metal plate with the deceased's name and dates on it, there were words scratched into the wood. We didn't have time to read them. The sun was coming up and we needed to get the grave filled in properly before the world was up and about. All I saw was, 'Herein lies the body of Lampwick the Robber, dare not to disturb.'

I didn't catch any more, not just because we were busy getting the coffin out of the ground, but because something distracted me. Out of the corner of my eye, I thought I saw movement. Nothing much, just a shadowy rustle of the bushes, probably a cat or a fox. But it gave me a chill down my spine and suddenly I wanted nothing more than to get out of that graveyard!

We got the coffin loaded up and drove it, and the others we had done earlier that night, all the way to St Peter's.

There, Steve went to speak to the vicar and the lady – you, Susan – who was helping organise the coffins. We unloaded them and you showed us where to put them in the crypt. Lampwick the Robber was first out of the van. I remember *that you tapped the top of his coffin when directing us. It was the lightest of touches, but I was already so spooked it made me flinch.*

We put him in the corner of the crypt. A quiet corner. But by then I reckon he had already been disturbed more than I care to think about.

❀

'So you think that's it, then? That all this is down to some kind of dreadful curse, put on us by a dead man called Lampwick the Robber?' Marsha frowned. 'It's like something out of a horror novel!'

Susan drew a slow breath. 'And yet . . . there was something about the way the crypt felt not long after that coffin was brought in. As if . . . some creature was there, watching me.'

She looked over at Fish, who nodded. He would have bet everything he had that he knew exactly which creature had been there, watching Susan as she made a few last checks and then locked up to go home. The demon of Lampwick the Robber's curse. He understood now what the creature was doing – it was making sure the curse happened properly.

'Yes,' said Jon. 'That is what I think. I don't care for myself any more – everything I had is gone – but I'm here to help you and Fish. And you, ma'am,' he added, looking at Marsha. 'If the curse was confined to just the people directly connected with the exhumation, then it would be the vicar, Steve, me and Susan who would be dead or facing death. But we have seen that it goes further than that; it includes our loved ones too, our close family. Right through from wives,' his voice trembled, thinking of his beloved Emily, 'to brothers-in-law, as Reg was to Susan. So if I'm right, everyone around this table is on the list.'

In the corner, Grimshaw scribbled in his notebook. He was having a very interesting time. He had found another human who was behaving with great dignity in the face of misfortune. He wrote: 'Unselfish Desire to Help Others'.

'So what do we do?' asked Marsha helplessly.

They gazed at each other in silence for a moment.

Grimshaw waited, pencil at the ready.

Then Jon Figg said, 'We run.'

7

SILVER KNIVES, FOR EXAMPLE

Grimshaw snapped shut the notebook and stuffed it back into his pocket, then lodged his pencil behind his ear. He frowned at a small dirt demon that had climbed on to his back paw – probably generated by the grime gathering where the sink unit met the floor. Such things were the lowest form of Avatar and Grimshaw was glad the stupid creatures only hung around the properly alive (and the mess they created) and couldn't exist in Limbo. He brushed it off irritably and looked at his chronometer. He had things to do and it was time to be getting on and doing them.

A curse demon's chronometer could take the shape of anything from an hourglass to an armillary sphere. Originally, when Grimshaw had come into existence over a hundred and fifty years ago, his chronometer had appeared as a pocket watch. So, because he had been born without clothing and had no pockets to put it in, his first task had been to find a pair of trousers. Later, to keep up with the times, Grimshaw had thrown away the chain and had strapped the watch to his wrist with a leather strip. He kept the trousers because he liked them, although, after a century and a half of wear, they were more darn than trouser.

As well as the time and the geography, Grimshaw's chronometer also read the constellations and the seasons, including human holidays like Christmas, Easter and so on. In addition to that, it highlighted special events on the Spirit calendar, like various approaching catastrophes (earthquakes, tsunamis, vast floods or landslides and the like), or the births and deaths of religions.

Right now, Grimshaw set the geography hands to outside number thirty-three, Whitefield Drive, under the rhododendron bushes. Then he pressed the send button. Then he disappeared from the kitchen.

✄

Outside the house, life was going on as normal. The sun was shining and there was a light breeze to cool the air and rustle the leaves. Grimshaw thought it made a nice change from Grey Space. He was well positioned on the other side of the road so that he could see the front door of Marsha's house and the view up and down the avenue (slightly obscured by a pink rhododendron flower, but not so that it was a problem).

Grimshaw studied the page in his notebook dedicated to Jon Figg, the Man Who Helped. By now there were ticks through dog, car, house, job and wife and the page was covered in notes. He reviewed the ones relating to last night, when Jon Figg's wife Emily had died in hospital. He frowned. He had written, 'Miserable Collapse with Despair and Sobbing', but somehow, thinking back, that didn't seem quite fair. After a brief inner struggle, Grimshaw crossed the comment through and replaced it with, 'Heartfelt Collapse and Dignified Weeping', then got on with the job in hand.

He scratched an ear and turned his inky gaze up the road, to where a small boy was kicking a ball around a front garden. The boy's mother had told him to play in the back garden, but he had decided to ignore her because he had been made to eat porridge for breakfast instead of chocolate krispies and was in a rebellious mood.

Next, Grimshaw looked the other way, to where a couple of men had pulled up in a truck. They got out and began unloading equipment.

Whitefield Drive was a pleasant avenue, lined with tall houses and trimmed with leafy trees that cast cool shadows in the bright sun. Mostly this was a good thing, but every few years the trees grew too large and the council sent out some men with a truck, some yellow tape and a couple of electric saws to cut off a lot of branches and thin the trees out. This was one of those years.

Grimshaw watched with interest as they fixed up their safety equipment outside Marsha's house, calling cheerfully to each other as they worked. The boy in the nearby front garden kicked his ball about more slowly as he spared some attention to see what they were doing. When the safety harness was in place, two of the men shouldered the electric saws, hopped on to the mechanical ladder on the back of the truck and rose swiftly to the leafy heights where they clambered into position. A second later the morning was split by the grinding whine of the saws and the cracking of branches.

Being a creature born of spirit rather than flesh, Grimshaw was able to see a little way into the future. It was a very complicated place. Humans had free will, and so, although there was a *most likely* course for them to take, they might change their minds and do something different instead. So each human's future was actually several possible futures running alongside each other. When a person made his or her choice about what to do next, then the several futures melded together into a single present. As their decision might affect everybody else's possible futures, it could be difficult to get a forecast exactly right.

Opening his inner eye, the one that could look forward in time, Grimshaw investigated the various futures that spanned out over the next few hours. Jon Figg left the house at around 10.30, just as a youth on a motorcycle sped down the road and disappeared around the corner. The men chopped branches until 1.00, when they stopped for lunch. The boy got bored and went in some time between 10.45 and 11.30. If he stayed out until the later time, his mother called to him from the window. There wasn't a lot of variation, apart from the time the kid got bored.

Flipping his ears, Grimshaw pulled off his backpack. Then he fished out an old school ruler and a battered copy of *How to Be a Dutiful Housewife* by Eliza Minchin and set to work. He had taken Mrs Minchin from the bookshelf of his first ever Sufferer to use as a prompt. The way it worked was this. First he held up the book and dropped it so that it fell open at random. Then he picked up the ruler and placed it anywhere on the page. Next, he looked along the line made by the ruler and wrote down the first words that caught his eye. Then he did it all again.

After a few goes he had written down a string of haphazard phrases. They said:

... silver, knives for example ...

... always chop the vegetables into small pieces ...

... look for materials that ...

... the stone should be scraped free of ...

Then he closed his actual eyes, opened his inner eye and looked again. This time he saw:

Falling knives chop into small pieces. Look at the stone.

He grinned, showing a row of small, yellowish stumpy teeth. He returned the book and his ruler to his backpack, stuffed his notebook into his pocket, then went to look for the stone as suggested by Eliza Minchin.

He found it very quickly, and when he found it he changed its position by one centimetre to the north and three to the west. It took experimentation to get the right place, moving it a little, checking the most likely futures, moving it a little more, checking again and so on, but eventually he found the right spot.

Then he went back to the rhododendrons.

❈

Fish couldn't believe it when the curse demon fiddled with the oversized watch on its wrist and disappeared. Especially as it vanished right about the time that Jon was telling them about the cottage on the moors.

'Nothing for miles but empty heath. If you can get lost anywhere, then it's in Crow's Cottage! Time itself would pass you by in that place. My parents liked to go there when they felt life was rushing by too fast. When my father died he left the place to me, but what with one thing and another, Emily . . .' he paused for a moment, his face twisting briefly, '. . . and I haven't been up there for a couple of years.'

'And you think we might be safe there?'

'If you can be safe anywhere. It's been deserted for a while so it will be in a state, but we can clean it up and stay there for as long as we need to.'

Susan glanced at Fish, who nodded. 'It's worth a try, Jon,' she said. 'Besides, what have we got to lose? If what you say is true, then every moment that passes, our lives are in danger here. We might be under this horrible threat wherever we go, but then again, we might outrun it.'

'We can take Reg's van,' said Marsha. 'Load it up with as much food, clothing and bedding as we can and off we go. Won't take long. We can be on the road by this afternoon.' She clasped her hands together and her cheeks looked flushed with determination. 'Don't worry, dears, we'll manage somehow.'

Susan smiled. 'I have to say, Marsha, you are coping with this far better than I would have thought.'

Marsha shrugged and sent a glance at Fish, the memory of his stern glance yesterday afternoon suddenly fresh in her mind. 'I think I finally woke up, Susan. This is really happening. I've lost my beloved Reg, and the only family I have left in the world, the people I care about, are in danger. If living in a fallen-down cottage at the end of the world will save us, then my best china, my chandeliers and my upholstery can go hang!'

Jon smiled at her, the first real smile Fish had seen from him. 'That's the spirit! Now, I'll give you the address and the keys. Here, I've already drawn you a map.'

Fish reached out, took the map from his hand and began to study it.

'Aren't you coming with us?' asked Marsha.

'Not till I've seen Emily decently buried. If I survive that long, I'll follow you, OK? And if I'm not there in a week . . . well, you'll know it's got me.'

As they headed to the front door to wave Jon off, Fish noticed a loud whining noise that he hadn't registered before, though he got the feeling that it had been going on for some time. When he opened the door he immediately saw what it was. Some men were high up in the tree outside Marsha's house, busily shearing off branches.

Jon shook hands and said goodbye, giving Fish a long look and a thoughtful smile. Fish knew that look; it was the one he got from people who had worked out that he knew things that they didn't, and who felt that what he knew was somehow *important*.

'Whatever happens to me, I wish the three of you well,' he said. Then he turned and walked down the path and out of the gate.

They watched him go. At least Fish did until he caught sight of a by now familiar shape lurking under a rhododendron bush. Horrified, he turned his eyes back to Jon and saw death gathering over his head in a silver cloud.

It all happened very fast.

In a nearby garden, the boy kicked his football for the last time. Instead of going over the hedge to land in next door's flower bed, it hit a stone at exactly the right angle to bounce left, strike the gatepost, hurtle through the air and land smack in the face of a youth on a motorcycle coming down the road. The startled youth lost control and the motorcycle went into a short skid, crashing into the back end of the truck, which in turn shunted into the tree. Happily for the men from the council, they were attached to the tree by a safety harness, but unhappily for Jon Figg, both of them, simultaneously, lost hold of their electric saws.

The ragged-toothed, shining blades swooped through the air, arcing over one another as Fish yelled, 'GET DOWN, JON!' at the top of his voice.

He was just a fraction too late.

8

THE GREAT BOOM

Fish sat quietly, watching while Susan answered the policeman's questions. In between consoling Marsha, the policewoman checked on him once or twice to see if he was all right. He smiled at her and nodded, though he was not all right at all. Fish's world had always been a strange and difficult place, alive with things that nobody else could see, but now it had become more than that. It had become full of death and the terrible fear of loss.

And more. Since Jon's death a faint shadow had begun to coil around his mother's body like a misty scarf. He knew what it was. Despair, or at least an Avatar of despair. If it was allowed to grow, it would darken and thicken until it became a demon in its own right, a cold, grey shadow-snake twined so tightly around her that it would crush her soul. He had seen them before, woven around, *and through,* people in the street. The people with dead eyes and lonely faces.

At least the creature didn't have eyes yet. He hated it when the things he saw could *see him right back*. He worried that when it had grown enough to have eyes, it would have got such a firm grip on his mother that it would never let her go.

On top of all this, Fish was keeping a careful eye out for the curse demon. He knew instinctively that it would always be there at the kill, so that meant they were safe as long as it stayed away. Even so, every unexpected movement made him twitch inside and whenever he had to do anything he kept bumping into the furniture because he was so busy trying to watch everywhere at once.

When the police had gone and Marsha had come out of the bathroom, they all sat for a moment.

'Right,' said Marsha eventually. 'You two had better get a move on if you are going to the shops.'

'Why? Why, Marsha?' cried Susan. 'It's too big, too far beyond our understanding. Wherever we go, it will find us. We could keep running and running until we die of exhaustion, but we will never escape. You can't get away from fate, everybody knows that.' She ran her fingers through her hair and gazed hopelessly at the table.

Fish watched in agony. He knew what was tearing her up inside most. Because she had helped to disturb the bones of a dead man, her son was going to lose his life. She would see Fish die and know that by her actions, however innocent they had been, she had killed him. And that knowledge was just too much for her to bear.

Twined about Susan, the shadow-snake thickened. Fish shuddered, wanting to stop it growing, but not knowing how. For a moment he thought he might tell his mother the truth about the things he could see, about the curse demon and the shadow-snake. But what good would it do?

And then Marsha came to his aid.

'That's dying talk, dear,' she said firmly, leaning forward to look Susan straight in the eyes. 'You might as well tie a noose around our necks. I mean it! Maybe you're right, but all we can do is try, and right now we haven't got a moment to lose. What just happened to that dear man is proof of that, if nothing else! We must be on the road by the end of the day. It's the only chance we've got!'

Susan blinked and looked over at her son. The shadow-snake was still there, draped around her shoulders, but she gave him a crooked smile and as she smiled it seemed to fade a little.

'Are you up to it, Fish?'

Nodding, Fish stood up. He could have cried with relief. Marsha was right. If they were to survive, they had to swallow their horror and sadness, and act.

❋

While Fish and Susan were at the shops getting the things they would need, Marsha first gathered together enough clothes and bedding for them all. Then she went into the kitchen to pick up a kettle, some saucepans and a few odds and ends. As she worked she talked to Reg, sometimes in her head and sometimes out loud. If Fish could have seen her now he would have noticed that the silvery shine around her grew brighter as she worked.

Sitting on the windowsill, his gently waving tail draped out of the window that he had pushed open just a moment ago, Grimshaw watched patiently.

Thinking that a hot meal before they set out might do them good, Marsha tried the gas again, but there was still nothing. As she turned the knob to full to see if anything came out, a gust of wind blew in through the window, ruffling the leaves of the lemon plant that lived on the kitchen windowsill. It was right on cue. Grimshaw considered it one of the great mysteries of human existence that *they were never able to get the weather forecast right*, even though the weather's future was one of the easiest to predict. He twitched his tail back inside and tucked it safely round his paws.

Feeling the draught, Marsha frowned. She didn't remember opening the window, but maybe one of the others had. Distracted, she went over and shut it, wondering if she should go around the house and make sure everything was locked up and switched off, ready to be left until they could come home again.

She made a mental note to do exactly that as soon as she had loaded up the van, then picked up the first armful of things to carry out. Unfortunately, she forgot all about the gas ring, still switched full on.

It took a long time to load the van up with all the things she had gathered together. While she was doing it, the gas people finally sorted out the fault.

In the kitchen Grimshaw sniffed, wrinkling his nose and flattening his ears. The gas was back on all right, just as he had anticipated. He could hear it hissing as it poured out of the gas jet that Marsha had left on. The horrible smell would reach Marsha's nose eventually, but not until it was far too late.

When she had finished with the van, Marsha remembered about checking the windows and lights. She started in Reg's attic-room study, working her way down through the second-floor bedrooms, heading towards the stairs. The ground floor and the kitchen would be last.

Grimshaw set his watch to the fourth branch up in the tree across the road, and pressed the send button.

❈

It was nearly five o'clock when Fish and Susan arrived back at the house and they were both worn out. Fish was looking forward to the time when they were on the road. Even though there was no certainty that running away would help, he hoped that the demon wouldn't follow them. After all, the thing had disappeared before Jon had given them the cottage details, so it couldn't know where they were going. But then it was a supernatural being, so perhaps it would know instinctively where its prey was.

'Come on, Fish, let's get this lot unloaded,' called Susan, interrupting his thoughts. She smiled at her son, but her voice was weary and her eyes were dark.

As Fish turned to help, his heart plunged. He felt rather than saw the demon in the tree nearby, and a glance up through the leaves revealed its hunched shape overhead, tail twisted around a branch. A ripple of fear scurried down his spine and he turned to run after Susan, who had just slammed the boot shut and was heading for the house, laden with bags. Suddenly, the upstairs window slammed open and Marsha appeared, her face deadly pale. Fish sprang at his mother.

Susan dropped the bags. 'Marsha!' she cried, just as Fish's arms closed around her. 'Let go, Fish, LET GO! She's in danger!'

Marsha waved her arms wildly. The smell of gas had just that minute reached her and she knew what happened next. There was no time to stop it.

'NO! Go back! Save yourselves! Farewell, my darlings!'

In the kitchen the boiler clock clicked to 5.00 and the pilot light came on with a pop. Instantly, there was a tremendous boom and a brilliant light so huge that for a second Fish thought they had been struck by a thunderbolt. The world was lit up and a wave of heat sizzled around them. Susan screamed, but her voice was lost in a wall of sound that knocked them off their feet and sent dustbins careering down the road. Up in the tree, Grimshaw was blown off his branch. Only his coiled tail anchored him and kept him from being flung over the houses behind. Glass, dust and splintered wood showered everywhere.

When it was over, Fish lay quivering against the trunk of the tree, his head ringing with the aftershock. Susan was motionless on the ground. When the world steadied enough, Fish crawled over to her, too faint to stand up properly. He felt as if his heart had stopped with fear for her, but she looked up and groaned just as he got there. There was blood on her forehead and cheek.

Even though he felt numb with the weight of Marsha's death, Fish knew that he could not pause to grieve. Any minute now the road would be swarming with police cars and ambulances, not to mention onlookers.

The car was still upright and on its wheels – unlike a couple of others closer to the house, including Reg's van. Grabbing Susan's arm, Fish slammed the boot shut then pushed his mother towards the door of the car. She nearly fell as she scrambled in, but she turned the key in the ignition and the engine ticked over. As Fish ran around to the passenger side, he glanced up. The demon was dangling from a branch by its tail. It wasn't paying them any attention.

Fish threw himself into the car, buckling up the seat belt as Susan took off, swerving to avoid the scattered glass and rubble. Her breath was coming in short gasps and her hands were shaking, but her eyes were clear and fixed on the road.

Fish stared at her, relief washing through him. The shadow-snake that had cast its length around her shoulders had gone, dissipated in a breath as her despair was shattered by something far stronger. Love for her son. Despair was something she couldn't afford right now. The curse had come a step closer and her choice was clear. Act, or Fish was sure to die.

'Sorry, Marsha,' she whispered, 'I have to go. I have to do the best I can for Fish.'

They got to the turn into Park Avenue just as the wail of sirens split the air. Susan put her foot down until they reached the main road and joined the traffic heading north, out of the town.

For better or for worse, they were on their way.

✤

Hanging from his branch, Grimshaw was experiencing exhilaration. He had felt a glow of satisfaction before, when some intricate arrangement had gone with the ease of clockwork, but never in his half-life had he felt such a rush of heart-stopping power as he felt now, after the explosion. It burned through him like white fire, making him tingle to his very core. It was amazing!

He opened his eyes and the devastation around him brought back that wonderful moment of BOOM. The blast had been so . . . so . . . CATACLYSMIC!

Grimshaw was certain in his heart of hearts that even Tun had never done anything quite like that, and he was the second most famous of all curse demons (the most famous being the awesome Mighty Curse). Yet he, Grimshaw, the third-rate demon of a curse thrown by an ordinary everyday non-magician, had created all that wonderful BOOM!

Squinting down the road, which was currently the sky as he was still hanging upside down, Grimshaw watched the car drive off in a hurry. He didn't need to guess who was inside. They had made a run for it, even while the ashes of Marsha's funeral pyre were still burning. He had to admit he admired their guts. Some of his past Sufferers would have just given up and accepted their fate.

Happily, Grimshaw rearranged all the hands on his watch to point to zero. Then he pressed send.

It was time he reported back to his Architect.

9

AN EVENING IN LIMBO

'Tell me about the knives again,' said Lampwick.

Grimshaw tried not to look bored.

'It's no good making that face. I know it means you're trying not to look bored. It's all very well for *you*. *You* can get out. I'm stuck forever in the same place.' Lampwick's voice took on a petulant note.

'The crypt is better than the ground.' Grimshaw closed his notebook with a snap. Any minute now he was going to start with the twitching. He could feel the charge building up inside him.

'True. True.'

Grimshaw's Architect was of average height, with brown hair and a cadaverous face, the last being due to his having died over a century ago. In life Lampwick had been full-cheeked and irritatingly rosy, and it had always annoyed him that he didn't look like the magician he pretended to be. His only satisfaction in half-death was that he had finally achieved a suitably gaunt look. Unfortunately, no one but Grimshaw was there to see it.

Lampwick folded his arms across the magician's robe he had been buried in, as per the instructions in his Last Will and Testament, scribbled in haste on the back of an arrest warrant seconds before he died. The robe was made of the best deep blue velvet and embroidered all over with stars and moons. The half-dead were technically non-physical in a substantial sort of way, like solid ghosts, but the human view of how things ought to be had a large impact on the way they looked. This meant that over the decades the non-physical embroidery on Lampwick's non-physical robe had begun to take on a frayed look. Most of the nap had worn off the velvet, leaving it threadbare in places.

'But the point I was making,' the Architect continued, 'had you been bright enough to follow me, is that *you* can get back *there* whenever you want. I can't. I have to stay in Grey Space!'

'Not whenever I want. Only when I have a Litany. When they're all done, I'll have to stay here with you. Like before.' The feeling of electricity under his skin was getting worse and worse and Grimshaw couldn't stop it. He yelped, as an all-over-body twitch got him so badly that he dropped his notebook and had to scrabble to pick it up.

Lampwick sighed. 'Why I couldn't have created a curse with more . . . more pizzazz, I don't know.'

'Because you aren't a magician. You're just a common thief who pretends to be a magician.'

'Someone I could have had a discussion with . . .'

'Curse demons don't do discussions, they do curses.'

'And that twitch is getting worse.'

'No, it's not!'

'Something with intelligence . . .'

'I'm as clever as you are,' snapped Grimshaw, flattening his ears and flicking his tail indignantly. 'Cleverer!'

'. . . and style.'

Grimshaw shut up. He could claim to be bright, but he certainly couldn't put his hand up to style. Now Tun, he had style. Even more than the Mighty Curse, who was just the most powerful curse demon ever made. Grimshaw flipped his ears thoughtfully. On reflection, maybe the Mighty Curse won on that point too – the total annihilation of all living things did have a certain flair.

'Anyway, tell me about the knives again. I liked that. Tell me about how they looked falling through the sky, all bright in the sun. And about how whatsisname . . .'

'Jon Figg.'

'. . . was right underneath. Tell me about the blood spurting all over the pavement and the bits—'

'They weren't knives; they were saws, electric saws.'

'Oh, electric.' Lampwick waved a hand airily. 'That silly modern invention you're always going on about. We had gas in my day, that was good enough for us. Nothing like the atmosphere of a couple of turned-down gaslights. Or candles! I suppose they've forgotten about candles . . .'

Grimshaw listened while Lampwick rambled on. He had heard it all before. Having spent over a century in his Architect's company, there was nothing that Lampwick could say that was new to Grimshaw.

Back in the days when he was alive, Lampwick had pretended to be a master magician who could see into the future. Even real master magicians couldn't do that because no human being could see into the future, they just weren't built that way. But Lampwick used a crystal ball and some clever lighting to make more than one rich woman believe him. His best trick was to 'foresee' his poor victim's death, but claim that he couldn't quite make out the details of how it happened. The victims then paid Lampwick a lot of money to keep trying because they wanted to be able to avoid it when the time came. He wasn't called Lampwick the Robber for nothing.

'The funniest was young Mrs Carroll. Her husband kept a tight rein on the money so she had to find other ways to pay. Did I ever tell you . . .'

'Yes.'

'. . . about the things she could do with a couple of carrots and a boiled potato?'

'Definitely.'

'Wonderful cook she was. I remember the time . . .'

Grimshaw flicked his ears as the sense reached him that Mrs Jones and the weird boy had stopped moving. He had been going to leave it until morning to take the next step, but that would mean hanging around with Lampwick all night. An idea occurred to him and he almost chuckled out loud.

'Got to stop you there,' he said quickly, holding up a claw tipped paw.

Lampwick glared at him. 'I was telling you about—'

'I gotta go. Mrs Jones has stopped running . . .'

'I do wish I could do something about that twitch.'

'. . . so I can go and do the weird boy.'

'Ahh, yes. You never did tell me what makes him so odd.'

'He hardly ever says anything.' Now Grimshaw came to think about it, that seemed like a really good character trait. He paused for a moment, trying to find the right words to express the boy's oddness. It was as if he was somehow more linked in to what was going on around him. Take the way he had shouted a warning to Jon Figg *almost before the chain of events had begun.* As if he had sensed or seen something . . . Grimshaw hunched his shoulders and gave up.

'And he's kind of small with thick white hair and hazel eyes,' he said instead.

'Hmm. Odd colouring, certainly.'

'And he's called Fish.'

'Fish?'

'Yes! Fish. That swim in the sea.'

'Oh! Fish! That's a funny name. Why do they call him that? Is it his real one?'

Grimshaw shrugged. Frankly, he didn't care. The

boy was just a name on his Litany. Unlike his mother, who had turned out to be quite interesting, with her admirable behaviour in the face of disaster.

'Quite a little character! It's almost a shame . . . Oh well, the woman disturbed me . . .'

'Good thing too! You were bored silly.' Grimshaw wrinkled up his nose disdainfully. 'Anyway, I gotta go.'

Lampwick scowled. 'You can retell it all when you get back then. There'll be plenty of time.'

'You said it,' muttered Grimshaw. He twiddled the hands of his watch, hoping that Lampwick wouldn't see what he was doing and cotton on to the fact that Grimshaw wasn't going to leave Limbo just yet.

The only way for a curse demon Avatar to get into Limbo from Real Space was to set all the dials on his chronometer to zero and return to his Architect. In a way, Lampwick was Grimshaw's gateway into the grey world. But once he had crossed over, he could travel around Limbo by setting the geography hands to a place and leaving all the other hands on zero.

Mrs Jones had stopped running, which meant that Grimshaw could go and do the boy. But Lampwick wasn't to know that Grimshaw wasn't going to do the boy *right now*. Instead, Grimshaw was going to visit his friend Tun. He wanted to tell Tun all about the wonderful moment of BOOM! and how it had made him feel.

So he pressed the send button and disappeared from the crypt.

76

10

HORSEMEN

Tun was rarely with his Architect these days. This was because his Architect thought that Tun was creepy and said that he would rather be on his own than be stared at by a mad bathrobe who'd make Death look like Santa Claus. Secretly, Grimshaw thought the description was a good one.

As a result, Tun had a habit of roving around Limbo more than curse demons usually did. This meant that it could take Grimshaw a little while to find him, and sometimes he failed to track his friend down at all. To his dismay, this was turning out to be one of those occasions. When he had nearly exhausted all the usual places, he tried the Lock-Out Club in London, Limbo. Tun didn't often go to the Lock-Out Club because he wasn't very keen on company, but it was worth a try.

Heads swivelled in his direction as Grimshaw popped into existence in the middle of a group of second-rate demons who were hanging out in the club lounge. If there had been any conversation, it died on the spot.

'It's that odd little creature again,' said one in a voice like broken glass. 'The one that's always in the books.'

Books in Grey Space might look dull on their outsides, but even Limbo couldn't control their insides, which had a half-life all of their own. The Lock-Out had a library, which was one of the reasons that Grimshaw liked the club best of all the curse demons' meeting places. Well, the only reason really. The Lock-Out Club chairs were like slippery rocks, having left all their squashy comfort back in Real Space, and there was never a fire in the fireplace because fire didn't work in Limbo. But the library, though small, was chock-full of adventure stories, and Grimshaw had experienced all of them at least twice.

Grimshaw sent a quick glance around the room, looking for Tun. It was always easy to pick him out because, although the Avatars who hung out in the club tended to be the sort with dark robes, cowled faces and a stare that could turn hot coals into ice cubes, Tun was bigger and more terrifying than any of them.

'Hmm,' said another, with a voice like hissing snakes, 'let's take him into the library. We could throw him into an encyclopaedia and see if his head explodes!'

Under the combined gaze of five Avatars, Grimshaw swallowed nervously.

'You've already done that,' he said. 'You know it does.'

As the demons began to drift towards him in a menacing kind of way, he spun the dials on his chronometer and hit send. Clearly, Tun wasn't at the Lock-Out Club, which left only one place to look. The Limbo desert.

Tun hardly ever went to the desert, because he didn't get on with Hanhut, the leader of the Ancient Egyptian Avatars, who usually hung out there. At least, a lot of them actually lived in the Limbo version of the British Museum, where all the Architects had been moved to as exhibits. But it was so crowded in there these days that most of the Architects took it in turns to banish their Avatars to the desert so as to make a little space.

Many of the Ancient Egyptian demons were mere second-raters, but Hanhut was the Avatar of a first-rate curse and every bit as famous as Tun. He had been created for an Ancient Egyptian queen with the impressive words 'Death shall come on swift wings to him that toucheth the exalted one'. As a result, Hanhut was a study in terror, tall, jackal-headed, with massive wings and eyes that struck fear into any heart. Including Grimshaw's.

When Grimshaw landed with a thunk on the sand that was sand-coloured but with a kind of grey quality about it, Hanhut turned his fearsome head and stared. Some of the other Ancient Egyptian curse demons were there too, sitting amid the dunes that rose against the grey sky like blocks of powdery concrete. In the distance Grimshaw could see the pyramids, their grey, triangular shapes jutting against the grey sky.

'It's that odd little creature again,' said Hanhut in his low voice that seemed to have a lot of snarl in it. He knew Grimshaw's name perfectly well, but pretended not to because he thought he was too important to address a third-rater by name.

Three over-tall figures in slightly unravelled bandages turned to peer at Grimshaw with the dark holes that served them for eyes. For some reason, second-rate Ancient Egyptian Avatars often came out looking like old horror-movie versions of revenge-crazed mummies.

'The third-raters are all odd,' said one in a bored voice.

'Some are odder than others, though,' said another. 'Have you seen that weird one like a lopsided pig?'

'His name is Wimble,' muttered Grimshaw, a little crossly. If the Mighty Curse was top of the curse-demon tree, then Wimble was the bottom – so lowly that even a demon of Grimshaw's standing could look down on him. Grimshaw was so relieved it wasn't him at the bottom, that he tried to stand up for Wimble whenever he could.

Hanhut took a step forward and put on a reassuring look that nearly made Grimshaw throw up with fright.

'Tell me, O cat creature with no fur, how does it feel to be so . . . mediocre?'

Grimshaw didn't know what mediocre meant, but he could take a pretty good guess. He flipped his ears and swished his tail, making ripples in the sand.

'Um . . . kind of . . . depressing.'

Hanhut nodded his jackal's head and ruffled his wings in a sympathetic way that made Grimshaw think he was about to be ripped apart. He swallowed hard, but managed to say, 'What does it feel like to be so . . . amazing?'

The other demons burst into laughter that sounded like somebody choking horribly to death.

Hanhut raised a hand and they fell silent. 'No, no. I will answer. Let the creature hear me.' He took another step forward.

Grimshaw shuffled back, getting slightly caught up in his tail. The other demons had stirred jerkily into life and were moving in different directions. Grimshaw had a nasty feeling they were positioning themselves around him. It didn't bode well. He twitched, then flattened his ears nervously and crouched a little closer to the sand.

His eyes glowing like yellow fires, Hanhut stepped closer. He raised a hand heavy with shining claws and reached out slowly towards the cowering Grimshaw.

'Now, let's see. How does it feel to plunge your hand into a man's body and pull out his entrails? To see the life go out in his eyes and know you have ended all that he was and all that he might have been? To fly on wings of flame and see men pale and sink to their knees before you?' Hanhut shook his head thoughtfully. Then he bared his long teeth in a smile that was more snarl. 'It feels . . . POWERFUL. That's how it feels.'

Hanhut smiled. Grimshaw wished he hadn't.

'But if such a lowly creature as you,' Hanhut continued, 'can never know how it feels to wield great power, I can at least show you how it feels to be . . . *the victim.*'

Grimshaw gulped as the others closed in. He could feel them looking down their bandaged noses at him. Now he was keeping one eye on Hanhut and one on a darkening of the sky over to the right. There was only one thing in Limbo that could spread shadows in that way. The Horsemen. Hanhut and his friends hadn't noticed yet because they were all focused on Grimshaw.

'I was just . . . erm . . . looking for Tun,' Grimshaw gasped, 'but he's not here so . . .'

Quickly, he spun dials at random and reached for the send button. He didn't care where the chronometer was set for, pretty much anywhere in Limbo had to be better than the desert right now. Grimshaw had never met the Horsemen and didn't want to. One look at their terrible shapes moving across Limbo, surrounded by darkness and the sound of screaming, was enough to tell him all he wanted to know.

'No, you don't!' A heavily bandaged hand took hold of Grimshaw's arm and plucked him from the ground, dangling him in mid-air so that he couldn't reach his chronometer without dislocating something.

'Look!' said Grimshaw urgently. With his free hand, he pointed at the Horsemen heading towards them. In Real Space their arrival would blot out the light, casting shadow across the land. But in Grey Space the light just stayed, well, grey.

'You won't catch us like that!' Hanhut didn't even

turn his head to follow Grimshaw's pointing finger, he just laughed. It sounded like the baying of a terrible hound. The other Avatars joined in, making a hideous clamour that hid the distant sounds of the approaching Horsemen.

The darkness arrowed down, swooping out of the sky. It was close enough now for Grimshaw to make out the huge shapes of the four Horsemen within it, wielding great fiery swords and clad in chain mail over bloody rags. He could see the night-black gloss of the horses too, their eyes full of flames and their lips rolled back to show teeth like tombstones.

Grimshaw shut his eyes and whimpered.

'Look, he knows what's going to happen to him,' sniggered the most unravelled-looking Avatar in a voice thick with the dust of death.

'Yes,' mumbled Grimshaw, 'but I don't think *you* do!'

As he spoke, Hanhut turned his head, hearing at last the sound of tortured screams that followed the Horsemen wherever they went. He gave a hoarse cry of rage and fear. The others caught on and tattered hands everywhere flew to dig out their chronometers.

They were too late. The Horsemen were upon them, flooding the air with the stench of blood and hot steel. It filled Grimshaw's nostrils, making him gag and splutter. Now, hooves were thundering on the desert sand and Grimshaw could feel the power of the horses' huge bodies as they surrounded the Avatars.

Still in the grip of Hanhut's crony, Grimshaw fought hard, desperate to break free. But he felt the sharp pull and the whoosh of air as the lead Horseman bent down, scooping up his Ancient Egyptian prey by its bandages and Grimshaw along with it. There was a moment of jerking chaos and noise as they dangled by the horse's side and Grimshaw caught a jumbled glimpse of a night-black flank, a steel-clad leg and some unravelling bandages. Suddenly the thundering grew less as the horses left the ground, their hooves now pounding on air rather than solid sand. The jolting eased too as they rose higher and higher into the sky.

There was a horrible scream from over his head and a lurch and the grip on his arm let go as Hanhut's struggling crony was hauled up and flung over the horse's back. Unnerved by the sudden release, Grimshaw made an instinctive grab and got hold of something firm, silky and horribly hot. A huge fiery eye rolled to look at him – he was wrapped around the horse's head!

With a horrified shriek, Grimshaw let go again. Feeling the wind and the chaos whirl around him, he shut his eyes, knowing it would be a long way down. But he'd be free too, which was the main thing. And then, just as he began to fall in earnest, a blackened fist closed around his backpack and held on. Now Grimshaw really screamed. The Horseman had got him!

Almost faint with terror, Grimshaw felt his captor lift him by the backpack and turn him. He caught a terrifying glimpse of the Horsemen flanking his and shut his eyes. He braced himself, waiting for the limb-rending to begin.

Hmm, said a voice heavy with the sound of grating steel, *did we mean to bring you along?*

Grimshaw knew that the Horsemen were angel Avatars, but anything less angelic than that voice he couldn't imagine. They were levelling out and speeding up now, the wind whipping about them, the air filled with the horrible screaming of the other demons as they pleaded for mercy. But Grimshaw could hear the voice perfectly, as if it didn't need to go through his ears to get into his head.

Daring to open his eyes again, he saw that he was dangling eyeball to horrible eyeball with his captor. He could see its skull face, barely covered with blackened flesh and with holes for eyes that glowed like furnaces. Flames flickered over its whole body, burning even in the gale that howled around them.

The furnaces were looking at Grimshaw with curiosity.

Answer, said the Horseman. He shook Grimshaw and then set him down carefully, placing him between the horse's ears.

Grimshaw grabbed hold of a chunk of mane, wrapping his tail around the horse's neck for added safety. Even in the air, the galloping motion was enough to make his whole body bounce with every swift stride. 'I'm an . . . an accident!' he stuttered, seeing an opportunity. He stared earnestly into the Horseman's glowing eyes. 'I was j-just looking for T-Tun. You know? The Curse of the H-House of Ombre?' He had to shout above all the wind and screaming, and what with the galloping motion his voice came out in bursts. He bit his tongue twice and tasted blood.

Indeed we do. And you? You are rather a small curse, aren't you?

'G-Grimshaw, Curse of Lampwick the Robber. Very unimportant. M-my Architect is a stupid thief. No class.'

Grimshaw was trying hard not to see what was happening to his fellow demons, though he could make out Hanhut in the background, shrieking wildly as one of the Horsemen turned his insides into his outsides piece by piece. Grimshaw's Horseman seemed to have forgotten the Egyptian demon slung carelessly in front of him, still struggling wildly as it tried to pull itself off the horse. It wasn't going to succeed as the Horseman had one hand placed firmly in the small of its back. Grimshaw was ready to bet it was a grip of iron.

'And you?' asked Grimshaw politely. 'Do you have a name?' This time he didn't shout and though his voice was lost in the gale, the Horseman heard him anyway. Grimshaw was picking up the horse's rhythm by now, enough to ease up a little on his tight grip.

King One.

'And your . . . er . . . brothers?'

We are all One, said King One. He chuckled and leaned closer to Grimshaw. Suddenly, the chaos and the darkness around them seemed to thicken, the

86

screams to become even more desperate, the stink of blood stronger. *Think of us as a single entity with as many bodies as we need.*

'That m-must be very . . . c-complicated,' gulped Grimshaw, through a fit of the shakes.

King One straightened up and the chaos settled back to its normal level of dreadfulness. *Not at all, once you get used to it. Now, what shall I do with you, eh? We don't normally deal with third-raters.*

Grimshaw felt a rush of hope. 'You're n-not going to rend me limb from limb, then?'

I won't, no. By rights, it is the job of the Sisters of Gladness to wake the small demons. We Horsemen ride the worlds seeking out the powerful ones, like the jackal-headed Avatar and his friends. Only the Mighty Curse, that lies buried deep and sleeping, is beyond our reach. It is the greatest of all curse demons, you know, created by the great wizard of the Clouded Land.

Grimshaw nodded.

But when we find demons that belong to us, we do unto them as they do unto others. It's supposed to make them think. Pain and suffering, the only means they understand, all to try and wake them up. King One sighed, making Grimshaw almost faint with fright at the sound of it. *A thankless task it is too, I might add!*

The cries of the Ancient Egyptians were hoarser now, as if their owners didn't have much left in them to scream with. Grimshaw tried even harder not to see their twisted, howling faces and the unravelled bandages and strings of innards flying in the wind like banners.

'But I think we're already awake,' mumbled Grimshaw nervously. He peered up into the staring furnaces that seemed to be growing hotter.

NO, said the Horseman, *you are not awake. You do not see.*

'See what?'

King One chuckled. A finger, blackened and raw, shook itself under Grimshaw's nose.

Oh no, we angel Avatars can only point the way. In the end you must work it out for yourself. Here we are.

'Where?' Grimshaw looked around wildly, then wished he hadn't.

I thought you wanted to find your friend? He is here, in the place where only he goes. It makes him feel powerful again. It's a shame he never looks beyond.

The Horseman whirled Grimshaw around his head and then let go. Flying through the air, the demon howled as he burst out of the darkness that surrounded the Horsemen into the grey Limbo nothing-light. He got a feeling of great emptiness and height, which rapidly turned to one of plummeting and pain as he hit the rocky ground and skidded several yards to end up at the feet of Tun.

11

BEYOND

'Hello,' said Grimshaw. He picked himself up and shook off the dust, then took a look around. As far as he could see, he was on the top of a mountain. Not just any old mountain either – this one was easily the highest in the world.

Tun ignored him. This didn't bother Grimshaw at all because, unlike all the other demon Avatars, Tun didn't just ignore Grimshaw, he ignored everybody.

'The Horsemen dropped me off. Wasn't that nice of them?' Grimshaw went on cheerfully.

Tun stopped staring over Limbo world spread out far, far below and turned to stare at Grimshaw instead. It wasn't a comfortable experience, and even though he was Tun's friend, Grimshaw couldn't help edging away.

One of the most impressive curse demons to look at, Tun stood nine foot tall and was robed entirely in a midnight black that was so dark it was almost not there. Only his pale, skeletal hands showed, and a hint of terrible eyes peering out from the depths of the cowl

89

that covered his head and drooped right down over his face (if he had one). The midnight robe was girdled by an age-blackened silver chain, each link shaped like a skull; and if all that wasn't enough, the demon's gaze was something that a Sufferer felt rather than saw. It pierced right through the heart.

Remembering Hanhut's screams, it dawned on Grimshaw that, as a more important demon, Tun's experience of the Horsemen was probably not a pleasant one. He flattened his ears anxiously.

'I had a very good day today,' he hurried on, by way of changing the subject. 'I blew up a house! BOOM! It was great!'

Tun went back to staring out over Grey Space from the edge of the precipice, his tall, night-black shape towering against the bleak sky. His silence didn't mean he wasn't listening, so Grimshaw went ahead and told him all about Marsha, doing sound effects and actions as well. He had played it down when telling Lampwick, because he hadn't wanted to share that wonderful moment of BOOM! with someone he didn't like. But he admired Tun, so he told Tun everything.

When he had finished, Grimshaw settled down to wait for Tun to answer. Although in Real Space it was so early in the morning that it would still be dark, in Limbo the light never got to be anything more or less than grey, like the light on a Real Space rainy day. This meant that Grimshaw could see the mountain laid out all around him. It was bare. In every direction was the same grey rock, some parts just higher or lower than others, receding into the distance where it was barely distinguishable from the sky. The only difference was on Grimshaw's left, where there was a cliff.

Grimshaw scratched an ear. He peered over the edge of the precipice to the dizzying drop below. It went down a lot. Then it went down some more. Then it went on going down until it met a shelf of rock that stuck out a little. After that it just got going again in a downwardly way, only this time it kept at it.

To be honest, Grimshaw didn't see the point. He certainly didn't understand the Horseman's comment about the mountain making Tun feel powerful again. Surely Tun was powerful enough already, without needing to see the world laid out at his feet in this way?

Not that you could see much of anything so high up – there was no view as such, unless you counted downwards as scenery. This being Limbo, there weren't even any clouds to look at. Grimshaw looked up to see if there was anything overhead. There wasn't. The grey Limbo sky just sat there.

Grimshaw yawned and scratched his ear again. It occurred to him to wonder what the mountain would be like in Real Space. He wondered what the Horseman had meant when he said it was a pity that Tun never looked beyond. Beyond what?

Tun stirred. Slowly, he raised and spread his arms and began to laugh. With his arms outstretched, the midnight robe that draped them resembled the wings of something vast and bat-like.

'Yes! BOOOOM!!' Unlike Grimshaw's annoyingly soft voice, Tun's was as clear and deep as a bell. The sort of bell that rings out when someone has died. 'Humanity seared and shrivelled before the terrible might of FIRE!'

'I . . . s'pose,' mumbled Grimshaw.

'Running, screaming, begging, pleading . . .' Tun bowed his hooded face and folded his arms again. He stood, silent and brooding. 'You did well, small one.'

'There wasn't any of that. The running and the screaming, I mean.'

'How many did you kill?'

'Just the one.' Grimshaw looked puzzled. 'The next one on the list.'

Tun's terrible eyes settled on Grimshaw again.

'Nobody else? You created an explosion and only killed ONE person?'

Grimshaw nodded, flattening his ears to his skull. He swished his tail in embarrassment, though he didn't know what it was that he had to be embarrassed about.

'What a waste of BOOM!' Tun sighed, then went back to staring at the grey swathe of rock and land far below. 'Still, it was better than sheep. And I have to say, the knives were interesting. I do like a good showing of blood. You'll have to tell me all about that one too.'

'But . . .' said Grimshaw anxiously, going back to the explosion, 'I couldn't kill all of my Litany, could I? That wouldn't be proper. You have to do them one at a time. It's more . . . ominous.'

'Of course! You pick them off one by one, that's traditional. But you don't only have to kill the humans in your Litany. You can kill other ones too, you know. Innocent Bystanders, I think they're called. Take out as many Innocent Bystanders as you like. Especially with a good BOOM. That's what it's for. Cataclysm. Catastrophe. Devastation. You can't have cataclysm with one death! I once used pestilence for a Sufferer – well, a whole branch of the family actually – and took out hundreds besides! Their precious city was a morgue by the time I finished.'

Grimshaw looked crestfallen.

'You were on the right track, though,' added Tun kindly.

'I didn't know you could do that.'

'Of course you can! That's what humans are all about. Blood, screaming, insanity, horrible death. That's why they are made so fragile, so easily broken. So . . . so . . . deliciously destructible.'

For the umpteenth time, Grimshaw wondered what it must be like to visit Death upon a Sufferer personally, not through some silly string of events. He shivered. It put BOOM in the shade all right, but the idea of personally visiting Death on someone like Susan Jones made him feel oddly churned up inside.

'I was wondering . . .' he said suddenly, even before he realised he was going to speak.

'Mmmhmm?'

'Do we have to kill everyone on the Litany? I mean, even the noble humans?' Although Grimshaw was talking about Susan Jones in particular, he thought that Jon Figg had been noble too, and Marsha's last words had earned her the phrase, 'Died with Courage!' in Grimshaw's notebook. But it was too late for them. Susan was still alive, although she wouldn't be for much longer. Soon she would see her only son die, and then there would be nothing left for Grimshaw to take but her life. In the back of his mind he was worrying about it. Somehow it seemed like a shame.

'Noble?'

'Yes, you know. Brave. Dignified in the face of calamity. That type of thing.'

Although Grimshaw couldn't see the expression on Tun's face, hidden deep within the cowl, his friend's silence conveyed only puzzled blankness.

'If we can kill humans not on the Litany, then maybe we can *not* kill humans who *are* on the Litany.'

'Don't understand you, small one.'

Grimshaw swished his tail urgently, wanting to make Tun understand, but not sure how to do it.

'You know. Choose . . .'

'Choose? We don't get to choose!' Tun's deep voice was scandalised. 'We are the Curse! We cannot decide which of our Litany is to live or die! It's death to all!'

'Sorry!'

Silence fell for a few moments. Tun stared down the

mountainside. Grimshaw watched him, fidgeting nervously, then switched his gaze elsewhere. Not for any reason other than that it was somewhere to look, he glanced up again. This time his eyes went wide with shock. He stared, trying to work out what he was seeing.

The sky in Limbo was always grey, apart from when the Horsemen were around, and nothing had changed, not really. The grey was still there. Except that suddenly Grimshaw had the feeling that he could almost *see through it*! As if, on the other side of the sky, something was shining. He knew that there was no sun in Limbo, just like there was no moon, no stars and no constellations, but he could sense a light that was like the sun only more so and without any sunburn. It was a light with warmth and gentleness, but bright too, bright enough to illuminate everything. It was the light of the brightest of days, and looking at it gave Grimshaw an ache deep inside.

'Besides, there are no noble humans,' went on Tun. 'It's a myth.'

Grimshaw dragged his eyes away from the sky and tried to focus on Tun.

'There are the powerful ones, the Architects, well, *most* of them are powerful anyway. And then there are the rest, those who are just the playthings of fate. Whose lives are as bright as the bloom of a flower and just as ephemeral.'

Grimshaw didn't know what ephemeral meant, but he got the general idea.

'Ours to pluck at will!' Tun stretched out a hand, bony fingers spread out in an open gesture, and then snapped it shut into a fist. 'Brief sparks to be snuffed out.'

He fell silent again. He sighed. It was a deep sigh, full of meaning that Grimshaw didn't understand. It puzzled him, but sometimes he got the feeling that Tun was unhappy. While he waited for Tun to say something else, he took a furtive glance upwards. It was still there, that strange brilliance on the other side of the sky. He wished he could see past the Limbo grey, see that light without anything in the way.

'What's that?'

'What?'

'That up there.' Grimshaw pointed. 'Behind the sky.' It dawned on him that this might be the Beyond that the Horseman had referred to.

Tun looked up, then peered down at Grimshaw. 'There is no up there, you foolish creature,' he said indulgently. 'This is the roof of the world. There is nothing above but sky.'

'I meant *behind* the sky.'

Tun shook his head. 'Funny little demon,' he murmured.

Grimshaw flipped his ears and gave Tun an agonised stare. It was as if Tun couldn't see what Grimshaw could see, which was a puzzle. But then, only a moment ago Grimshaw hadn't been able to see it himself. He flicked his tail to and fro, trying to work out what had changed, what he had said or done to make him suddenly able to see this hint of Beyond. They had been talking about noble humans and the possibility of choice, but surely that couldn't have anything to do with it?

Tun had turned away, his gaze roaming thoughtfully over the grey world of cloud and rock at his feet.

'Did I ever tell you,' he said, 'about William Frederick Ombre, the seventeenth son of the house? Of all my Sufferers he was the only one who came close to courage. He had the makings of a first-rate Architect, but he refused to practise the Art.'

Usually, Grimshaw liked to hear stories about Tun's reign of terror, about how he had tormented, driven insane and finally wiped out a whole dynasty, persecuting them down the years until their name was spoken with hushed horror and they were shunned by their fellow men. So he settled down to listen, while Tun cleared his throat and began to speak. But somehow the story wasn't as good as usual and part of Grimshaw's mind was elsewhere, thinking about Beyond, and about the existence of noble humans too. Deep inside, he was wondering if maybe, just maybe, Tun was wrong, though he didn't know how that could possibly be.

Still, he listened until his own Sufferers had started their day and it was time for him to go back to work.

12

ONLY SKY

But before he did, he took a short detour to see what the mountain was like in Real Space and ended up in a blizzard.

Grimshaw flipped his ears thoughtfully. He knew that mountain tops were often covered in snow, but hadn't realised that it would be quite so cold or quite so wet, or even quite so deep. He floundered about for a while, then found that he was sinking rather than moving so he sat still and peered up. His teeth were chattering, but he couldn't hear the noise they made over the howling of the wind. The sound of that wind gave him the willies. It was so . . . lonely. It chilled his heart even more than the sound of Tun's death-knell voice. If he hadn't already been shaking like a leaf from the cold, he would have trembled at its constant, eerie wail.

Up above he could see more snow that was whirling about in the air rather than lying on the ground. Hurled around by the wind, no doubt. Apart from the snow, there was little to see.

Just as Grimshaw was about to give up and go, the

storm blew over. With all the whirling white gone, he saw at once that here, in Real Space, the sky was full of only sky. There didn't seem to be any Beyond. It occurred to him that perhaps Beyond existed only on the Limbo side. Still, the mountain was interesting, so to find out a little more he checked the Acts and Facts.

This was what Tun called the web of common knowledge that all of the half-dead and half-alive shared with others of their type. Grimshaw had access to the knowledge web belonging to curse demons and their Architects, but not to that belonging to any other type of Avatar. The Acts and Facts provided a combined information bank and grapevine. So, as well as entries posted by other demons, any significant deeds done were also automatically recorded and circulated. What the Acts and Facts didn't do, however, was provide any colour or atmosphere.

So, now, it told him that this particular mountain, the one that Tun liked the Grey Space version of so much, was situated in the Himalayan mountains in the country of Nepal. It also told him that the mountain was known to be the tallest in the world, rising to a height of nearly nine kilometres above sea level. This information had been provided by Conick, a second-rate Avatar who had once visited death upon a Sufferer by forcing him from his path to wander lost and terrified on the lonely mountain until he fell screaming into a glacier.

Grimshaw thought it all very interesting, but noticed

that the entry by Conick failed to convey a couple of significant details. In Grey Space everything was static. In Real Space he was surrounded by the snow-topped mountain range with its awesome cliffs and distant plateaux. Below him, the ever-changing cloud was shaped by the wind into vast cathedrals of vapour. Here the snow and the rock and the hurrying cloud made a tapestry of shadow and light, of dark-gold and white and blue and indigo that made his head spin at the sheer size and beauty of it all.

But most amazing was the sky, even without Beyond. Although Grimshaw had set his watch for morning, the sky over the mountain was a strangely thrilling dark blue. He was truly sitting on the top of the world. It gave him a sort of buoyant feeling that was also bright, like he had a balloon of light in his middle. In Real Space, the mountain was beautiful.

Even so, Grimshaw felt it was time to go. He was turning blue and was so numb he could hardly feel his limbs. Floundering about, it took him a moment to realise that the snow had began to move around him, gathering pace as it slid towards the sheer face of the precipice. And over it.

Because there was so much down to fall through, he had plenty of time to admire the cloud-wreathed cliffs of brilliant ice, before he felt the need to reset his watch and move somewhere a little safer.

✤

Having zapped back to the gentle English countryside and taken a few moments to recover from his trip to the mountain, Grimshaw's next task was finding a way to polish off the weird boy. In his notebook, under the heading 'Sufferer 4: Susan Jones. The Woman Who Knocked', the list of things and people that he had to take away from her to cause her pain were all ticked through. Except one. Her son.

Using Mrs Minchin's *How to Be a Dutiful Housewife* to search for hints usually gave ideas that were in tune with Grimshaw's frame of mind. The falling sheep, for example, had been suggested when he was feeling rather frivolous. Now, with his head still full of sky and high places, Mrs Minchin gave him an idea that was astonishing in its unexpectedness and impact. Especially impact!

It was so brilliant that Grimshaw couldn't help laughing out loud. Then he packed away Mrs Minchin and went to look for a good place to hide his backpack.

It was time to kill Fish Jones.

❦

'We don't have Jon's map,' said Susan flatly. The sun was just coming up over the horizon, lighting up a clear sky with a few golden clouds scattered across its pale blue. Although they had stopped to sleep for a while in the car, they had been awake again and driving since dawn. Now, Susan had left the main roads and had parked the car in a small town while they took stock and maybe got some breakfast.

Fish sighed. The map was in the van that Marsha had been loading up. The one that had been parked outside the house and was currently a knot of mangled metal.

He dug in his pocket and found his dog-eared memo pad and a pencil. Turning to a blank page he wrote: 'Crow's Cottage, near Bone Mill, Yorkshire'. Then he began to draw, adding in the landmarks Jon had mentioned, like Menga's Tarn and the butterfly valley.

Susan glanced at him. 'You remember? All I can think of is a fallen-down water mill and a road into the moors.'

After some sleep, she sounded better, and to Fish's relief there was no trace of the shadow-snake. It had stayed gone. Instead, a faint silvery shine glistened on her skin. Susan had grown up with Marsha; they had shared their childhood and their youth. Even though they had drifted apart over the last few years, all that history still counted. Fish wondered if he had a glow of his own, but he thought that maybe, however much he cared for them and would miss them, neither Marsha nor Reg had ever been a central part of his life. At any rate he couldn't see anything, though he peered occasionally at his arms.

One thing though – he was beginning to feel very hungry.

'Anyway, let's get that breakfast,' Susan went on, as if she had read his mind. 'I could really do with a cup of tea! We'll get something to take away with us too, then we can just keep driving until we get there, OK?' She sent Fish a smile. 'We'll be all right. We've got to believe that.'

Fish nodded, sending an automatic glance over his shoulder to make sure the demon wasn't lurking in the back seat. To his relief, it still hadn't put in an appearance.

Susan gave him a worried look. 'Do you think we're being followed or something? I can see why you might, but curses aren't like that. They're not something tangible that you can see.'

Fish smiled at Susan in a way that said nothing, and then concentrated on sketching a map of the route to Jon's cottage in the heart of the fells.

When he was done, they left the car and headed into the town square. It was still early and all around them the shops and cafes were just waking up and getting ready to face the day. Together, Fish and Susan ambled slowly down the high street. Neither of them felt like hurrying, they had been on the road all night and right now they were both enjoying a moment of feeling normal.

'There,' said Susan, spotting a small cafe on the other side of the road, where a woman in a blue dress was reading the menu posted in the window. 'That's just the right place.'

And she stepped off the pavement to go and take a look.

13

JUNK

High above the Earth and clinging on to a portion of old satellite, Grimshaw went over his calculations again. Avatars had an excellent spatial sense and chronometer travel was pretty accurate, but even so, landing on a target this small and moving this fast had posed some problems. Grimshaw had spent some time pinwheeling dizzily in orbit, but on his fifth try had managed to zap to a position close enough to catch hold of the lump of space junk and pull himself on.

Grimshaw knew the Earth's orbit was filled with man-made debris ranging from nuts, bolts, gloves and other leftovers from space missions to defunct satellites and failed space probes. Some of it would fall harmlessly back to Earth, burning up in the atmosphere or landing in the vast amount of ocean that covered the globe. At the last estimate the blanket of junk wrapped around the planet totalled roughly one hundred and ten thousand objects, many zooming along at speeds of over seventeen thousand miles per hour. Grimshaw knew this, not because he had found it on the Acts and Facts, but because he had read his way through a copy of *Science Monthly* while waiting for the vicar to stop sobbing long enough to climb the church tower. He had thought the article very interesting, but now realised that it had not mentioned the sheer giddiness of all this whirling about so far above everything. Nor did it mention the general all-round amazingness of the world.

From this high up, hanging in the freezing vacuum, the sight of the Earth backed by the great void of space knocked the view from the mountaintop into a cocked hat and out the other side. To his left, one last slice of the planet was still covered by the blanket of night, but where day had cast its light the many hued greens of the forests and the golds and purple-browns of the land swam in an ocean of deep turquoise blue. The whole beautiful thing was wreathed with white clouds that swirled across its surface. It was breath-taking.

Shaking himself vigorously, Grimshaw turned his attention back to the job in hand. The particular piece of space junk that he was clinging to was due to fall to Earth any moment. When he felt the orbiting chunk graze the Earth's atmosphere, Grimshaw tensed, ready for action when the right moment arose. The piece of debris kept going on its downward course, plunging deeper into the pull of the planet. Now, instead of silence, the wind whistled in his ears as the junk fell so fast that it began to burn. He congratulated himself on having left his trousers and notebook in his backpack, hidden in a bush on the planet below. Grimshaw could survive the flames, but they wouldn't have.

The junk's death dive was magnificent. The heat became intense as he hurtled on towards the blue-green globe, which grew and grew until the swirls of colour became mountains, rivers, plains and deserts. Grimshaw would have yelled with the sheer exhilaration of it if he had had any breath left to yell with. The speed of his descent was so great that, had he breathed in, the oxygen would have ignited in his lungs, burning him to a crisp from the inside out.

And then the crucial moment arrived – the moment when Grimshaw had to act. The half-alive had substance, but not much in the way of weight. Using what little he had, Grimshaw leaned to the left, changing the junk's flight path in a small but significant way. Underneath him the metal glowed white hot, vaporising as it fell. When it hit its target it would be a fraction of its original size, but still big enough for Grimshaw's purpose.

Clouds were rushing up to meet him in cathedrals of blue-white vapour that looked almost solid. For a fleeting moment, Grimshaw felt their cool touch as the junk dived into them. Then the junk sizzled their towers, domes and twisting helter-skelters into steam as it tore through and out the other side. Grimshaw burst out into air that stung his skin with its fresh brightness. And now there was real landscape below, sea, sand, woods, fields hurtling past at a fantastic speed and all seen through a corona of fire. And then a town. The view narrowed to a high street and a boy in an overlarge T-shirt, walking along the pavement, studying something in his hand.

At this point, Grimshaw had intended to hit the send button on his chronometer and jump ship. But then something occurred to him. Something huge and terrifying.

If he stayed where he was, he would be clinging to the debris at the moment it plunged out of the sky and smashed the boy into raspberry pulp. It would be the nearest he could ever come to the sort of personal visitation of death that Tun and his like were allowed, and though he might not want to do it to noble Susan Jones, the boy was nothing more than an ordinary victim, a secondary Sufferer with nothing special about him. The thought sent shivers of panic and excitement running up and down his spine. Even if hitting the ground would hurt a little – well, a lot actually – it might just be worth the pain. His mind made up, Grimshaw hung on.

While Susan was heading over the road to investigate the cafe, Fish was working out that he had almost enough small change in his pocket to buy a couple of pastries from the bakery as a treat for them both later on. He was short by just one pence. He could ask Susan for it, but that would spoil the pleasure of producing them as a surprise, which would be a shame. And then, at just the moment he was wishing he had one penny more, he noticed a glint of shiny copper lying in the gutter. It was a bright, new one-pence piece! He frowned, puzzled, because he could have sworn that it had not been there a moment ago, that it had appeared all of a sudden. Then he shrugged, smiled and went to pick it up.

Bending to tuck his fingers around the small coin, Fish felt a scorching blast as something incredibly hot went past him. There was a terrific cracking thud and dust flew everywhere. Someone screamed. Although Fish didn't know it, the person who screamed was Susan.

It had all happened very fast. Turning to call Fish, Susan had seen the lump of junk hurtling out of the blue, heading straight for her son's head. When Fish unexpectedly bent down, the junk sailed through the empty spot where his head had been a second before and crashed, steaming, into the pavement. The impact sent fragments of hot stone flying everywhere.

One of them hit a passing car and smashed the windscreen. Out of control, the car spun in the road, hitting Susan with a glancing blow that threw her into the air like a rag doll. Her body turned a graceful arc and then slammed back to Earth with a sickening thud. The car went on, sliding in a full circle before it came to a halt, jamming itself into the back of a parked delivery van.

Fish didn't see any of this. He straightened up to stare in shock at the mess of steaming, mangled metal that had so nearly got him in the back of the head. Sprawling a little way beyond the junk was an equally steaming demon. Its skin was seared black and was still sizzling.

It shook itself dizzily, a pained look on its ugly face. It looked up.

Their gazes locked.

Fish saw the demon's evil-looking, all-black eyes widen for a moment as it realised two things. First, its prey was still alive, and second, *the human could see it!* Terror surged through Fish as he stood there, gaze to gaze with the horrible thing. The demon snarled at him, and arched its back as if it was about to spring. But it didn't attack. Instead, it reared up until its face was on a level with his.

'Run,' it sneered in a voice softer than Fish would have imagined. 'Run all you like, human. I will find you wherever you hide. And I will *GET YOU*.'

And then it vanished. And in that second, it dawned on Fish that something terrible was happening behind him.

His heart went cold as he realised that Susan wasn't there. She wasn't right beside him asking if he was all right. Turning, he saw confusion, people running and calling out and the wreckage of a car. There was a group gathered around someone lying in the road.

For a long, awful moment, Fish understood that his mother might be dead. Around him the world went grey and cold as the blood drained from his face. He struggled not to pass out and had to crouch down against the bakery wall, his head bent forward until the darkness passed.

Now the wail of sirens filled the morning. An

ambulance and two police cars glided to a halt. Uniformed men and medics scrambled out. Some ran to the woman and others to the car, where the shaken driver was trapped inside his crumpled vehicle, amazed that he was still alive. A policeman began talking into his radio.

Crouched against the wall of the bakery, Fish watched, his heart hammering and his mind in turmoil. The grey clouds had passed and now his blood sped around his body crazily, pounding in his head and making him feel hot and clammy. He wanted to run out, calling for his mother, but years of coping with a world that no one else could see had made him careful.

By now, Susan was being lifted on to a stretcher. Fish was sure that in the muddle of people nobody would pay much attention to a small boy mingling with the onlookers, so he took a deep breath, stood up and walked calmly out into the busy crowd. He pulled on the arm of one of the ambulance men, the one standing slightly back from the two handling the stretcher. The man looked round, then down. Fish could see himself reflected in tiny detail in the man's eyes. Just a kid with white-blond hair and eyes the colour of hazelnuts, drowning in a T-shirt far too big for him.

'Is the lady going to be OK?' he asked.

The ambulance man smiled. 'I reckon so, kid. She needs some care and attention right now, so we're taking her to the hospital at Blackheath, but my guess is she'll be fine.'

Fish nodded, as relief rushed through him in a tidal wave. His mother was going to be all right.

'Did you see anything?' asked the ambulance man. There was a shout and he looked away for a moment. When he looked back Fish had disappeared.

14

EXTRA-SPECIAL VISION

Perched on top of the cafe, Grimshaw flipped his tail irritably as feelings of confusion and anger fought for possession inside him. Not a single one of the possible futures that he had seen when arranging the Junk Event had shown the boy bending down to pick up a coin.

In doing so, the boy had set off a chain of events that had led to Susan Jones diving across the road to be mown down by a car! It was fortunate that the car had only caught her a broadside blow instead of hitting her head-on. Otherwise Grimshaw would have killed his main target before he had finished the loved ones! The thought made him go hot and cold all over.

And then there was the issue of the boy himself. It was incredible, but Fish Jones was clearly gifted with extra-special vision. He had seen Grimshaw plain as day, there was no doubt about that. Grimshaw wondered briefly if it was the extra-special vision that had caused Fish Jones to survive, but dismissed the idea. Extra-special vision was not responsible for the sudden appearance of a coin where no coin had been before.

He sat for a while, turning it all over in his mind, but could come up with nothing to explain what had happened. The only possible answer was that he had missed a potential future, overlooked it somehow. It didn't seem very likely, but what else could it be? He groaned wearily. He was never going to hear the end of this one.

'GET YOUR SCRAWNY RUMP BACK HERE AT ONCE!' screamed the voice of Lampwick in his head, right on cue. 'I WANT A REPORT, AND IT HAD BETTER BE GOOD!'

Grimshaw closed his eyes briefly, but there was no point trying to resist. Already, he could feel the command taking hold, making him shiver and twitch all over. He could fight it for a short while, but sooner rather than later the compulsion to obey would win out. So he gave in, turned his chronometer to zero and went back to Limbo.

❈

Leaving the ambulance man to get back to work, Fish had slipped away down a quiet side road. He kept looking around for the demon, but it had gone. He didn't know what he would have done if he had seen it. He wanted to scream at it, hurt it, damage it somehow as revenge for all it had done, but he knew those feelings were pointless. The creature wasn't made of flesh, nor could he make it suffer remorse. He was powerless to do anything but run.

As he stumbled on, shaking with fear and rage, he tried to think about what to do next. He knew that the accident had been meant for him, that the demon killed off the main target's loved ones first and then dealt with the main target. As long as Fish was alive, Susan would be safe, because the creature wouldn't attack her until she had suffered enough. Until she had seen her only child die.

At the thought, Fish clenched his fists, his nails digging hard into his palms. He couldn't let it happen. He *wouldn't* let it happen. Somehow he had to find a way to stay alive.

Fish had always looked after his mother, which was interesting because *she* thought that she always looked after *him*. But Susan couldn't see the creatures that Fish saw, and so there were some things that only he could do. And right now, even though he desperately wanted to be with her, he knew that the best way he could look after her was to keep out of the way of the demon. If he couldn't do that, then they were both dead. So his only real option was to keep going until he reached Crow's Cottage. The creature would find him there eventually, but he hoped that out in the wilds he would spot it coming. And with no scaffolding, electric saws, cars or any other number of lethal everyday things around, its options for a murder weapon would be limited.

With a new determination, Fish took stock. He had the clothes he stood up in, a pound coin and a few ten pences and coppers, and the map he had drawn of Crow's

Cottage. Feeling in his back pocket, he also found a fold-out road map that Susan had bought earlier. He wished he had thought to pull on his jumper before they left the car. It was warm enough now, but if it rained, or he had to spend the night in the open, he would miss it.

Turning a corner, he found a quiet road leading to a field. On the other side of the field he found a gap in the surrounding hedge and struggled through to another road, which he crossed. Then there were more fields, layered one after the other to the horizon. Shading his eyes against the early-morning sun, he thought he could see another small town nestling in the middle of the fields, so he headed for that.

After he had been running, then jogging, then walking for a while, Fish began to feel calmer. Although he couldn't stop thinking about Susan, his stomach began to tell him that he was hungry. He was angry with it because it had no right to go on behaving as if nothing had happened, but it rumbled at him all the same.

He had reached the next town by now and there were plenty of cafes on the high street advertising breakfast, but that would be too painful because eating breakfast in a cafe was where he should have been with Susan. Anyway, he had very little money and there were other things he needed more than food.

So Fish ignored his stomach and bought a postcard, a stamp and a phone call instead.

The phone call was to Jed. It was no use ringing Alice, because her mother had an answering machine and the chances of actually getting Alice to pick up were too slim to risk. So instead Fish gave Jed precise instructions.

'Go to Alice as soon as you can and repeat everything I tell you.'

'Uh huh. I can go now if you like.'

'As soon as we've finished talking.'

'Righto! What do you want me to tell her? Hey! They knocked your house down! I saw it! It looks awful, Fish. Are you all right? Were you in it?'

Fish shook his head out of habit, then remembered that he was on the telephone and had to speak.

'No, Jed. I'm all right. Tell Alice I need her to post me as much money as she can manage . . .'

'OK.'

'Jed!'

'Yeah? I was going now . . .'

'You need the address to send it to.'

'Uh huh. What's that then?'

'Have you got a pen and a piece of paper?'

'No.'

'Get some and come back to the phone, but be quick.'

There was a rattle and a clunk. Fish had a horrible thought that Jed had hung up and cut him off, but then he heard Jed asking his mother for a pen. In his mind's eye he could see his friend, still surrounded by that childish glow that most kids his age had already lost. A moment later Jed was back.

'I've got a pen and a page of Mum's notebook!'

'Write this down.' Fish spelled out the address, including spaces and commas, very slowly. He could hear Jed breathing hard as he wrote it down in his big, odd printing.

'Now take it to Alice.'

'Uh huh.' The phone clanked down and Fish was left listening to the empty wire, something he always hated. It never failed to give him the creeps.

'*Hello, little boy,*' whispered nobody. '*Stay and talk to me.*'

Fish hung up fast.

❈

'Well, I'm not surprised it didn't work!' Lampwick was saying for the umpteenth time. 'You tried to brain him by dropping a . . . a . . . lump of old junk on him! It's no wonder you missed . . .'

'It was a *piece of satellite* and it fell from the sky. Why don't you *listen* properly. The point is that the futures went wrong . . .'

'You missed one, you mean! You'll end up as bad as Wimble.'

'. . . and he's got *extra-special vision!*' Grimshaw looked hopeful. 'That might mean something.'

'So what? The boy's a freak of nature – it's got nothing to do with the futures. No curse demon with an ounce of gumption would let a silly little thing like that throw him. And why can't you STOP TWITCHING?'

'Because I was made by YOU!' snarled Grimshaw,

twitching so hard he had to scrabble to keep his perch on top of the tomb opposite Lampwick's coffin. 'And it didn't *throw me*, it's just *interesting*!'

Lampwick threw up his hands. 'Useless! Useless! A curse that can't even bash someone on the head! What happened to mysterious fevers, hearts exploding in the victim's chest, people torn limb from . . .'

'That's enough! I've had enough! You make a third-rate Avatar and demand first-rate delivery! And it was a *satellite* from *space*. It was a brilliant plan . . .'

'Pah!'

'. . . given the dumb *Rules* I have to put up with.'

'But your precious plan came to nothing, didn't it?' sneered Lampwick. 'Not so brilliant now, eh!'

Grimshaw screamed at Lampwick, lashing his tail furiously. By now, the twitching was so bad that every other moment he flipped several inches into the air. When the next spasm catapulted him off the tomb, he sprang to his feet and stomped off, heading for the worn stone stairway out of the crypt. Lampwick hopped down from the coffin and started after Grimshaw. Because Grimshaw wasn't used to walking anywhere – he normally travelled by chronometer – and because his legs were bent like those of a cat rather than straight like a human's, he tended to use his paws to help him get along. And Lampwick always lurched about like a zombie anyway.

'Making you was a waste of my breath, you pathetic little half-life!'

'If you were a real magician instead of a dumb thief, I might have been an Avatar to reckon with.' Grimshaw lolloped up the stairs, with Lampwick staggering at his heels so close that he trod on the curse demon's tail.

Grimshaw hissed over his shoulder, flattening his ears back against his head. Lampwick would have stayed firmly where he was, deliberately crushing Grimshaw's tail to pulp, but he couldn't keep his balance and pitched sideways, staggering into the wall. Grimshaw whipped his tail free and set off again. Lampwick righted himself and followed.

'You wouldn't know how to be a curse worth having! Space junk! Falling sheep! It's ludicrous.'

'And you're a fake with nothing but a few dumb tricks to your name. You . . . You CONJURER!'

Lampwick howled with rage.

Grimshaw reached the top of the stairs and bounded through the wooden door into the main body of the church. Lampwick tried to follow him. There was a screech as the robber's invisible tether kicked in. He howled again, teetering for a moment on the edge of the stairwell, then lost his balance again. This time he fell, tumbling head over heels all the way back down.

Grimshaw stood, listening happily to the howls of fury echo up the stairwell as his Architect ricocheted from one wall to another. When it was over, the demon grinned smugly and headed off down the nave of the church towards the main door. He pushed it open, using both paws to grip the massive handle, and then he was outside. The fight with Lampwick had vented his rage and had left him feeling keyed up and restless, but not angry. The twitches were beginning to let up too.

He was ready to bet that Lampwick would be too battered – and too sick of his demon anyway – to summon him back. So, halfway down the path, Grimshaw paused, wondering what to do. He didn't feel like having another go at killing the boy just yet; his failure with the space junk had made him wary. Although overlooking a possible future was the logical explanation, Grimshaw didn't want to believe that he had made such a stupid mistake.

Quickly, he searched the Acts and Facts, but came up with nothing else that might explain the unexpected survival of a Sufferer. Missed futures had happened to other demons, but usually they sorted the problem out on the next attempt and everyone just forgot about it. Except in the case of Wimble, the most hopeless of all curse demons, who was on his fifth go at killing one of his Sufferers because he kept overlooking some of the less likely futures and so didn't allow for them in his calculations. It was this constant failure that had earned him a place at the bottom of the curse-demon pile.

Grimshaw shook his ears. He knew he was a thorough demon and he was ready to bet that he hadn't overlooked anything. Something else had gone wrong and he wanted to know what it was. He wondered if, between his checking the futures and steering the junk, something could have changed. As if something had interfered in a way that *altered all of the possible futures.* But what?

As he disconnected from the web, a movement in the sky grabbed his attention.

Beyond the rows of blank tombstones and the graveyard gate was a street whose dominating feature was concrete. Concrete was the one thing that Limbo did well. Where stone, brick and tile lost some basic element of their nature, concrete stayed the same. Which meant that its drab, squalid all-over-the-placeness shone out like a used plaster in an empty first-aid box.

Beyond the street, Grimshaw focused on three distant figures circling in the dull sky. The Sisters of Gladness. They were called the Sisters because they were sisters, and as for the gladness part . . . well, it was probably meant as a joke. Nobody was ever glad to see the Sisters.

Remembering the Horseman's words – that small demons belonged to the Sisters, whose job it was to *make them see* (whatever that meant) – an idea began to form in Grimshaw's mind.

As he watched, one of the Sisters dived, swooping out of sight behind the houses then rising again to join the others. He thought he could hear some horrible screaming and a lot of laughter. He was ready to bet his trousers that the laughter part was coming from the Sisters.

As there were not that many small demons in Limbo, the Sisters spent a lot of time tormenting the other inhabitants of Grey Space. The Wanderers. Grimshaw had no time at all for Wanderers. To his mind they were just plain stupid. They were the humans who could not die properly because *they did not realise that they were dead in the first place*, and so could not go on to wherever it was they were meant to end up. Instead they had to wander Limbo until they worked it out. These Wanderers were the Sisters' favourite prey and he suspected that the screaming he could hear was coming from one of them.

The Sisters had singled out Grimshaw for attention a couple of times in the past and he knew how mean they could be. Once, they had pinned him under some rocks, all spreadeagled out so that he couldn't reach his chronometer, and he had had to stay there all day staring into the grey Limbo sky until a passing Wanderer had taken pity on him and let him go. Quite how that had been supposed to make him *see* anything he couldn't understand. For some reason, the thought of Beyond – the light behind the Grey Space sky – flitted across his brain, but he dismissed it. He didn't have time to think about that now.

Instead, he stared at the distant figures darting to and fro in the sky and wondered if they could answer the question of Fish Jones and his survival against the odds. After a moment, he found himself heading off towards the Sisters. It probably wasn't a good idea, and it would certainly hurt a lot, but it was worth a go.

15

SISTERS OF GLADNESS

In the street, four cars were arranged across the road. They were grey. Or at least grey with a hint of something that might have been a real colour once but had forgotten how to do it. The vehicles were also empty. Often, Limbo didn't bother with details like old sweet wrappers, CDs, window scrapers, A–Zs, last week's shopping still in the boot, etc., etc. It just copied the basic shell and left things at that.

The silent street rolled out before Grimshaw like a plaster model that no one could be bothered to paint. A double-decker bus stood just past the bus stop looking grey and forlorn.

When he was level with the Sisters, just a road away, Grimshaw realised that rather than walk up one street to go down the next, he could cut through the houses. So he dived across the road and headed up the garden path of the first one he came to.

Getting in wasn't a problem as locks didn't work in Limbo. Nor was there any glass in the windows, as glass, with its world of reflections and its magical near-invisibility, was far too exciting to exist in Grey Space. Inside the house, Limbo had taken care to reproduce some details while totally ignoring others. There were no ornaments, pictures or items of clothing. There were no toys or games, but there were books on the shelves, ready to trap the unwary. There were no DVDs or videos, but there was a dead-looking TV. There were carpets and sofas and so on, but they had long ago forgotten how to be cosy.

Pushing open the door to the patio, Grimshaw lolloped down the garden and over the end wall, using a plastic table and chairs as a step up. This brought him into the garden of the house backing on to the one he had just cut through. Here he found a plastic paddling pool. There was no water in it, just as there was no water in any of the taps, lakes or rivers. All the water in Limbo was where it belonged – in the sea. A sea which (predictably) didn't do waves or tides or anything active like that.

Grimshaw hurried down the garden, picking up a hoe as he went. He charged through the house, which was pretty much the same as the last one, burst out through the front door and headed for the street. This was the street in which the Sisters were having fun, attacking a Wanderer.

Ahead, Grimshaw could see the man waving his arms defensively over his head. It was a pointless exercise. The Sisters were only playing with him. If they wanted to, they would have him in shreds in a moment.

One of them darted at him, lifting him into the air, then dropping him on to the road where he lay stunned.

Dragging the hoe, Grimshaw stepped forward. He dropped his backpack to the ground to give himself more freedom to move and to run if necessary.

The Sisters spotted him instantly. They had better vision than an eagle. Although they weren't as terrifying as the Horsemen, the Sisters weren't pretty to look at. At least, their heart-shaped faces were lovely, so long as they didn't smile and show their pointed teeth. Their hair was long and silky and floated on the air like thistledown, and the skin of their arms was smooth and golden, until it reached their bony-fingered, hook-nailed hands. But from the armpits down they were serpent-like with rough yellow-green scales on a torso that went straight into a twisting tail, without bothering about legs or anything. Their large bat-wings were the same unpleasant colour as their scaly bodies, but the most frightening thing about them was their eyes. These were the colour of emeralds and shone like lamps, and being caught in their gaze was like falling into a vast green emptiness from which you might never get out.

'Ooh, look, Rage,' said the youngest, whose name was Lady. 'It's Grimshaw!'

'So it is,' sniggered Rage. 'We were talking about him only this morning and here he is! Poor little Avatar.'

'Third-raters always look so . . . pathetic, don't they?' said Flute. She was the middle one of the three and easily the most cruel. 'Remember the one like a pig with cramp?'

'Wimble is a very fine Avatar,' snapped Grimshaw, tightening his grip on the hoe. A little way off, the man lying in a bloody heap on the ground began to groan as consciousness returned.

The Sisters stared at Grimshaw. He stared back.

'I liked the pig one,' said Flute sweetly. 'He was fun. He squealed so much.'

Grimshaw swallowed hard, flattening his ears against his skull and crouching closer to the ground. Behind the Sisters the man groaned and raised his head.

'Oh, shut it up,' said Rage.

Flute darted forward, grabbed the man by the ankles and hoisted him off the ground. The movement revived him and he began to screech. Flute tossed him over a fence, where he hit a house, sliding to the ground with a strangled squawk.

'I'm going to ask you a question,' said Grimshaw firmly, looking at Rage, 'and you've got to tell me the answer, right?'

She burst out laughing, bobbing in the air above Grimshaw's head. The others joined in. Stabbing the hoe at them as threateningly as he could, Grimshaw inched around so that he had a solid garden wall at his back.

'The Horsemen told me it was your job to make me see . . .' He paused, not knowing how to finish the sentence.

'Oh, they did, did they?' Rage sighed. 'Really, they

are *so* indiscreet.' She folded her arms and frowned at him. 'Our main job is the Wanderers, so even if it's true, why would we want to help a pathetic little scrap of half-life like you?'

Lady yawned delicately. 'I'm bored,' she said.

'Because . . . it's what you're meant to do? It's the Rules!' snapped Grimshaw.

'Oh, *Rules*,' sneered Flute. 'There's no Rule tells us who to help. We've got *some* independence, you know, unlike you pitiful things.'

'But you've *got* to help me, it's your job! King One said so.'

The Sisters swapped a glance. All three turned to gaze at him steadily, their green eyes bathing his face with light. Grimshaw got the feeling they were impressed by something. At any rate, he had their full attention now, though the thought made him shiver with fright. He really didn't see why the angel Avatars' help had to hurt so much.

'Hmm, he told you his name, did he?' said Rage. 'That's nice. Well, he should also have said that we'll get to you when we're good and ready.'

'But I need you now!' yelled Grimshaw, hopping from paw to paw with frustration. 'You've *got* to because . . . because if *you* don't, nobody else will!'

'Funny little creature,' said Flute indulgently. 'It wants to be helped! That's kind of sweet – so few of them appreciate our efforts. All they do is scream.' She glanced at her sisters.

Rage gave a tiny nod.

'It's strange that you should want to ask us something,' said Lady, bobbing forward, 'because we've got something to show you too. Let's see if your question and our answer match.'

Cautiously, Grimshaw lowered the hoe. 'I want to know,' he said, 'why Fish Jones survived? What was it that messed with the futures?'

There was a moment of silence. The Sisters' emerald eyes were suddenly cold and cruel and Grimshaw shivered as if the temperature had dropped, although such a thing was impossible in Limbo. Technically, like the Horsemen, the Sisters were angel Avatars, but they didn't look to Grimshaw anything like the pictures he had seen in Real Space books and paintings. You certainly wouldn't put one on a Christmas tree.

'Wrong question,' murmured Lady. 'What a pity.'

Rage bobbed forward, her green lamps peering into Grimshaw's inky ovals. The demon shrank away.

'Tell you what – we'll answer two questions for you: the one you asked and the one you *should* have asked.' She stabbed a finger at him, nearly putting out an eye. 'We'll even show you how things really are, by way of a bonus.' She brought her face close to his, so close that all he could see was the glow of her eyes. 'If you have the wit to see,' she added, snarling the last bit.

Grimshaw shrieked as everything suddenly whirled and fell away beneath him. It took him a moment to realise that Lady had snatched him up and was rocketing into the sky with her captive dangling upside down, gripped by her twisting tail! Far away and getting further, he saw his backpack and the hoe lying in the dusty earth, along with his notebook that must have fallen out of his pocket.

Lady slowed down a little and, giggling, began to spiral as she flew, spinning Grimshaw round and round. It made him feel sick. Rage began circling around her whirling sister, going in the opposite direction. It made Grimshaw feel even sicker.

'Now, my little third-rate creation of a deceitful man's dying curse,' cooed Flute, flying so that she was keeping pace with Grimshaw, face to face. 'We'll get to the question you actually asked later. First of all, let's work on the question you *should* have asked. Bear in mind that we are already cross with you for getting it wrong. It's very disappointing because you were doing so well, you even got a peek at Beyond. Are you going to throw up yet?' She reached out and hit him in the stomach.

Grimshaw threw up. Not a nice thing to have to do upside down. Some of it came out of his nose.

Lady dropped him. They let him fall a little way before Rage grabbed him and began to fly upwards again. The ground receded further and further, the church of St Peter and St Paul disappearing into the distance as they went on and up, heading north-east.

16

TWO QUESTIONS

They were flying so fast that Grimshaw had to fight for breath. The land was already far behind and they were out over the flat, grey expanse of the Limbo sea. Flute was screeching in his ears as Lady hauled him along, flapping in their wake like a torn pennant in a gale. When they were high over the sea, they stopped flying and a game of toss the demon began. By now, Grimshaw was too busy screaming to worry about questions.

'Ooops,' said Lady, missing him for the second time.

Flute dived, catching him by an ear. She twisted it hard and shook him.

'Yaaargh! That hurts!'

'Upside down is best. They throw up more.'

'Sorry.' Flute threw him to Lady, who got him by the legs again, wrapping her tail tight around him. She began to drift in slow circles, with Rage in the centre, humming to herself. Rage hovered, turning on the spot with her arms folded, listening to Flute as she spoke.

'Come on then, addleshanks,' cried Flute cheerfully.

She was flying upside down in front of Grimshaw, her luminous green eyes inches from his inky ones. He shut his tight so as not to see. 'What *should* your question have been? What else has been bothering you lately? Let's see if you can guess.'

Grimshaw struggled to think. 'If your job is to help us see the truth, why are you so mean about it?' he yelled crossly.

'Are you trying to distract us?' smiled Flute, flying closer. 'It won't work. We are mean to the Wanderers because no human sees as clearly as when he thinks he is about to die – even when he's already dead! And we are mean to you, little demon, because you are a nasty thing and you deserve it.'

To demonstrate, she reached out a hand, but before she could claw him, Grimshaw's madly scrabbling brain put together what she had said about something that had been worrying him and that moment of seeing Beyond on the mountainside. He spoke hurriedly, feeling a little sick from all the drifting in circles.

'The other thing I've been wondering about is noble humans. There never were any before, but now I keep seeing them everywhere.'

'Good demon,' said Flute, drawing back her hand. 'That's the *right* question.'

Grimshaw gave an inner sigh of relief. If he was on the right track, maybe things would hurt a little less. 'But I thought I must be wrong,' he went on, 'because Tun says . . .'

'Oh, what does he know?' put in Rage. 'He's only a demon Avatar like you . . .'

'He's a first-class one.'

'You mean, not a foolish little skinned thing that can't kill its boy Sufferer and hasn't yet worked out why?' Rage snorted. 'Huh, that doesn't mean he's not just as dumb as the rest of you.'

From above him, still holding him by the ankle, Lady giggled. 'How does it go?' She put on a doomy voice. 'Until my name is writ upon the tomb of my ancestors, the House of Ombre will be hounded unto death through every generation.'

'Honestly,' shrieked Flute, 'only a real dimwit would kill off the *last family member* with a curse like that! Now it can NEVER be fulfilled!'

'Never?' mumbled Grimshaw, puzzled. Personally, he thought it was a pretty good curse.

Flute rolled her eyes. 'Tun's Architect,' she said with exaggerated patience, 'Rudolphus Ombre, was cast out by his family. When he was dying, Rudolphus asked for his name to be added to the list of ancestors carved on the walls of the family vault. But they refused outright, didn't want to know him, see? So, with his dying breath, he put a curse on the family name that would last until they relented.'

'The curse that Tun is Avatar for?'

'That's right. But now Tun has killed them all, there are no family members left to want Rudolphus Ombre's name carved anywhere, let alone on the ancestral vault, see? Although everyone is dead, Tun is still connected to the curse.'

Grimshaw winced, and not just at the idea of never ending. With no more House of Ombre there could be no more Sufferers. So Tun was stuck in Limbo forever, never able to go into Real Space! Maybe that was why he seemed so unhappy at times.

'Unless,' Flute went on, 'he can find another way out, which I very much doubt! Anyway, my point was, your great Tun isn't bright enough to know a noble human if it stood up and bit him.'

Just to demonstrate, Flute bobbed forward and sank her razor teeth into Grimshaw's shoulder.

Blood flew into the air in scarlet streamers. Lady had stopped drifting and was flying on, picking up speed as she went so that Flute had to raise her voice as she flapped alongside.

'OW!'

'Come on, O small creature born of a sick man's spirit,' Flute shouted. 'The answer to the noble-human question is easy. You just need to take a good long look at things and see how they really are.'

She stabbed a finger in Grimshaw's direction and began to spiral as she flew alongside him. Her hair whipped about her like golden snakes. Grimshaw groaned and shut his eyes, feeling sick and giddy.

Rage darted in and gave him a whack. 'Name a Sufferer from the past,' she yelled in his ear.

Grimshaw's original Litany of Sufferers, the one he

had been created with, had included all the policemen (or Peelers as Lampwick insisted on calling them) who had tried to arrest the Robber on his deathbed. There was also Mrs Boldheart, who had told the policemen all about the sorry affair of the pawned necklace, the physician who had been present at the time of the arrest, and the families and loved ones of all of the above. It had been a long list. But Grimshaw didn't need to refer to his notebook. He had gone through the stories so often for Lampwick that he pretty much knew them all by heart.

'Emily Boldheart,' snapped Grimshaw. 'Screaming and Sobbing followed by Collapse and Medication.'

'And that's true, is it?'

'I have an excellent memory for detail,' yelled Grimshaw coldly. He tried to fold his arms, but it didn't work very well at velocity. Lady was curving round now, far above the great grey blanket of the ocean. They were so high that Grimshaw could make out the rougher grey edges of the land on both sides of the sea.

Flute darted closer, peering into his face. 'Mmhm? You don't look too sure. But I expect you are right. I expect she screamed and sobbed as if her heart were broken. After all, her son had just been trampled to death. Very bloodily too, I believe.'

Grimshaw swallowed nervously.

Flute smiled, baring her teeth like needles of bone. 'What about at the funeral? I bet she made a right fuss at the funeral.'

Grimshaw opened his mouth and then shut it again

as an image flashed into his mind. The cabby, his face red with shame and misery as he begged Emily Boldheart's forgiveness for killing her son. And Emily as she took his hand in hers and said:

'My dear, good man. You were sober and awake and did all in your power to control the horse when it bolted. Never think that you are to blame for the cruelty of fate. But if you feel that you need a word of forgiveness from me, then you have it. I forgive you with all my heart, as would my son also.'

Thrusting her face into his, Flute snarled. Grimshaw screamed as she raked her claws down one side of his head from chin to scalp. Then she hit him so hard that he felt his neck crunch. Lady began to fly even faster and the wind whistled about his ears, sounding bleak and cruel.

And suddenly other images were flicking through his mind in jerky technicolour. The policeman who went to rescue his wife from their burning home and nearly died in the attempt. The policeman's daughter who sat up night after night, patiently watching over her mother as she lay at death's door from her injuries. The physician who . . .

Somewhere in the middle of all his screaming, Grimshaw finally understood that Susan Jones was not the first noble human that he had come across, *she was just the first that he had noticed.*

'It's working,' cried Flute, happily. 'Amazing how fear can sharpen the perceptions. I think he's beginning to look outside himself at last, to see humans as people, not just victims! We'll make a better being of him yet, you'll see.'

'We're here!' called Lady. 'Look, Grimshaw, we've brought you back over land. Aren't we nice? We know you can't swim. We may be cruel, but don't ever say we aren't thoughtful!'

She slowed to a halt and hovered. Grimshaw risked a look. It was true. Right down below him, dizzyingly far away, was the familiar sight of England. Limbo style.

'We're very . . . high . . .' mumbled Grimshaw, trying to shut his eyes against the spinning landscape of undulating grey far below. It didn't help. He yelped as Rage whacked him round the ears.

'Eyes open, if you please. This is the part where we show you how things really are. You can't adore the glory of the world with them shut.'

'Hardly glory,' snapped Grimshaw crossly, squinting down at the grey expanse stretching out beneath him.

'Try to see it as we do.' Lady tossed him high in the air where he hung for a few seconds, while Limbo's dodgy gravity thought it over.

Flute spun away from Grimshaw. She hovered for a moment, looking at him, her emerald eyes unfathomable in their depths. 'And now for the answer to the *other* question, the one you asked. The one about Fish Jones and why he's still alive.'

'Yes?' said Grimshaw eagerly.

'Destiny,' she said.

As he began to fall, Flute dived towards him one last time. For a fleeting moment her lips touched his cheek.

'That's for the question you got right,' she said. Then her hand darted out to snatch at his wrist. 'And this is for the one you got wrong.'

For a second, Grimshaw didn't realise what she had done. Then it hit him. Her sharp-tipped fingers had closed firmly around his chronometer, tearing it from his wrist!

'Yaaaah! Give it back! Give it back NOW! That's mean!'

Flute laughed, keeping pace with him as he fell. Then she held out an arm and let the chronometer go. It vanished from sight in a moment. 'Bye, Grimshaw,' she said sweetly, and with a flick of her wings she was gone.

Screaming with panic and rage, Grimshaw plunged to Earth. He struggled as if he could somehow reach his chronometer. He didn't know why. It had already disappeared from view.

His howls were lost in the vast emptiness of the Limbo sky, and through the whistling gale around his ears he thought he could still hear Flute laughing.

17

DESTINY

Someone cleared his throat. Grimshaw squinted up as best he could from his spreadeagled position on the ground.

He was keeping still while his skeleton, shattered by the fall, got on with the business of reorganising itself to be the right shape again instead of just lazing around in a jumble of splinters. It felt like he had been waiting forever, even though he knew it could be hardly more than an hour or so – in Real Space time – since his mortification at the hands of the Sisters of Gladness. He had stopped bothering to scream at the pain because his throat was getting sore from all the yelling. He was just lying there listening to the grinding and crunching as his bones worked hard to put themselves together again. In addition to all this, the spot on his cheek where Flute had kissed him glowed warmly, as if trying to get his attention. He ignored it. It made him think about noble humans, and frankly he wasn't in the mood.

'Hello, small one. What are you doing down

there?' Tun was standing next to him, tucking away a complicated chronometer made of wood, glass, sand and a lot of carving.

'Mending,' snapped Grimshaw sulkily.

Tun nodded, understanding. He settled next to Grimshaw, his inky robes spread around him, looking like a pool of midnight on the ground. It was the first time Grimshaw had ever been face to face with his friend, as they were usually separated by Tun's great height. Not that he could see any face as such, but he could sense Tun's dreadful gaze issuing from the depths of his cowl. It dawned on Grimshaw that, for the first time ever, *Tun* had come to find *him*. Any other day he would have been pleased, but right now pleased was not on Grimshaw's menu.

'Well, small one. You are in a bad way! Your Sufferer has a destiny and you have lost your chronometer!'

'The Sisters took it . . .' Grimshaw halted, unable to talk with the shame of it. He took a deep breath in an effort to calm himself, but it didn't do a lot of good. He knew that there had never before been an Avatar who had been so utterly, unbelievably stupid as to lose his chronometer. The thought that it might be gone for good made him dizzy with terror.

'It's just so . . . awful!' he finished miserably. 'It's nearly as bad as Wimble missing futures.'

'I fear it is worse than that, small one. You are probably the most shamed curse demon in history now. But still, try not to dwell on it.' Tun reached out a skeletal hand and patted Grimshaw's shoulder gingerly, as if he wasn't quite sure how to do it. 'The Sisters love to torment. Look at Wimble! They took that uncouth raincoat he wears and threw him starkers down the chimney in the Lock-Out Club! Amusing for the rest of us, mind you.' Grimshaw didn't think Tun sounded at all amused. 'The main thing for you now is to get your chronometer back.'

'It's . . . It's my connection to the universe! I don't even know where I am any more!' Grimshaw's voice rose to a wail of panic. He heaved a quivering breath, then struggled to sit.

'Much better. You'll get nowhere if you give up.'

Under Tun's piercing gaze, Grimshaw flexed a paw. He winced. The limb worked, but the movement sent needles of pain up his arm. Tun was right though; it felt better to be sitting up.

'I have to get back to Lampwick.' Grimshaw's voice quivered again. Without the chronometer his spatial sense had gone west, or would have if it had known which direction west was. He had no idea where he was relative to Real Space time, or to geography either, he couldn't work out how to find Lampwick, and he hadn't a clue what his Sufferer was up to. It felt horrible, as if part of his brain had turned to porridge.

'Which way do I go?' he asked anxiously.

'There I can help, at least.' Tun waved a pale hand. 'That way. Keep going as straight as you can. If you pass a big stone cross, you'll know you're going in the right

140

direction. Eventually you'll hit the motorway, and it's easy from there.'

'Oh, thank you!' Grimshaw got painfully to his feet.

Cautiously, he tested his legs. There was no help for it, he was going to have to walk all the way back to the crypt. Miles and miles. And miles. He set off, limping painfully, with Tun strolling at his side, stopping every so often to let the smaller demon catch up. Now he had a direction to go in, Grimshaw's mind turned to the other huge problem.

Destiny. The possibility that Destiny was involved blocked out all the other things the Sisters had said – like the reality of noble humans – pushing them to the back of his head. Grimshaw paused to rub his cheek, wishing the kiss would stop stinging. It felt angry now, as if he was doing the wrong thing. But it was weaker too.

'The Sisters said that my Sufferer has a destiny,' he said anxiously. 'Do you think that's true?'

'It's an interesting theory. But the Sisters are very lowly angels, so you don't have to believe everything they say. It's not like the Horsemen.' Tun leaned towards Grimshaw and whispered, 'It is said among us first-rate demons that the Horsemen know . . . *everything*!'

'Everything?'

'They are in touch with the Highest Orders of Avatar, the ones we cannot even see!' Tun straightened up and raised his voice again. 'So, just because the child is proving hard to kill, doesn't mean that the Sisters are right, that he has been chosen by fate for some higher purpose. Although I'll agree that his extra-special vision may point to some great meaning in his existence. That certainly makes him a creature apart from the rest of his kind.'

'Yes.' Grimshaw nodded agreement.

'Tell me, is he one who is strange to the eye? Who does not behave as others of his age and position?'

Grimshaw thought of the boy's virtual silence. 'Yes.'

'Shunned by most, save for two trusted friends.'

'Yes.'

'Downright odd?'

'YES!'

'Hmm. In that case, small one, I fear you are stuffed.'

'Stuffed?'

'Stitched up like a kipper. The Sisters, lowly as they are, have spoken the truth. Your Sufferer has a destiny. There is some deed of significance assigned to him, that he must live to carry out.'

Grimshaw stopped his limping progress as the significance of all this sank in. All curse demons knew that Destiny trumped curses. And if Fish Jones had a destiny, then one of the mysterious Higher Orders would be looking after him to make sure that the destiny was fulfilled.

'He has a guardian angel,' said Grimshaw slowly, twitching his ears. 'That is who messed with the futures and planted the coin in the gutter.'

He stood for a moment, taking in the fact that his Sufferer was protected by powers so great, so far above a mere third-rate curse demon that they were out of his sight. Then he tipped back his head and howled with anguish and misery.

Killing Fish Jones had just become impossible.

❧

'You can't be the first curse demon to come up against this,' said Tun, when Grimshaw had finished howling. 'Perhaps a little research will show you that it is not as uncommon as you think, small one. Why don't you trawl the Acts and Facts? Maybe there will be a solution. It'll be something for you to do on the long journey home.'

Grimshaw sighed. 'Everything was going so well,' he said, 'right up till I got to the boy. Horrible boy.'

'Do not be cast down. You will not be the only demon in history with a Survivor . . .'

'Wimble,' snapped Grimshaw. 'He is the only one. And now me.'

'But Wimble's Survivor is still alive because Wimble cannot read the futures properly. All the other humans just think the man is accident prone. In your case it's because the boy has a destiny, and you can't be blamed for that.'

It wasn't true and Grimshaw knew it. They'd sneer at him and look down on him. Well, they did that anyway, but they'd do it *more*. Add a long-standing Survivor to the loss of his chronometer and Grimshaw would be bottom of the curse-demon pile for years and years. Possibly forever. There would be no redemption. Curse demons were an unforgiving lot.

It crept into Grimshaw's mind that maybe Tun had come to find him out of a desire to gloat rather than to be supportive.

'Roll up, roll up,' he mumbled, 'see the most useless demon in everlasting history!'

'Sorry? Did you say something?'

Shaking his ears, Grimshaw asked grumpily, 'So why did you finish off your last-ever Sufferer? Surely, if there is no one left from the House of Ombre, then your Architect's name will be forgotten, certainly not carved among those of his ancestors.'

Tun didn't flinch, even for a moment. If there was any stiffening of the tall dark form walking next to him, Grimshaw didn't pick it up.

'Do you know what happens to a curse demon when the curse is complete?' Tun said, his voice cool. 'We are all aware that the Architect, being a human soul, moves on to Whatever Comes Next. But what about the Avatar of the curse? Hmmm?'

Grimshaw turned it over in his mind. It was true that he had never really thought about it, but he knew from the web that spent curse demons vanished from Limbo.

'They cease to exist, that's what,' went on Tun. 'Gone.

144

Snuffed out like a candle. They have no everlasting soul, so they cannot live beyond their purpose. See?'

'But not you?'

'Not me. Because my curse will never end, I will live forever.'

In Limbo, thought Grimshaw, but he didn't say it. He wondered briefly if Tun was wrong about the ceasing to exist thing too, as well as noble humans.

Tun stretched out his arms and shook himself, his night-black robes rippling on the still Limbo air. 'I'll leave you to research possible ways to redeem yourself, hmmm? If such a thing can be done for one who has sunk so low.' There was an edge to his voice, a little stab. Revenge for Grimshaw's question, perhaps.

'OK,' said Grimshaw humbly, hoping he hadn't annoyed Tun too much. He needed his friends.

'I'll watch you through the Acts and Facts,' said Tun, sounding more like his usual self. 'I can catch up with you later, when you have your chronometer back, and maybe we can put our heads together.'

'Thank you,' said Grimshaw, but Tun had already disappeared.

❧

In Real Space, Fish felt as if he had been on the run forever, even though he knew that it was only mid-morning, just under four hours since his near-death by space junk and since his mother had been taken to hospital. He had slept a little in the car the night before, but it had been edgy sleep full of anxious dreams, so now he was feeling tired to his core. The memory of the demon's words and of its horrible, cruel eyes kept on coming back to him, making him feel cold and frightened inside and lonelier than he had ever been in his life.

He had long since left the town behind and was following the dark strip of the road as it headed north, bordered by fields, hills and woods. He struggled through hedges and barbed wire as cars whined past, sounding like giant wasps. Fish was ready to bet that none of the drivers, and hardly any of the passengers, even saw him. And if they did, what was he to them but a scrawny boy-shape trundling across the scenery?

And if anyone did stop to offer help, he had no story to give them that would make sense and there was nothing they could do for him, save to take him all the way to Crow's Cottage and leave him there, with no questions asked. And what person would do that?

When he ran out of breath or got a stitch in his side, he slowed down to a brisk walk, but mostly he kept at a steady jog, looking only ahead. By now he was hollow with hunger and dry with thirst. He still had a few pence left and he began keeping an eye open for a place to stop. Somewhere he would be able to use the bathroom, get something to eat, and rest for a while without anyone paying any attention – although he wouldn't stay for long in case the curse demon caught up with him. It was an age before he saw the large sign up ahead with its knife-and-fork symbol announcing a place to eat, and even longer before he finally got there.

He began with the bathroom, then headed for the restaurant. The smells grabbed his attention as soon as he got in the door. It was only just gone ten and they were still serving late breakfast. Metal trays of sausage, bacon, mushrooms, eggs and beans stood waiting to be piled on plates by hungry travellers. The place rang with the clatter of serving spoons, the chink of plates and the busy hum of voices. From no people at all, suddenly Fish's world was full of them.

He looked around anxiously, assessing the life. There was a man on the other side of the room crawling with so many dirt demons that he must have smelt really bad. Funnily enough, the tables on either side of him were empty. Elsewhere, a thin man in a suit had bright red wasps darting around his head. Fish always stayed away from people like that, people ruled by their violence or anger.

A middle-aged couple to the left of Fish shared a misery-snake so strong that it had twisted itself into a complex knot around the pair of them. It had two heads and two bodies and would become two snakes when the couple weren't together, but for now it was one, locking them firmly into whatever hell their relationship had become.

Fish shuddered and looked away. Apart from that, the diner was full of normal, everyday people who washed, were reasonably OK with their lives, kept more or less healthy and weren't guilty of anything too horrible. One or two of the children shone the way only the really innocent could.

He dug out his money and gazed at it ruefully. Then he turned his back on the hubbub and went to the newsagent instead. Keeping an eye on the prices he picked up a chocolate bar, because he had read somewhere that chocolate was good energy food, and a small carton of apple juice and took them to the till.

Where he froze.

18

ANGEL

The man behind the counter looked at Fish with eyes like chips of ice and smiled. Around his head dark lights flickered like splashes of night on the air, small black stars that sucked in light instead of giving it out.

'You buying that, son?'

Fish nodded and put the chocolate and the carton on the counter. He could feel the blood draining from his face. Still smiling, the man rang the items up on the till.

Fish ignored the dark sparks and kept his eyes on the man. The sparks were frightening, but it was the man, their Architect, who was dangerous. Those anti-lights flickering around his head were a sign of the bad things he had done and that were now part of his soul. They told Fish that here was a man who enjoyed inflicting pain, wielding power over the helpless. Because dark sparks were made by cruelty.

Fish dropped his money on the counter without waiting to be asked.

The man scooped it up.

'Quiet, aren't you? The silent type, eh?'

To Fish, the sparks looked like holes into some other place, a lightless universe in which there were things that could look out and *watch*. He held out his hand for the bag with his purchases in it. The man didn't hand it over. Instead, his eyes lingered on Fish's face. Inside the sparks, things began to stir.

'On your own, are you?' The man leaned forward over the counter and lowered his voice. His face showed only concern. 'Come a long way too, by the look of you.'

Fish went on holding out his hand, his eyes fogged with strands of fear, real fear, that he was weaving around himself in a net of shadows. No one else would be able to see it, but Fish could and, because he could, he understood that if anything trapped him, it would be his own fear. So he took a deep breath and a step back. If necessary he would leave without his purchases.

'Look, son, you're worn out, I can tell. Why don't you come round the back here and sit quiet for a few minutes. If you're on your way somewhere, maybe I can help. Give you a lift or something. Won't ask you any questions. Just a helping hand and something to eat and drink, eh?'

The man smiled again. It was a reassuring smile that spoke of understanding and help. Fish didn't need to wonder how the man had worked out that the boy in front of him was a runaway. The things watching from that dark universe were waking up, and although the man didn't know they were there, he was still listening to their whispers in his brain. The feel of their presence made Fish weak with fright.

'No need to worry, son. I'm not gonna ring the police or anything. I know a boy in trouble when I see one . . .'

There was a sound at the entrance to the shop and the man's eyes darted up once and then down to Fish again. A woman in a blue dress had come in, bringing with her an air of sunlight and life. She went straight to the newspapers ranged on the shelves beside Fish. Her presence was enough to spark him into action.

'Can I have my things, please?' said Fish as loudly as he could. He was trembling, but tried not to show it. The woman raised her head and glanced over.

The man felt her eyes turn in his direction and automatically put the bag down on the counter. Fish grabbed it just as the woman came up behind him, clutching a daily paper. Then he ran.

Fish kept going for an hour, his breath huffing in and out like hot knives and his heart pounding like hammers on an anvil. He paused only once, to eat half the chocolate and drink half the juice, but even so he was still thirsty and hungry. He wanted to keep something for later, so he put the rest of the chocolate in his pocket. He tied the plastic bag round the juice as tightly as possible so that it wouldn't leak through the straw and jammed the carton in the other pocket. Then he got going again, wanting to put as much distance between himself and the newsagent as possible.

The day was turning into a scorcher. Fish kept to the shade where he could, but his T-shirt was already damp with sweat and his scalp prickled with it. He was jogging along in a kind of daze. It was as if the dark sparks had given his fear fuel, and he was weighed down by so much of it that his brain had to protect him somehow, to build a wall between him and the ocean of terror that threatened to overwhelm him, or he would crumble. The faint grey strands that dimmed his vision were still there, weaving a misty web around him. The more frightened he was, the darker they would grow.

He did not think that the curse demon would suddenly attack him, for he had begun to believe that it could not catch him up while he was on the move. It would wait until he had stopped, and then it would know instinctively where he was and it would find him. And then the battle for his life would begin.

But more immediately he was horribly afraid that the man from the newsagent would come after him, would cruise up and down the motorway until he saw Fish struggling along the banks. Then he'd stop and get out and no one would come to help because no one paid much attention on a highway. And before he knew it, Fish would be crammed into the man's car, stolen away to be tortured and killed for fun, and the things watching deep inside the dark sparks would really be awake then! The thought turned his insides to liquid.

His other terrible fear was for his mother, but all he could do was cling to the words of the paramedic, repeating them over and over to block out the fear that her injuries were worse than they appeared. Or that at this very moment doctors might be hurrying her to an operating theatre for vital surgery, that she might . . . might . . . He stopped, overtaken by a fit of the shakes.

Well, anyway, the paramedic had said that she would be all right. She needed some care and attention, but she would be *all right*.

When the trembling calmed down he started to jog again, but it was a loose, wobbling jog, as if all his joints were rubber.

And then, on top of all that, he was afraid for himself. Not just because all this running away might simply end in death at the hands of the demon, but because he would have to face it all on his own. Since Susan had been rushed off in an ambulance, Fish had come to understand what it felt like to be alone. Not just lonely for company, but truly alone, with no one to go to for help, or to talk things over, or simply to be there, a buffer between him and the universe. It wasn't just that he had no friends to help him, it was more than that. He couldn't go to the police or any of the network of support organisations set in place for lost children or people in danger. Even the help of strangers was out of reach. Right now, the universe was vast and dangerous and ganging up on Fish. It was an unfair fight.

All he could do was try his best to survive. And he didn't know how long he could go on surviving for. Surely the demon would get him eventually? It had said it would, and its words had a ring of certainty. He couldn't evade it forever, and it clearly wasn't going to give up and go away. The knowledge filled him with despair.

Which brought him to his last and most personal fear, the one he didn't even want to think about. So he didn't. He stopped again and stood, head down, gasping for breath.

A car pulled over into the lay-by. The door opened.

'Hey, are you all right?'

Fish jolted upright. He stared, his shaking legs forgotten.

'You don't look so good.' The woman stopped a little way away from him and smiled. She was wearing a blue dress and Fish wondered hazily if it was the same woman who had come into the newsagent's at exactly the right time.

'I was just driving by, you know, and I saw you and thought, That kid looks sick. So I thought I'd stop and check you were OK. I can get help if you need it.'

Fish opened his mouth to speak, but his eyes were wet and he couldn't say anything.

'I've got some water.' The woman turned back to her car, her blue dress cool against the hot grey road.

Fish stared at her. In the sunlight she was so radiant it hurt his eyes. As she moved into the shadow of the trees he could see that most of the shine was her own.

'Here.' She handed him a bottle of water, one of

those with the top designed to drink from. Fish took it, his hand still shaking. She watched him gulp it down. The water tasted unbelievably sweet.

'Don't take too much at once, right.'

Fish nodded and paused, a trickle running down his chin.

'Where are you going?'

Fish thought quickly. He didn't want to tell her about the cottage because it was a long way away and she might feel like she had to give him a lift or something. And however much she shone, however bright she was, Fish didn't want to accept a lift from her. She would ask questions and the answers would be lies. And she would know. In fact, Fish thought, she might already know, even though he hadn't said a word.

'Stoney Cross,' he said, picking the next landmark on his journey. He knew the name from the map and it didn't look far.

She nodded. 'Well, you don't have to walk to the next turn-off. I know Stoney Cross, and once you leave the duel carriageway the road doubles back. You'll save yourself a hard slog if you cut across the fields from here.' She pointed to the dip and rise of the land on Fish's right.

While she talked, telling him the way, Fish drank some more. He still couldn't take his eyes off her. She wasn't a child obviously, or one of those people who were still children inside even when they were grown-ups. She didn't look like someone bereaved either, and she was older than he would expect a newly-in-love person to be. Besides, the shine was brighter than all of those. Brighter and whiter.

'I'm on my way to pick up my husband,' she said, almost as if answering his questions. 'Every year his work sends him off on some training course or another, as if he didn't know pretty much all there is to know about banking by now!' She smiled at Fish as he finished drinking and held out the bottle. It was empty.

'Sorry,' he said.

'You needed it.' As she reached towards him, the silver bracelet around her wrist glinted in the sunshine. The sunlight combined with her own radiance made her look translucent, a woman of crystal. Light made solid.

Fish shivered and was glad that she didn't touch him when she took the bottle from his fingers. She may not have been a demon, but she was just as terrifying in a different way.

She walked a few steps and then turned back. Standing there in her blue dress with her yellow hair and the shine flooding through her, she looked as luminous as an angel in a stained-glass window. Her eyes fixed on him. They were so full of sapphire light that being caught in their gaze was like falling into a vast blue infinity from which you might never get out. She smiled.

'Remember now – go across the fields until you see the barn, then get on to the road and you'll be there.'

Fish nodded, but she was already in her car. The engine roared into life, drew forward a little way, paused for a moment then was gone, swept into the river of traffic.

He stood and watched for a while, puzzled. But then there was no reason why he should be. After all, he was only a kid. He could hardly have seen everything that the hidden world had to show him. Look at the curse demon. He had never seen one of those until yesterday. Maybe she was just one of many something elses.

He turned it over in his mind, wondering what other strange and terrifying things might be out there that he hadn't met yet. Then he turned his face to the fields and started to run all over again.

Ten minutes after he had gone from view, a car cruised up the road, going as slowly as it could. Inside it was the newsagent, his eyes like chips of ice, scanning the roadside as keenly as if he were looking for a favourite toy. He didn't guess that his target had taken a different route and was well away across the fields by now. So he found nothing.

This time.

19

STONEY CROSS

The fields went on for a little way after the barn, but eventually Fish got back on to a narrow, winding road in the middle of nowhere. A mile or so down it he spotted a large monument to one side, surrounded by grass and overhung by tall trees.

He veered towards it and dropped to the ground. Leaning against the rough stone, he dug out the last of the chocolate, which he finished quickly. He saved the juice as the water had quenched his thirst enough for now.

Next, he pulled out the road map and studied it. From everything the woman had told him, he should be near the village of Stoney Cross by now. He craned his head backwards to look at the monument. Sure enough, it was a huge cross, roughly hewn from some grainy golden stone and standing about twelve feet high from the ground. The actual cross part rose from a solid base that was taller than Fish and it was this base that he was leaning against. Fish stared up at the monument for a few seconds, then smiled. This was Stoney Cross, all right! The village must be further on down the road. He studied the map, getting an idea of the land and which way he should go after the village.

Glancing at his watch, Fish saw that it was exactly midday. Everything was quiet and peaceful and nothing moved, apart from a lone aeroplane speeding towards the horizon. He stared up through the green and gold canopy over his head, his mind moving on to Susan. This time he could see that his mother was where she needed to be, in hospital with doctors and nurses who would do everything they could to make sure that she was safe and cared for. So, in the dappled shade of Stoney Cross, Fish faced his last horrible fear. The personal one, the one that made him feel faint with terror.

He looked down at himself.

Seeing nothing but his own skinny chest wrapped in a T-shirt that was torn and dirty and far too big for him, Fish drew in a wobbly breath full of relief. He must not let himself sink into despair and be crushed by a shadow-snake, or they would both be lost.

Now, gazing at the fish outlined on the no-longer white material, Fish smiled for the first time that day. Leaning back, he kicked off his trainers to let his sore feet feel the air. Sitting here in the dappled shade under the trees, he realised that he was feeling a lot better. The fears that had dogged him since this morning hadn't all gone away, but they seemed more like things he could deal with rather than things that would crush him. It had something to do with the peacefulness of Stoney Cross and something to do with the shining woman and the long, cool drink of water. All of it had stolen the fire from his fears and damped them down to a manageable level. Closing his eyes, he let the soft air flow over him. He had no idea how long it would take him to reach Crow's Cottage, but he wanted to get there before nightfall. The cottage, unlived in for some time now, would be showing the signs of neglect, and he wanted to face any lurking demons of dirt or decay while it was still light. So he wouldn't stay long at Stoney Cross, however nice it was to sit in the warm with the gentle sounds of the world buzzing about his ears and to keep his nightmares at arm's length for a while.

But he could afford a short rest and so he stayed for five minutes, and in that five minutes his eyes closed and Fish fell asleep.

❋

For the thousandth time Grimshaw asked himself why a lost chronometer didn't automatically return to its Avatar instead of its Architect. It was a stupid question, because he already knew the answer.

It was punishment. Punishment for being a pathetic no-hoper who couldn't kill his Sufferers and who even went so far as to actually LOSE the main instrument of his craft. An Avatar without a chronometer was like a bus driver on a bicycle, a dentist with a toothpick, a . . . a . . .

He stopped and groaned out loud, this time with

the pain of an injured spirit rather than injured flesh. On top of his spiritual misery and his still aching bones, Grimshaw's paws were cut to ribbons and hurting horribly. He just wasn't designed for walking. Still he kept going.

At last, after what seemed to Grimshaw like several lives' worth of walking, he found what he was hoping for. A huge lump of grey stone by the road, looking spectacularly slab-like in its dullness. Its top half was roughly hacked into the shape of a cross. Too weary to feel relieved, Grimshaw dropped down on to the dry cracked earth. He needed to rest, and this was as good a place as any. Just as he leaned back against the base part, underneath the cross, everything blinked as Limbo updated itself. Which meant it had to be midday.

Grimshaw squinted up at the grey sky. Because anything in the Limbo sky usually meant trouble, it soon got to be a habit for curse demons and Wanderers to check regularly just to make sure they weren't missing anything important. Especially after a Blink. This time, far in the distance, he could see the grey smudge of an aeroplane as it drifted to Earth, bereft of passengers and pilot and with its engines suddenly as good at flying as a metal brick. Any moment now Limbo's dodgy gravity would notice the thing and bring it crashing to the ground. Fortunately it was too far away to be a problem to Grimshaw. Almost as he thought it, the plane stopped drifting and began to plummet.

Satisfied that he was in no danger, Grimshaw looked

over the vast stretches of dusty earth on either side of the road. In the distance he could see a single Wanderer trudging across the land towards the horizon. He couldn't tell if it was male or female, but he could hear the faint echo of its voice as it sang a determined-not-to-give-up type of marching song into the empty waste. It sounded very lonely.

Then it stopped and silence fell.

It was a flat silence, the sort of silence that really gets going on any nearby ears until they start making sounds up just to maintain a little sanity. It got on Grimshaw's nerves almost at once. In the silence, an odd feeling came to Grimshaw. He felt as if Fish Jones was there, somewhere nearby but unseen. Normally, a curse demon knew where his Sufferer was at all times, but that knowledge was tied in to the possession of a chronometer. So, having this strange sensation when his chronometer was not strapped firmly to his wrist as usual was kind of spooky. Grimshaw shivered and looked around anxiously. Not surprisingly, there was nothing there, but the feeling persisted.

Although Grimshaw didn't know it, as it was not the sort of information available on the Acts and Facts, there were rare times when Grey Space and Real Space could be drawn closer together.

Demons didn't sleep, but Grimshaw was worn out by all his misery and anger, so he stopped thinking and let his mind drift. Sinking into a kind of daze, he found himself seeing the Jones boy as if he was *right there*, next to Grimshaw. The boy looked peaceful, with sunlight on his face and a faint breeze ruffling his hair.

At the thought of the sun and the breeze, and of the boy's right to live in Real Space and enjoy all those things which were denied to Grimshaw, the demon felt a surge of jealousy so fierce he thought he would break in two. At first, the boy had been just another Sufferer. Then he had turned into something more – a problem case with a destiny. He had become a frustration, an obstacle in Grimshaw's way, when all the demon wanted to do was finish the job. But seeing the boy lying there bathed in the sun of another dimension, Grimshaw's feelings changed again. At this exact moment, right here and now on this spot, he began to hate Fish Jones.

The boy stirred and woke up. He looked at Grimshaw, his eyes wide with shock, and then scrabbled backwards, away from the demon.

Grimshaw puffed up at once. He shook himself and bared his teeth in a snarl, glaring at the boy with his corner-to-corner black eyes, trying to look as fierce as possible. Shaking with fright, Fish stayed where he was, half crouching, his face level with that of the demon.

'Please,' Fish said suddenly, 'please let us live.'

It was the first time Grimshaw had heard the boy speak and his voice was softer than he had expected.

'Your mother disturbed the sleep of the dead,' Grimshaw snarled, making his own voice deeper than usual, hoping it sounded more like Tun's. 'She deserves to suffer.'

'I know we are only humans,' said Fish, the words tumbling out of him now. 'We aren't powerful like you. I know we are nothing special, we're not going to do great works or . . . or make great discoveries, but neither are we evil. My mother didn't wish to disturb the dead, she would never have wished that, she just didn't understand. Please, let us live and enjoy the world, that's all we want.'

Grimshaw howled. He hadn't meant to, but at that moment his jealousy and rage got so huge they boiled over. The boy's attempt to reach out across the vast space that separated the living from the half-alive, even though he was in mortal fear for his life, was too much. How dare the boy be noble on top of everything else!

'I'LL GET YOU,' Grimshaw screamed, his voice a harsh, spitting roar. 'NO MATTER WHERE YOU HIDE, I'LL FIND YOU, FISH JONES. I'LL FIND YOU AND I'LL KILL YOU.'

The demon sprang, his claws spread, ready to break the Rules and visit death on the human with his bare paws. But the connection between their worlds had been broken and Fish Jones had gone, and Grimshaw, fully alert and seething, was burying his claws in nothing but dry earth.

He lay there for a while, huffing miserably, while rage and frustration tore him to pieces. Then, silent and grim, he got to his feet and started once again to limp on towards home.

❀

In Real Space, Fish Jones woke up with a start. He had been dreaming about the demon, as if it had been right there, next to him. It had glared at him with its terrifying, all-black eyes, and had leapt at him as if meaning to tear out his throat. Fish shuddered. For some reason it had never occurred to him that the demon might attack him with its bare ha . . . paws. Images filled his head of having to fight it, of touching the horrible thing. It made his blood run cold.

He shook himself. It was just a dream – what else could it be? The demon wasn't here, he would know when it arrived. Still, the things it had said and the look of hatred and fury in its eyes stayed with him.

Getting to his feet, Fish brushed the grass from his jeans and T-shirt. Then, his face set with determination, he turned towards Crow's Cottage and started on his way again.

20

KILL FISH JONES

Some hours later, Grimshaw was making real progress, his paws hardening up as they healed so that he could walk faster. Fired up by the dream of Fish Jones that had made him so angry, he connected to the Acts and Facts looking for any hints about how to deal with Destiny.

The curse-demon information web was vast, encompassing the deeds done by the Avatars of all curses everywhere throughout history, plus any interesting snippets of information that they felt inclined to post. The easiest way to find anything was to think about the demon or the subject that you wanted to know about and see what turned up.

Focusing on Destiny got Grimshaw absolutely nothing. Not a bean. It was annoying, because Grimshaw was sure that Tun must be right. He couldn't be the only demon ever to have come up against this problem. Clearly the Acts and Facts wasn't allowed to hold information on such lofty matters. He couldn't even find a firm reference to the fact that Destiny trumped curses, even though everyone knew that!

What he did turn up was a list of curses where there had been a significant delay in the killing of one of the Sufferers. It was a short list. In most of those the delay was due to missed futures, or a Sufferer who didn't stop moving – one of them got around the world *twice* before the second-rate demon Juniper finally caught up with him; and then only because the man had collapsed from nervous exhaustion. In one case a Sufferer holed himself up in a single room, waited on solely by his faithful servant, and managed to survive for some years before the third-rater Ansifar finally managed to arrange a (slow) death by poison. It took a huge amount of planning, searching the possible futures, more planning and so on, and Ansifar was granted a kind of honorary second-rate status for his efforts.

But most interesting of all was a failed attempt by a first-rate demon to kill off his third victim. The failure was followed by a delay of *three years* before the Sufferer was finally dealt with. The first interesting thing about this case was the lack of any recorded explanation for either the failure or the delay, and the second interesting thing was the demon's name. Hanhut.

Grimshaw paused as a sign loomed up in front of him, the words meaningless because place names didn't work in Limbo. Limbo wasn't a world with direction. Even so, Grimshaw was pretty certain that he should leave the roadway here.

So he left the highway with its untidy rows of dead

cars and lolloped on to the smaller network of roads that would eventually lead him back to the church of St Peter and St Paul. He barely noticed the change of surroundings as dead houses and shops took the place of dead earth, and his mind kept going back to the odd case of Hanhut's third Sufferer. Instinct told him that the reason there was no reason given for the failure and the following delay was that it involved something that could not be recorded on the curse-demon web. Destiny.

And yet Hanhut had succeeded in the end! Of course, Hanhut was a first-rate demon where Grimshaw was only a third-rater.

Grimshaw paused to snarl quietly to himself. He felt angry at everyone and with everything. He was furious with Flute for being so spiteful as to steal his chronometer. With Tun and Hanhut and their like for being so superior. With himself for being such a useless Avatar. With Lampwick for creating him in the first place. With Fish Jones for having a destiny. And for being noble. And for being human.

Especially with Fish Jones.

After a short detour to pick up his dropped notebook and abandoned backpack, Grimshaw turned wearily into the gate of the church. He really, really didn't want to do the next hour or so. With a sigh, he pushed open the door and went in.

'Utterly disgraceful!' Lampwick was striding, or rather lurching, up and down the crypt, waving his arm occasionally for emphasis.

Slumped in the middle of the floor, Grimshaw stared at his toes. His chronometer was laid out on the top of Lampwick's coffin and he was itching to grab it and put it on, but he had to wait until Lampwick gave it back to him. Unfortunately, the magician was enjoying himself too much to bring the lecture to an end.

'I can hardly believe that even you would do something so . . . so . . . farcical!'

Grimshaw didn't know what farcical meant, but he got the general idea and shuffled his paws.

'What were you thinking of! Putting yourself in the way of the Sisters of Gladness! Going to chat to them like Grey Space was a tea party!'

'They had things to tell me,' mumbled Grimshaw. 'Even if they were nasty about it.'

'Losing . . . and this I really cannot believe . . . *losing your chronometer*!!'

'They took it!'

Lampwick gave him a shrivelling gaze. He was pretty good at shrivelling gazes. When he was alive, he had used them a lot on anyone who dared to question his honesty.

'Well, they did!'

Lampwick ignored him. '*Losing* your chronometer! You've always been a joke, barely fit to do your job, but that is shameful. Quite shameful. You're the laughing stock of the demons!' Lampwick paused and looked at him steadily before delivering the deepest cut. 'Even Wimble.'

Grimshaw closed his eyes in pain. He had been hoping that it wasn't so, that in spite of his disgrace his not-quite-bottom position in the demon hierarchy hadn't changed, but there it was, Lampwick had said it. Grimshaw was the lowest of the low. Even Wimble could look down on him now.

'Not to mention,' went on Lampwick, his voice heavy with scorn, 'that you appear to be incapable of killing a small, defenceless boy!'

'He has a destiny,' snarled Grimshaw. 'Destiny trumps curses.'

'Always an excuse,' sneered Lampwick, waving a hand dismissively. 'It's not my fault,' he whined, putting on a high, wavering voice, 'it's not my fault I'm useless . . .'

Grimshaw raised his head and fixed his corner-to-corner black eyes on Lampwick with a look of intense hatred. For a brief moment the magician faltered, but it passed.

'I suppose you will just have to join the roll call of shame, those few dismal Avatars who have *Survivors!*' Lampwick sighed and shook his head.

'Wimble. Wimble is the only Avatar to have a Survivor.'

'We will have to wait until they rebury me and you have a new Litany,' went on Lampwick, talking over him. 'Let's hope you can work on that without messing up.'

'I'll do it!' snarled Grimshaw suddenly. The hatred and rage were too much to bear, and inside, something snapped. 'I'll kill the boy one way or another, you see if I don't!'

'What happened to Destiny trumps curses?' snorted Lampwick.

'I DON'T CARE,' screamed Grimshaw, rearing up on his back paws as far as he could. A twitch was building up in his body, he could feel his muscles crackling with it. When it struck, he leapt with it, landing on the tomb next to Lampwick. He leaned forward and looked into his Architect's pale eyes.

'I don't care about flaming Destiny,' he said, hissing the words, 'I'll do it somehow. I'll kill Fish Jones, you'll see.'

'Hmmn! I'll believe it when it happens.' Lampwick stalked erratically over to the coffin and picked up the chronometer. He threw it at Grimshaw.

'Go on then! Get out of my sight!'

Sticking out a hand, Grimshaw caught the chronometer and slapped it on his wrist. Then he spun the dials as fast as possible and hit send.

He ended up back in Real Space on a tuft of grass in the middle of a field. A cow raised its head and looked at him. Avatars were hidden from human eyes, it took an effort of will to make themselves visible, but animals could see them all right.

The cow chewed thoughtfully, then looked for another mouthful. It took a step forward, interested in the succulent clump that Grimshaw was sitting on. Grimshaw snarled at it. It lowered its head and gripped a chunk of grass practically underneath Grimshaw, then pulled hard, forcing him to move.

With a scream of rage, Grimshaw flailed around, tearing up chunks of grass and throwing them at the cow. It ignored him. He bounced towards it and landed a kick on its solid flank, then bounced back, turning to face it with a howl. The cow began to eat the grass.

It was intolerable. Even cows treated him with disdain!

He stopped howling and stood, heaving in great, deep breaths of air. His corner-to-corner black eyes smouldered with an inky heat. He would show them. He had meant what he said, all right. A little thing like Destiny wasn't going to get in his way. If Hanhut had done it, so would he.

Persistence, he thought, *that's the key. Determination. Hit the boy with everything I've got and leave Destiny standing.*

Grimshaw dug out his copy of Mrs Minchin, and his ruler, and got to work. Destiny or not, Fish Jones was as good as dead.

�֎

Later that same afternoon, in a small town some miles beyond Stoney Cross the sky was filled with leaden smoke that twisted and heaved in oily clouds. Sirens wailed and from everywhere rose the clamour of screams, crying voices and running feet. Broken glass crunched underfoot and the stench of petrol and greasy flames hung in the air. Behind a barrage of fire engines, a row of firemen struggled to control the blaze consuming a petrol station. Paramedics ran all over the place and policemen shouted directions, organising people and vehicles to safety.

A short distance away at the corner of the street, an old man stood watching, his face covered in dust and soot and his hat clenched in one hand.

'Excuse me,' said a voice at his elbow.

The old man looked round and then down. He cocked an eyebrow that looked like a shaggy grey caterpillar against the dark skin of his face.

'Can you . . . um . . . tell me what's going on?' said the new arrival. 'I just got off the train, see. I was meant to catch a bus from here, but everything's delayed.'

'Been an accident,' said the old man. He looked bemused, like a man who was trying to work out something complicated, something possibly unbelievable. 'Well, several, actually. Someone died too. See, there was this boy . . . Odd-looking kid. Fair hair, almost white, and eyes like hazelnuts. Wearing a T-shirt far too big for him. Had a drawing of a fish on the front.'

The girl stared at the old man with fixed attention.

'Fish?'

'Yes, like I said. And the word fish.'

The girl blinked at him. Then she cleared her throat

173

and dragged a battered notebook out of her pocket. 'Tell me everything,' she said firmly. 'The name's A. J. Craig and I'm a reporter . . .'

❧

When the old man had finished his story of death and mayhem, A. J. Craig nodded. She had long since stopped writing it all down. She looked over to the houses with their broken glass and tattered curtains billowing in the air, hoping that no one had been in there, sitting in front of the TV or reading, when it happened.

'So the boy was unharmed, right? Even after four near-fatal . . . accidents! But someone *did* die – the man in the truck, the one that ran into the petrol pump?'

The old man sighed heavily. 'Yes. I wish I was not there then. I wish I had stayed at home, but I saw it all. A scarecrow of bones and ash, still burning inside the truck. Horrible it was. And . . .'

'Yes?'

'And I will tell you this – there was something else too. I will tell you because I must tell someone or go crazy. Just for one split second, when that young fellow went off his head and crashed into the pump, I saw *something in the truck with him*. Something that flicked into view and then disappeared again. Something . . . *horrible*! Like a skinned cat with extras.'

He looked down at the scrawny figure with the notebook, the carrier bags and the shocked expression. 'You do not have to believe that. But it was there.'

'Thanks,' said A. J. Craig, stuffing the notebook back into a tatty pocket. 'Thanks very much, you've been ever so helpful, but I've got to go now. I've got to hurry. But I'll tell you something – about the thing you saw in the truck.'

The old man swivelled his gaze from the scene of chaos around him to the grubby-looking would-be reporter. 'Mmm?'

'I believe you. I really do.'

21

ALICE

Fish was still running as evening began to draw near. He didn't care which direction he went, as long as it was away from the doomsday town and the demon. He could barely keep upright, and his foot was hurting so badly that every step was like treading on knives. His face was wet, though he couldn't remember crying, and his head was filled with the effort of keeping on the move. He wasn't even looking forward to arriving at Crow's Cottage, because all he would find there was an abandoned house full of the demons that came with dirt and decay.

The road was empty. He had just left the last small village behind and was facing a long walk up a hill to the rocky wilds ahead. After that would be a long walk downhill. And then he had moors to cross. Above him, the sky pressed down in a darkening bowl, filling his vision in all directions. Silence blocked his ears and cool air stirred around him in silky currents. It made him feel like he was at the bottom of a deep sea.

Although he had escaped alive, the barrage of attacks

had left his head full of chaotic images. Of these, the one that came back to him the most, more than all the damage and the fire and the frightened people, was that of the demon as it snapped into existence right in front of him on the High Street. It had reared up as tall as it could on its back paws and had looked at him, stared him in the eye, and the look it had given him was one of exultation. It had revelled in his terror, it was as simple as that. And it was Fish's terror that had stopped him in his tracks and sent him fleeing to the other side of the road, right where disaster was waiting to strike in the form of shattered glass, falling tiles, flying pottery and exploding pumps. Any one of those accidents could have killed him, *would* have killed him but for a series of freak events (the unravelled shoelace, for instance) that delayed him right at the crucial moment.

But if it was the demon that had sent him into the path of danger, then it was the thing that he had seen at the petrol station that had caused him to veer away just as the explosion happened. And that thing was death.

Death, in Fish's view of the world, arrived in the form of silvery light. Inside the silvery light was *something*. Fish had only once been close enough to see the something and it freaked him out far more than dirt demons, or even misery snakes.

Death could be quick or it could be slow. When it was quick, as in the case of Jon Figg, the light arrived fast and went as swiftly. Right over the petrol pump, Fish had seen the light appear and he had run away because he was afraid it was meant for him. As it happened, the poor man in the truck . . . well, anyway, the death hadn't been there for Fish after all, but seeing it arrive had saved his life. Odd that.

Fish glanced at the sky again. By now, the sun was sinking fast and he knew he wouldn't make it before dark. He also knew that he could no more stop and sleep than he could fly. He would just keep walking until he couldn't walk any more and then he would fall down and if he was lucky he'd live until the morning. Then he'd have to hope that he could get up again.

A long way behind him a black dot appeared in the middle of the horizon. As it drew nearer it became a car. It was nearly on him before he heard it. Startled, Fish turned to look.

It was more than just a car. It was a taxicab. Right out here in the middle of nowhere. Fish stared at it, bewildered. It drew level with him and then it stopped.

The door opened and someone peered out.

'God, Fish, you look like death! Seems I got here just in time.'

Fish smiled. It was hardly visible beneath all the dirt and blood on his face, but it was a big smile.

'Come on then!' A small and grimy hand reached out to grab him. He stumbled with it, falling into the cab. The door slammed.

'You can drive on now.'

The taxi driver, who had been staring at Fish, faced front again and put the cab back into motion.

'Well,' said Alice J. Craig firmly, 'I brought some money like you said. Hadn't you better tell me exactly what kind of thing is out to get you?'

✤

Fish sank back against the well-worn leather of the taxi and thought that he had never known such comfort in all his life.

'I suppose it's something weird,' said Alice. There were two large shopping bags at her feet, along with a smaller plastic bag from Sainsbury's. As usual when she wasn't at school, she was wearing a skirt with a torn hem, a corduroy jacket with frayed cuffs and a dirty top with a sequin butterfly on it. The butterfly was missing a lot of its sequins. Her shoes were scuffed on the toes and hadn't been polished since they were bought. She had smudges on her tanned face, grub under her fingernails and had forgotten to brush her hair, but she looked like heaven to Fish.

He nodded.

'Why doesn't that surprise me! The moment Jed told me about your call I knew it was something to do with all that stuff. It's why I decided to bring the money myself instead of posting it like you said. What is it this time? Worse than the dirt devils, obviously. Worse than the death things? The ones that hang around old people and sick folk?'

Fish nodded again.

Alice stared at him, shoving her mop of dark hair

back behind her ears. 'It's something to do with your mum and them dug-up coffins, isn't it? Judging by the trail of wreckage you've left behind you, I'm guessing a . . . demon of . . . revenge? Like a curse demon?'

She took one look at Fish's expression and sighed. 'Right, so we're going to this Crow's Cottage to hide, yes?'

By now the taxi had gathered speed and was sailing up the hill. Around them the landscape unwound in a vast expanse of heather and darkening sky. Fish took a moment to appreciate its beauty.

'Nice up here, isn't it?' Alice leaned forward and tapped on the window between them and the cabby. He reached up and pulled it open.

'Are we nearly there?'

'Not yet, love. 'Bout ten miles.'

'Thanks.' Alice waited until he'd closed the panel again before she spoke in a low voice. 'I've got plenty of money. I took everything out of my savings and nicked some more from Mum's wallet – she always says I can take what I need. Got a train easy. Had to change at that place you devastated, which is when I realised that something really bad was going on. You should've seen the mess! So I thought I'd better get a taxi. Figured we'd pick you up on the way. There's only one road going in the right direction. Good thing too. You'd never've made it on foot, not in the state you're in.'

Silently, Fish reached out and squeezed her hand.

She blushed. 'That's OK. Anything for a mate. And

Mum won't even see I'm not there for a day or so. You know her – back from work after I've gone to bed, and off again before I'm up.' She gave a snort of laughter. 'Dad left over a year ago, now, and I don't reckon she's noticed yet.'

They drove in silence for a while through the steadily gathering dusk that covered the land like shadowy silk. On the far side of the hills was a small town where yellow lights glinted in windows, suggesting warmth and hot dinners and TV. But they drove through it and out the other side into a darkness broken only by the taxi's headlights.

They drove for a long time, deeper into the growing night, and then at last the taxi drew slowly to a crawl.

'We're about the right place, love, but I dunno this Crow's Cottage. Can't be that one there.' The cabby jerked a thumb towards a dark hump against the pale moonlight. 'It looks deserted.'

'Next one along,' said Alice smoothly.

He drove slowly down the road for about a mile before Alice said, 'There, that's my auntie's house.' She pointed towards a light in the darkness. 'Come on, Fish, out you get. Go round the back – she'll have left the door open for us. Let's get inside quick.'

She pushed open the door, shoved Fish out and climbed down behind him, dragging the bags with her. Fumbling in her pocket, she brought out a wad of notes and peeled off a bunch from the top to hand to the cabby, who pulled open the window to take it.

'You've given me too much, love!'

'Keep it.'

'But . . .'

'Look money's no problem, right? Money I've got in spades. And you've been awful nice and patient and everything, driving all that way. And you've got a long way to go back too, so keep it.'

The driver smiled in the darkness. 'Ooo am I to argue, love?'

Alice picked up the bags and headed fast towards the light. Bewildered, Fish followed her. She let them in the gate and hurried up a path through a neatly kept garden. The taxi was taking its time to leave.

'Round the back,' she whispered to Fish. 'He's a nice man, so I'm betting he won't go till he thinks we're safely inside. And try not to be seen!'

Behind the cottage, Alice flattened herself against the wall. So did Fish. They listened until finally, with a deep rumble, the taxi pulled away. While they waited for Alice to be completely sure it was safe, Fish's eyes adjusted to the lack of light. Slowly, the landscape took shape in silhouette against the dark blue of the night sky.

'OK,' said Alice.

Carefully, they crept back around the cottage, trying to make as little sound as possible. As they went past the front window, Fish heard the murmur of the TV, which explained why nobody had been paying attention to what was happening outside.

On the road again, Alice set off back the way the taxi had come.

'It's not too far, Fish,' she said gently. 'Can you make it?'

Fish nodded. He'd had a rest now, and besides, a mile up the road from here was nothing compared to the long, long walk he would have had if Alice hadn't picked him up.

The night air was soft and still with a smell like cool water. Overhead, stars pricked the sky with brightness and a thinly sliced moon cast a pale light. There was no sound but the soft pad of their feet on the road and the rustle of the carrier bags. It didn't take them long to reach the dark shape that had to be Crow's Cottage. The iron gate had a crow on it, which kind of clinched things. Fish paused, looking anxious.

'Come on,' said Alice. 'It can't be that bad. Let's go and see.'

She pushed open the gate and they crunched up a gravel path with weeds poking through the stones. When they got to the front door they stopped.

'Fish, how do we get in?'

Fish screwed up his forehead, then groaned as he remembered that Jon had given Susan the keys to the cottage. She had put them in her handbag, which meant they were either lying by the road where she had fallen, or else someone had found her bag for her and the keys were in Blackheath hospital, nearly thirty miles away.

'I'm guessing we'll have to break in, right? Come on, let's find a back window or something.'

Alice dumped the bags on the doorstep and set off around the house. Reluctantly, Fish followed her. He was not good at adventures and liked to do things in a proper, orderly fashion. Breaking windows did not appeal. Alice, on the other hand, took keep-out signs as an invitation, never did as she was told and liked to climb on things. It was part of the reason Fish liked her. The other part was the way she understood him without him having to say much.

She pounced on a chunk of brick at the side of the path and a moment later the night was filled with the tinkling sound of broken glass. Fish glanced around, worried that someone would hear. Alice took off her jacket and wrapped it around her hand.

'Seen them do this in films,' she said. 'Stops you getting cut.'

Along with some swearing that made Fish blush, Alice reached in carefully, found the knob and pushed open the back door of Crow's Cottage.

22

CROW'S COTTAGE

Alice pulled a torch out of her pocket and directed the beam into the darkness on the other side of the door. They peered inside and Fish shuddered.

'Where?'

He pointed to the dirt demons on top of a pile of old rags. They had turned their heads when the door opened, and their eyes, reflecting in the torchlight, glared up at Fish irritably. One of them bared teeth like tiny needles. To the left, he could see more movement out of the corner of his eye, but he made sure not to look at it.

'Uh huh. Well, I can see spiders.' Alice was looking up at a knot of webs near the ceiling. 'Oh yuk.'

Hanging on to each other, they edged through the kitchen into the hall. It was narrow, with a tiled floor and a couple of doors leading from it, both shut.

'Going to get the bags,' said Alice, 'then we'll look upstairs.'

She handed Fish the torch, walked to the front door and opened it, then pulled in the bags that were still sitting on the front step.

Fish looked around carefully, playing the beam over the floor, walls and ceiling. There were no dirt demons in the hall. It was dusty and some thin cobwebs floated from the ceiling, but there was no rubbish and nothing to decay. The floor was bare boards and the walls were painted straight on to the plaster rather than being papered and heaving with demons, which was a relief. Paint was hardwearing. It got dirty, but it didn't decay like paper.

When she had the bags, Alice put them in the middle of the hall, closed the door, took the torch back and went warily up the stairs. The bare boards creaked under her weight, sounding horribly loud in the night silence. After a moment's hesitation, Fish went after her.

At the top, Alice headed for the only open door. It led to a small, empty room at the back of the house. It was lighter here as a pair of ancient curtains were pushed half open, letting in the pale light from the night sky.

'Right,' said Alice, looking at the curtains, 'I'm betting those rags are crawling with things?'

Fish nodded. Whatever colour the cloth had been once, it was now a faded grey-brown, and it was heaving with demons. They were small and (unlike the dirt demons in the kitchen) blunt-toothed, with eyes like pale disks in the half-light. Alice grabbed the curtains and pulled. Demons rained to the ground where they thrashed about for a second and then vanished. The material tore, but the curtains stayed in place.

'Bum. I'll have to get up there somehow. Or do you want to look in the other rooms . . . I'll take that face as a no, shall I? You'll have to give me a lift up then.'

Fish squatted on the floor to let her climb on his back as if he were a footstool. Alice kicked off her shoes and stood on him, wobbling a little.

'C'n just about reach, right. Difficult with the torch though. Keep still!' The light bobbed about as she struggled to get the curtains down.

About two inches from his nose a small, rather faint demon glared at Fish. It eyeballed him angrily and bared its stubby teeth. It looked like an angry frog and made Fish feel like laughing. It was a good feeling.

'Got 'em!'

A second rain of demons bounced to the floor where they squalled furiously and evaporated. The curtains followed, dropping into a heap on the boards. New demons began to wriggle out of the fabric almost at once. Because they were coming from something so rotten they developed fast, opening their eyes seconds after they formed. They immediately swivelled to stare at Alice, who was throwing the second curtain down on top of them. She climbed down from Fish's back. Then she screamed.

Fish uncoiled quickly. Alice grabbed his arm.

'Sorry. Spider. Big. There.' She aimed the beam of the torch.

It was toiling diligently along by the skirting. Fish went over to it and cupped it in his hands. It tickled.

He carried it to the window, which Alice opened with a hard shove.

'Good,' said Alice with relief, as he dropped it to the ground below. 'Right. I'll deal with these then, shall I?'

She scooped up the dirty material and headed for the door. Left alone, Fish took a look around the room. It was still and quiet, and with the curtains gone, the bare walls and floor were burnished with silver light. He nodded and felt something inside him unknot.

A moment later, Alice was back, carrying the bags she had brought. She upended the largest, shaking out a small, thin quilt and a crocheted blanket.

'Mattress topper and a baby blanket. We can make a bed. And two blow-up pillows.' She dug in the other bag. 'Lemonade, biscuits and a loo roll. Not that I'm suggesting we look at the bathroom tonight, but there are some nice bushes outside.' She beamed at him. 'We'll be all right.'

Fish smiled back. 'You're fantastic,' he said.

✄

At last they curled up on the quilt, still in most of their clothes and with the blanket laid over them. Outside the window, a tree brushed the glass with its leafy fingers and somewhere Fish could hear a soft hooting that he thought must be an owl. It was a lifetime away from Nightingale Row, with its street lights that banished the stars and the purring of engines late into the night. He drew a deep lungful of air and let it out again in a long sigh. Already, Alice was asleep. He could hear her steady breathing and feel the warm centre that was her, resting next to him. And for the first time since yesterday morning, when he and Susan had come back from the shops to find their lives changed forever, he felt peaceful.

Closing his eyes, Fish slept and the night went on in silence.

23

NOTHING LEFT

Grimshaw was standing in the middle of the town, seething. By now the ambulances, the police cars and the fire engines had left the scene. Everyone had gone, even the sightseers, and a sort of calm had been restored to the village centre. The wreckage was still there, of course, surrounded by police tape, but the fires were out and the body of the poor man in the van had been taken away. Everything was quiet. Stars came out overhead.

But Grimshaw still seethed.

After Destiny's interference in the deaths he had set in place, Grimshaw had been forced to improvise, showing himself to the truck driver and causing the vehicle to smash into the petrol pump. For a single glorious moment, when he saw the boy flying through the air like a kicked ball, he thought he had won. But all demons know instinctively when they have made a kill, and he soon realised that against the odds the wretched boy was still alive.

Not long ago he would have revelled in the cataclysm,

but that marvellous feeling of BOOM had been lost in his desire to win. Grimshaw had scarcely noticed the boiling clouds overhead or heard the screams of the people. It hardly registered that he had killed an Innocent Bystander. All he could think about was that Fish Jones had got away again.

At last the silence and the emptiness got through. There was nothing left to see, and nothing left to do but face Lampwick.

The knowledge that the only way into Limbo was through zero, which automatically took him to his Architect, only increased the fury in Grimshaw's heart. Typical of flaming Limbo that every stupid Rule was designed to make half-life worse.

Still, he wouldn't stay in the crypt any longer than he could help. Standing here, stewing in his anger, it dawned on Grimshaw that there was something he should have done before he even thought about attacking the Jones boy again. He should have asked Hanhut about the strange case of his third Sufferer. He should have made Hanhut tell him how to cheat Destiny.

Savagely, Grimshaw spun the dials of his watch back to zero, hit send and vanished.

❋

Lampwick brightened up as Grimshaw snapped into being in the middle of the crypt floor.

'Aha! There you are! I was waiting for you to come crawling back.'

Grimshaw snarled at him. Before Lampwick could get going, he turned his back and began rearrange the dials on his chronometer. He hesitated for a second, wondering where Hanhut was most likely to be – the British Museum or the desert.

'. . . so pathetic . . .' Lampwick was saying in his most scornful voice, '. . . you really thought you'd done it that time, eh? But the kid just walked away without a scratch . . .'

It was just too much. Grimshaw stiffened.

'He. Has. A. DESTINY!' he screamed, spinning around to face his maker. 'Don't you get it? It's nothing to do with me, the boy's protected . . .'

'Oh, *that's* right,' sneered Lampwick, gearing up to do the whole 'any excuse' rant again. 'I remember, it's not poor little Grimshaw's fault, it's all down to *Higher Beings* . . .'

His voice was cut off as Grimshaw twisted the dials and hit send as fast as he could.

Lampwick watched him go, sniggering quietly to himself. He considered summoning the creature back, but decided against it. It was always more satisfying to have the useless thing come slinking in of its own accord. In the meantime, he could wait. It would give him an opportunity to think up some juicy insults.

After all, there was plenty of time. All the time in the world, in fact.

Far away, on top of the Limbo mountain, Tun was also thinking about time.

He had gazed over the grey panorama below him so often that although it would look like a dust-coloured nothing to anybody else, Tun could see that the grey was etched and swirled with the faint outlines of countries and kingdoms stretching to the horizon in all directions. It was the world and it lay at his feet, reminding him of days when he had held the lives of men in his hands. He stood, motionless, understanding that this was all he had left to him. Forever.

Of course, in Tun's case forever meant until the tomb of the House of Ombre ceased to exist.

Tun bowed his head, shuddering. A curse, and its Avatar, could only end when it was either completed or became meaningless. Tired of the endless round of still-beating hearts and so on, he had thought that the death of the last family member would be enough to end his curse and bring him freedom. But the dying words of Rudolphus Ombre hadn't specified that it had to be *the family* who must carve his name alongside those of his ancestors, only that they were the ones to be persecuted for so long as the job wasn't done. Technically, anyone could do it, but with the family gone, who would even think to? With the passing of centuries, no living human even remembered the name of Ombre, let alone where the ancestral vault was!

No, the tomb was the key to the curse, the tomb waiting for all time for that one last name to be added to those on its dark walls. And as the tomb in question was the size of a marble mansion and was built where wind, fire, flood and earthquake were extremely unlikely to damage it, that pretty much meant forever. Until the Earth fell into the sun, if that was how planets died.

Hidden deep within his cowl, Tun's terrible eyes closed as he struggled with the knowledge that he had condemned himself to forever in Limbo. Now, he would do anything to be able once again to travel to Real Space and feel men's hearts beating their last in his clenched fist. But there was no undoing what he had done.

Over the last few centuries since he'd driven his last-ever Sufferer insane, goading him to horribly murder his young wife and daughter, and then terrifying him to death afterwards, Tun had been over and over the problem of how to escape the nightmare that his half-life had become. He could think of only one possible way to end it all and it was a fearful way indeed. But he was unable to put it into action because to do so would mean travelling to Real Space, which he couldn't do without Sufferers. At times he was almost glad, because the idea was so terrifying he wasn't certain that even he had the nerve to do it.

But then, standing there on the mountain, contemplating his long and deathly future, Tun had a revelation!

The demon's eyes sprang open again, and if this had been Real Space the expression in them would have turned a summer's day into a winter's night. Maybe there was a way after all! Grimshaw.

With Sufferers still to kill, Grimshaw *could* travel to Real Space. More than that – inside Grimshaw burned the desire to redeem himself, to claw his way back from the pit of shame he had been cast into by the loss of his chronometer and the survival of Fish Jones. The small demon was angry, but was he angry enough to carry out Tun's fearful plan for him? Strangely enough, Tun didn't think to question Grimshaw's courage. Anyone who could hand themselves over to the Sisters of Gladness and their like had to have courage in spades. It might be enough, or it might not. That was the gamble.

So, maybe, if Tun played his cards carefully, if the idea was explained to Grimshaw in the right way at the right time . . .

The demon smiled a terrible smile. Fortunately, no one was there to see it. He stood for a while longer, designing a plan so twisted that it warmed his cold heart. Then he went to find his friend.

�֎

Grimshaw popped into existence in the middle of the Limbo version of the British Museum. It was bedlam, as usual. Even though the Architects took it in turns to banish their Avatars to make a little space, the two large rooms that housed the museum's collection of mummies teemed with the half-alive and the half-dead. Here, the Avatars were outnumbered by the Architects. Often there was more than one Architect for every demon, as that role belonged not only to the Kings or high-born persons whose body was protected by the curse, but also to the priests who had set the curse in place. For the most terrible demons, like Hanhut, a whole team of priests had been employed in their creation.

''Scuse me,' Grimshaw mumbled to a demon so ancient it looked like a heap of crumpled bandages. He had materialised on its foot.

'No problem,' it said politely in Ancient Egyptian. 'We're used to it in here.'

Fortunately, language wasn't an issue in Grey Space, so Grimshaw thanked him equally politely in Victorian English and glanced over at the demon's Architect, an Egyptian king so wizened he was barely recognisable as once-human. He eyed him coldly. Grimshaw ignored him and set about looking for Hanhut.

Everywhere he looked were demons in bandages, demons with heads like predatory birds, or demons like sleek and hungry cats. Demons with hides and teeth like crocodiles, or in priestly garb with eyes like black pits and carrying some very nasty-looking hooks and knives. Of the Architects, many were still in their bandages and almost indistinguishable from their demons. Others were unwrapped, revealing their dried-out, shrivelled bodies, and some of them (the really powerful ones) looked as impressively jewelled and garbed in death as they had in life. It seemed to Grimshaw that they were all arguing, and the racket was tremendous.

He reached out and carefully tweaked the bandaged arm of the Ancient One whose foot he was trying not to stand on again.

'Excuse me, but I'm looking for Hanhut?'

'Oh, are you? Grimshaw, isn't it? The Curse of Lampwick the Robber? Shame about the chronometer, but damned good effort even so. I particularly enjoyed the sheep. Plus, the explosion at the gas station was a corker – showing yourself to that driver was a stroke of genius, though I'm not sure you weren't breaking the Rules just a little!'

'I didn't reveal myself to a Sufferer,' Grimshaw pointed out. 'The Rules only say that I can't reveal myself to a Sufferer. Don't say anything about humans generally.'

The Ancient One nodded. 'Well, it certainly made up a little for . . . you know.'

Grimshaw sighed inwardly. He knew all right. Everyone would be on about the curse demon who lost his chronometer.

'I'm surprised,' he said a touch irritably. 'I didn't think anything would make up for that.'

'You've a long way to go yet, true. But it was a good start. Anyway, it's made a nice change, talking to you.' The Ancient One pointed with a ragged arm. 'If you want Hanhut, head for the middle of the room. Try not to tread on anyone or there'll be an awful row.'

'Thank you,' said Grimshaw again, and set off,

weaving his way through the crowd of irritable demons and hoping he was too small to be noticed.

As soon as he had rounded a sarcophagus or two, he spotted Hanhut. The tall jackal-headed shape, its dark wings neatly folded, was standing at the side of its young owner-Architect, who in turn was surrounded by a gaggle of her priests. The Egyptian queen who owned Hanhut's curse had once been beautiful as well as powerful. Even dead, her kohl-ringed eyes were lovely, and her slim body was decked with ropes of precious gems. She was sitting on top of her sarcophagus, kicking her heels in a bored way. Because Limbo didn't do glass, the displays of coffins were not enclosed as they would be in Real Space, so Grimshaw was able to squeeze through the surrounding throng until he was close enough to stand at the queen's feet.

She spotted him at once and immediately brightened up.

'Oh, look, Han,' she said. 'There's that funny little third-rater! The one who lost his chronometer.'

A pair of burning eyes swivelled to look at the new arrival. Grimshaw tried not to faint with fright. He squared his shoulders and did his best to meet Hanhut's gaze head on.

'I need to know,' he said as firmly as he could manage, 'about your third Sufferer, the one it took you three years to kill.'

He had to raise his voice a little to be heard over the

argument that had just broken out between a couple of nearby crocodile-like demons who had trodden on each other's tails.

Hanhut's glare intensified. His snout wrinkled back in a snarl that showed his long, pointed teeth. Grimshaw could feel him tensing, getting ready to deal out punishment to this miserable scraping of an Avatar that dared to ask him questions.

'Oh, Han, wasn't that the weird one who didn't die first go? You know, the one with the hunched back and the limp?' The Queen clapped her hands and giggled. 'You made a right hash out of that – the way his pet pig ran out and tripped you up just as you materialised made me hoot!'

Hanhut winced. Grimshaw could hardly believe it, but there it was. A wince.

'You got him in the end though!' Hanhut's Architect giggled again. 'I did like the way you skinned him first – really fun that was! I think you should do that more often. When . . . *if* we get another Litany, of course.' She sighed and stuck out her lip in a pout.

The two demons, big and small, exchanged a long look and for once it was a look of total understanding. By way of direction, Hanhut made a small triangle in the air with a claw, then, as one, they reached for their chronometers.

'Remember when you had to go all the way to Paris to get that one on top of the metal tower thing with the holes . . .'

Again as one, the two demons pressed send and vanished from the museum . . .

. . . to reappear in the Limbo desert at the foot of a pyramid and right in front of Tun.

24

TUN'S DESIGN

'Oh, there you are, small one,' said Tun, ignoring Hanhut as openly as possible. 'I've been looking all over the desert for you – I was going to try the museum next. Thought you might want to find out more about the odd affair of the third Sufferer.'

Grimshaw nodded eagerly. 'You spotted that too?'

Hanhut sighed loudly. It sounded like knives scraping against stone, probably being sharpened. Tun did a mock start and said, 'Oh, you're here, are you? Didn't see you against all that sand! You do kind of blend in.'

The jackal-headed demon glared at him irritably and ruffled his wings. For the first time Grimshaw registered that Hanhut's all-over deathly grey colour did rather match his surroundings. He also realised that after their sudden exit, Hanhut's Architect might decide to summon him back before they had a chance to talk. He'd better move fast. Taking a deep breath, Grimshaw went for it.

'Look,' he said. 'You are the greatest demon . . .'

'Ahem,' coughed Tun meaningfully.

'. . . *one* of the greatest demons in history, apart from

the Mighty Curse which is most powerful of all, and yet your third Sufferer survived the first time you tried to kill him. Then you didn't try again for *three whole years*. And then you got him. So my questions are: why did he survive? Was it Destiny, like Fish Jones? And how did you get him in the end? Please tell me. I know I'm only a small curse, but I lost my chronometer, my Sufferer keeps surviving and I'd really *really* like to know.'

Aloof and chilly, and with his arms folded in a forbidding, headmasterly kind of way, the jackal-headed demon studied Grimshaw. Tun hummed tunelessly, making patterns in the sand with a bony toe and trying to look disinterested.

'Why?' asked Hanhut finally. 'Do you, pathetic little failure that you are, truly have the nerve to challenge Destiny?'

'Yes!' cried Grimshaw. 'I did already! I tried and tried, though it didn't work. But if there's a way, if you know a way, then I'll try again till it does.'

Hanhut glared at him some more, but there was a hint of curiosity in the look.

'You are a strange one,' he said, 'I'm almost tempted, but . . .'

'He won't tell you,' put in Tun. Deep in his cowl, his unseen eyes were alight with cunning design as he steered events in the right direction. 'He wants you to go on thinking that he's a powerful Avatar who bested Destiny in some mysterious way, when for all we know he failed the first time because he made a mistake.'

There was a furious roar from Hanhut, 'You . . . you moth-eaten BATHROBE!'

Tun sneered. 'Everyone knows that one, it's not funny any more. But if it's the best your dog-brain can come up with . . .'

Hanhut threw back his jackal head and howled at the sky, making Grimshaw cower. In response, Tun raised his arms, his night-dark robes swirling. Around him the air shimmered, and Grimshaw knew that if they had been in Real Space it would be growing dark and chill. Hanhut spread his wings, casting a shadow on the air, even in Limbo, which was no mean feat. The two demons faced each other, poised as if ready to strike.

Grimshaw glanced nervously at the sky. Such a display of power was likely to attract attention.

'Stop it!' he yelled. 'The Horsemen will hear you!'

The warning got through. Tun and Hanhut stopped glaring at one another and sent worried looks up at the sky. Hanhut abandoned his angry pose and reached for his chronometer of carved alabaster, intending to zap somewhere else just to be on the safe side.

'TELL ME!' howled Grimshaw.

'If there's anything to tell,' murmured Tun.

The Egyptian demon paused. Tun's point had hit home, and Hanhut couldn't bear for anyone to think he had failed to kill a Sufferer because of a mistake. He glanced up, checking the sky once more. It was empty save for one tiny dot far in the distance. It wasn't the Horsemen, so he ignored it.

Tun was almost sure he knew what Hanhut was going to say, and if so then it would push Grimshaw further in the right direction. Of course, he might be wrong. If it wouldn't have been beneath him to do so, he would have held his breath.

'It was Destiny,' Hanhut said at last in his rasping voice. 'My third Sufferer was protected by the Higher Orders.'

'But you killed him in the end!' cried Grimshaw.

Hanhut laughed, ignoring the intensity of Tun's gaze that would have bored holes in steel.

'I was lucky. The man's destiny came upon him while I hesitated, wondering what to do next. He made the scientific discovery that he was born to make and then his days of protection were over. He was mine for the taking. And I took him.'

Grimshaw stared at Hanhut in dismay. 'You mean I have to wait!'

'It's the only way,' said Hanhut. 'Destiny trumps curses, even curses as great as mine. Only the Mighty Curse, the most terrible of us, would be strong enough to overcome it.'

'But how long will I have to wait?' cried Grimshaw.

'Who knows?' put in Tun quickly, well satisfied with the way things were going. 'The boy could be an old man before he does whatever it is he's destined to do. You will just have to bear the disgrace for a few . . . well, probably many . . . long years. Still, what does it matter? You are only a small demon, after all.'

'IT MATTERS TO ME,' shrieked Grimshaw, his anger rising through him in a flood.

'Well then, what are you going to do about it?' said Tun, cheerfully. On Tun, cheerful sounded like the crack of doom, but there was something in his voice that made Grimshaw glare at him accusingly.

'You know something!'

Poised to press send, Hanhut paused, his curiosity getting the better of him. In the sky, the distant dot grew larger, flying purposefully towards the group at the foot of the pyramid.

Tun cleared his throat. 'I have been thinking about your situation a lot, my small friend, and it has occurred to me that there is one possible solution. If you were daring enough to carry it through. As you know—'

'Get on with it,' snarled Hanhut. 'We can do without one of your monologues.'

Tun glared, but got straight to the point anyway.

'You could wake the Mighty Curse,' he said, his voice a deathly whisper in the still Limbo air, 'and call its doom upon the world and everything in it. *Including Fish Jones.*'

There was a stunned pause, then Hanhut threw back his head and howled with laughter.

'Idiot,' he sneered. 'The Mighty Curse is lost and no one knows where. Besides, you would destroy the world!'

'Exactly,' murmured Tun to himself. 'And more than

that.' Deep in the shadows of his cowl, the terrible eyes gleamed.

Still howling with laughter, Hanhut vanished. Grimshaw barely noticed him go. True, the Mighty Curse was lost, but Tun's idea filled him with restless excitement and he wanted to talk about it. Neither of them had spotted the shape on the horizon, close now, looking like a small winged serpent flying swiftly their way. But not all serpent. Its long hair flew out behind it in a golden veil, bright against the dull grey of the sky, and even from this far away the green glow of its eyes was visible.

'But . . . I mean . . . how would we find out where the Mighty Curse was? It can't be in Limbo with its Architect or we'd know.'

Tun waved an arm airily. 'That, my friend, is a point I have often considered. And I believe,' he spoke softly, his dark monk-shape leaning closer to Grimshaw, 'I have at least half of the answer. Imenga the Mighty made his curse to act once and once only and then to come to an end. So, when he died, his soul was sent on to wherever it is that immortal souls go when they have tried to kill the world.'

Grimshaw flattened his ears back against his bony skull. Tun stepped back, giving Grimshaw time to work it out.

'So . . . what you are saying is . . . it's with its Sufferer? With the World! It's in Real Space, isn't it?'

'Exactly!'

'But *where* in Real Space?'

'That is the half I don't know. But I was wondering . . . You were brave enough to ask the Sisters for answers before. Perhaps you could try them again. They are angel Avatars, even if they are lowly ones, so surely they will know.'

Grimshaw smiled up at Tun gratefully, but inside something was bothering him. A frown began to creep over his brow. 'It's very good of you to come up with all these ideas,' he said slowly, 'when it could have such consequences for you too.'

'Whatever do you mean, small one?' Tun turned his cowled head and Grimshaw felt his friend's terrible gaze settle on his face.

'Well, with no one left alive in Real Space to invoke the curses, won't they all be broken? Our Architects will die properly and will move on to Whatever Comes Next. And all of the Avatars, angel or demon, well . . . who knows what will become of us?' Grimshaw flicked his ears and glanced up into the depths of the cowl that hid Tun's cold eyes, watching him so steadily.

'Especially,' he went on slowly, 'when you went to the trouble of making it so that your curse, and you, could never end.'

And then, out of the blue, Grimshaw saw the full truth of it. He understood why Tun always seemed unhappy, and why he had really killed the last family member of the House of Ombre – not to live forever, but in an attempt to end his curse!

'It's what *you* want me to do!' cried Grimshaw. 'End all the curses so that you can end too.' Hunching his bony shoulders, Grimshaw hissed at Tun as the hurt went deep. 'You're using me!'

The words hung in the still Limbo air. All the concern, all the help, was nothing more than Tun's plan to break free of his doom.

Tun gazed at Grimshaw steadily, then gave a dismissive wave of his hand. 'So, small one,' he said coldly, 'do you want to discuss tactics or not?'

'NOT!' cried a familiar voice over their heads.

'Flute!' Grimshaw screamed as a lithe body swooped down from the sky and two clawed hands grabbed him by the shoulders, jerking him from the ground. Startled, Tun took a moment to react, but then reached out and seized one of Grimshaw's disappearing back paws.

'He's mine!' howled Tun. 'I had him just where I wanted him! Let him go you . . . you harpy!'

Flute shrieked with laughter, still pulling Grimshaw away. Tun held on, while Grimshaw yelled and struggled, wanting them both to let go. But for all that Tun was a fearsome demon, Flute was stronger and had a better hold. Feeling Tun's cold grip on his back paw slide away, Grimshaw yelled even louder.

'Find me,' commanded Tun as the Sister tore Grimshaw free. His deep voice rang on the air like a death knell. 'Find me, small one, and I'll tell you what to do next to give us both our heart's desire!'

25

THE GLASS OCEAN

'So, this is cosy, isn't it?' said Flute's cool voice above Grimshaw's head.

She had dropped him on his front on a rock at the foot of a cliff, looking out over the Limbo ocean. Scrabbling upright, Grimshaw looked round to see her settling on the rock next to him. The lack of legs made it difficult for the Sisters to land anywhere as they had to lie on their middles and prop themselves up with their slender arms. Mostly they stayed in the air, hovering ceaselessly or flying high against the grey Limbo sky. But here was Flute, perched next to him with her wings folded and her lamp eyes studying his face.

Any other time, Grimshaw would have been impressed that one of the Sisters wanted to talk to him. Now, he just glared at her. The memory of his exchange with Tun still seethed in his head.

'I thought you might have some questions for me,' said Flute.

Grimshaw shrugged irritably and looked away, over the ocean that rolled out beneath him. The sea in Limbo was always grey and totally still. There were no waves or even ripples, and certainly nothing as exciting as a tide. It looked like an endless expanse of lifeless grey glass, a mirror of the sky. The only mirror that existed in Limbo.

Flute pinched his arm to get his attention.

'My sisters don't want me to be here,' she hissed. 'We had quite a row about you. They think you are a dismal disappointment who should be left to moulder away in the company of your tiresome Architect until his remains are dust and your curse ceases to exist and you along with it. They think you are a sad, pitiful, pointless waste of half-life. I, on the other hand, don't.'

Grimshaw flicked his ears. He didn't want to listen to Flute, he didn't want to listen to anything but his own anger snarling away in his head, but he couldn't help going back to the problem of Fish Jones. He turned his inky gaze to look at Flute.

'Here's a question for you,' he said, 'my Sufferer has a destiny and I want to know when his destiny is going to happen so that I know how long it will be before I can kill him.'

'Oh,' said Flute, sadly, 'you don't want to know anything about noble humans, or Beyond, or Choice or any of those things?'

'No,' said Grimshaw coldly. 'They don't really matter. Not in the way that killing my Sufferers and being a great demon matters.'

'Oh,' said Flute again, and Grimshaw thought he saw

something like disappointment in her glowing eyes. It made him even angrier. He was only trying to do a good job, to be the best demon he could be, so what right had she to be disappointed? He glared at her, letting the rage well up inside him, driving out all the terror he would normally feel in the presence of any of the Sisters.

'Well,' she said after a long moment, 'humans of that kind can have one destiny or many. Or they may have a destiny that takes them a lifetime to complete.'

Grimshaw kept glaring straight into her green lamps, his paws clenched. She blinked at him.

'And Fish Jones . . . ?'

'Has many tasks over many lives to perform in the service of Fate.'

Hunching his shoulders, Grimshaw turned away to stare out over the sea.

'So here's another one then,' he said softly. 'Where in Real Space is the Mighty Curse?'

Flute sighed. Her voice dropped to a soft whisper and her lamp eyes bathed the side of his head in their light as she leaned closer. 'We knew about Tun's plan to use you, and we guessed long ago that you would try asking us about it sooner or later. My sisters made me promise not to tell you where the Mighty Curse sleeps.'

'Doesn't surprise me,' snapped Grimshaw. 'I may only be a small demon, but I'm not stupid. I worked it out. Everything would be destroyed, including all the Avatars.'

'Possibly, nobody knows for sure. But still,' Flute went on, 'even though I don't know what will become of me and of my sisters, I am here for a reason. I will give you what you wanted long ago when all this was just beginning. I will give you the gift of choice. You can choose to unleash the Mighty Curse and destroy every living morsel of humanity and all the curses with it. Or you can choose to step back and let Fish Jones carry out his destinies, while you accept your disgrace and live out your half-life to its natural end.'

Grimshaw turned back and glared into her emerald eyes again. 'What choice is there,' he snarled, 'if you won't tell me what I need to know?'

Flute shrugged. 'Work with me here – I'm taking a big risk for you. And do you know how hard it is to give my sisters the slip! Look, just because we're cruel, doesn't mean we aren't good. I'm sure in my heart that you will choose to let the noble humans live. I believe you have it in you to be a better being. But I could be wrong, and if I am . . . who knows what I will have unleashed? What we will all have to face?'

The angel leaned even closer, so that her cheek brushed the demon's forehead and her lips tickled his pointed ear. 'I promised my sisters not to tell you where the Mighty Curse is hidden,' she whispered, 'but I don't *need* to tell you. You are a half-life and have it in you to divine the answer for yourself. You do it all the time. So do it, *if you choose.*'

She drew back and peered into his corner-to-corner

black eyes. 'Just one last thing before I go. You were given a glimpse of Beyond, remember? There was a promise in that, a promise of something more than all this, and that is a rare thing for a curse demon to have. So now, a warning. *Look. Down.*'

Unfolding her wings, Flute shot upwards in a flurry of air and a wave of tail and was gone, leaving Grimshaw staring after her. He hissed quietly, his brain turning over what she had said.

A choice. Kill the world and Fish Jones with it. Or let the humans live.

And a warning.

Almost without thinking about it, Grimshaw turned his eyes to look down. There was the Limbo sea, as blank and dead as ever. Except . . . His eyes went wide with shock.

Except that now, suddenly, Grimshaw could see *through* the grey glass surface of the ocean. As if there were something beyond the still, dead water. And what he saw made his flesh crawl and his insides tie themselves in knots. What he saw beneath the glass ocean was a darkness so deep and so endless that he could feel the chill of it in his blood. It was the darkness of the darkest of nights, and looking at it gave Grimshaw a gaping hole inside, even though he didn't understand what it had to do with him. He stared, horrified, for a long moment, all thoughts of the Mighty Curse and Fish Jones temporarily suspended.

But slowly they came back, and when they did he

spun the dials of his chronometer and went to Real Space to think things through.

Grimshaw drew in a long breath of sharp, salty air. Above him, the Real Space sky was clear and filled with stars, and a sliver of moon cast its cold light over the heaving waters. The whole effect was about as far away from the glass sea in Limbo as anything could get. Although there was no endless dark beneath the waves in Real Space, still the sense of mighty depth and sheer size was breathtaking. Watching it with his unblinking eyes, Grimshaw thought that he had never seen anything so amazingly lonely, or so amazingly beautiful. Or for that matter so amazingly powerful. It was far, far better than BOOM.

He was sitting on the same rock that he had just left in Grey Space, but here the waves broke and frothed around his perch, dashing icy spray across his skin. Behind him, the great cliff reared darkly against the night sky, towering over the cluster of rocks at its feet. Grimshaw's was the one furthest out. The one nearly on its own, surrounded by the restless energy of the water that seethed about him with barely contained power.

He shivered, coiling and uncoiling his tail. His clawed paws dug deeply into the seaweed, grazing the rock beneath. The smells of night air and salt filled his nose and the ceaseless calling of the waves roared in his ears. It all matched his dark, unsettled mood so perfectly. He could feel the ocean seeping into him, reaching deep into his heart and filling him with its deadly power.

In Grimshaw's head, thoughts and feelings churned and boiled. If he could find the Mighty Curse and wake it, he could achieve his aim and kill Fish Jones. But the world might end and every human with it.

He curled his tail thoughtfully. For all Flute's certainty that he cared, noble humans seemed like something he had worried about a long time ago and now the thought of wiping them out didn't bother him at all. He wanted to be worth noticing; he wanted to be different. Angels and demons alike, he wanted to *show them all*.

And what about the curse demons that he would also bring to an end? Grimshaw curled his lip in a sneer. What of it? He owed them no loyalty. All he ever got from them was mockery and scorn. He'd end himself too, of course, but so what? If he did this, if he awoke the Mighty Curse and wiped out everything for his own ends, he would no longer be some third-rate scraping of a demon. The instant before they were snuffed out they would know who it was who had bested Destiny against the odds. They would know who had killed them. And that would be enough for Grimshaw.

Gazing out across the heaving, restless mass of the ocean, Grimshaw felt again its pull on his heart. His all-black eyes glittered darkly as the power of it worked into every inch of his being and made him want things. It made him want to be vast and eternal and mighty. It made him want to be MORE.

Why care about death, he thought, when I can be *great*!

Looking up, he saw that the sky was beginning to lighten. He watched it while it changed to turquoise silk and then pale green and then gold. And then the sun rose.

And when it did, Grimshaw went to find the Mighty Curse.

Book Two

THE CURSE OF IMENGA
THE MIGHTY

26

CALM

When Fish woke up he was alone in the room. Not in the house though, for Alice had left the bedroom door open and he could hear her downstairs. He lay for a while, listening to the sounds of morning. Normally, he was woken up by early risers heading off for work in their cars, or by the milkman, or the smell of toast. Today, apart from Alice, all he could hear were birds singing. Nothing else. Not an engine sound anywhere.

He yawned, stretched and sat up, then looked around, fearful that the demon would be crouched somewhere, watching him. Planning his death. It wasn't.

Getting out of bed, he pulled on his jeans and limped downstairs. His foot hurt too much to be put back into a shoe just yet. It was still wrapped in his handkerchief, which looked as if it might have stuck to the wound as the blood dried. He wasn't looking forward to pulling it off.

In the kitchen, Alice had emptied the contents of the Sainsbury's carrier bag on to the table and laid them out. There was a packet of plastic knives and forks, a small jar of strawberry jam, a loaf of bread, two tins of soup, a small bottle of water and some chocolate. The lemonade and the biscuits from the night before were still upstairs.

As Fish came in, she looked up. She was holding a bottle of kitchen cleaner in one hand and a cloth in the other – bought along with the food, Fish guessed – and she was covered in coal dust.

'I got the stove going! And don't think it was easy! I made a bit of a mess. And I even managed to get rid of the spiders!' Through the dirt, her face shone with triumph. 'Anyhow, I figured that since I couldn't see the demons to worry about them, and since you needed a rest, I'd sort out the kitchen first thing.'

As she spoke she sprayed the work surface next to the stove with a good dose of cleaner. A couple of demons that had been rolling about in some unidentified grime, hissed and spat, then rapidly dissolved under the fine drops. Another scrabbled out of the way and fell to the floor, where it evaporated. Fish laughed. Alice rubbed the surface vigorously with the cloth, sweeping up one last squalling demon.

'I found some coal in the outhouse, only it was a bit webby in there and I'm not going anywhere near it after dark, and I had some matches in the bag and there were even some firelighter things to get it started, in the outhouse, I mean, and look . . .'

She went to the sink and turned a tap. After a lot of spluttering, water came out.

'The cottage has got a well. There's a pump and I pumped for HOURS.'

They looked at the brownish water.

'We can boil some and use it to wash, but I don't think we ought to drink it. We can have the rest of the lemonade and bread and jam for breakfast. I forgot butter. But we're gonna have to get more food and something to drink from somewhere. We'll have to find a shop.'

Fish thought it might be a long walk.

'Could be a long walk, mind you,' went on Alice grimly. 'Not a lot around here, as far as I can see!'

They ate breakfast sitting on the back step where there was a paved area, trying to be a patio. It ended in a couple of steps down, a strip of grass and a low wall. Beyond that was open moorland, rolling out before them, decked with heather and shrubs and wild flowers. In the distance and nestling behind a couple of trees, they could make out an old farmhouse.

'That must be the place we stopped at last night.' Alice pointed with a jammy finger. 'I wonder who lives there. Better go and say hello when we've eaten.' She looked at Fish's foot. 'At any rate, after we've done something about you. That looks a right mess!'

She got up and went inside, taking the plates. A moment later she was back with the third bag, the one that didn't contain food or sleeping equipment, which she dumped on the ground next to Fish. She began taking things out of it.

'Right. Spare money.' She took out an old sponge bag and pulled open the tie ends. It was stuffed with a roll of banknotes. 'Matches, rope, scissors – cos I didn't have a knife – torch, spare batteries, alarm clock, emergency chocolate and spare knickers.'

Fish blushed.

'And . . .' she triumphantly pulled out an old tin that used to hold fancy soaps, '. . . first-aid box. Nicked it from our bathroom. I better get a bowl of water and we'll see what we can do. Oh, and Jed sent you this.' From the bottom of the carrier bag she pulled something red. Jed loved red. It was his all-time favourite colour.

Taking it carefully, Fish held it up. It was Jed's jacket. His favourite jacket, the one he always wore. Fish looked at Alice.

'He wanted to come too, but his mum would have noticed. He said you probably needed something to keep you warm and dry. You're not going to cry, are you? Good. It was nice of him, though.'

It was more than nice. And it was at that exact moment that Fish understood what friends were all about. Alice and Jed. That was friendship. One had rushed to Fish's rescue at the drop of a hat and the other had given Fish the thing that he valued most in the world as a token of support, just because he couldn't be there too.

Alice had already gone to the kitchen. He could hear her cranking the handle of the pump and the sound of water splashing. It went on for a while. He was glad of the moments alone so that he could rub his eyes a few times and wipe his nose on his sleeve, as he didn't have anything else to use. At last Alice came back with a bowl of hot water.

'Sorry, took forever to boil. But the water's coming out cleaner. Here, stick your foot in that and soak the hanky off.'

She opened the first-aid box and began to sort out bandages and ointment. Fish turned his face up to the sun and closed his eyes. He was still feeling that peaceful feeling, like there was no need to run just now.

'Feels kind of safe here, doesn't it?' said Alice, thoughtfully.

'It's the calm,' said Fish.

Alice looked at him.

'The one before the storm,' he explained.

She nodded and went on bathing his battered foot.

❧

'We've just arrived in Crow's Cottage,' said Alice, 'only Mum's not feeling well so she sent us to see if there was a shop around here we could get some stuff.' She looked at the woman innocently, as if it wasn't obvious that there was no shop for miles.

The house they had borrowed last night to convince the taxi man they were safe turned out to belong to Mr and Mrs Dunnet. Mrs Dunnet, Penny, was a youngish woman, rather plump with a lot of bright copper hair and a large smile. She immediately invited them into the kitchen where she was baking huge quantities of cakes. Alice nudged Fish hopefully.

'I'm sorry to hear about your poor mam,' said Penny, 'but there's no shop round here. Tell you what, why don't you take some fresh bread and some milk and eggs from us?'

Alice opened her mouth, wanting to be polite and say not to worry, but knowing that this was just what they needed. 'That would be really great,' she said, honestly.

Penny was already putting things into a bag for them. 'Arthur goes into Knockton on a Thursday, so if your mam's not better tomorrow, you can give us a list and we'll get you whatever you need.'

She put the bag on the table next to Alice. It looked very full.

'Um . . . Should we pay you for this?'

'No!' Penny winked at them. 'Just take it as a sample of our famous Yorkshire hospitality.' She went back to mixing dough.

'You make all your own bread then?' asked Alice.

'Oh yes, and cakes . . .'

'They look really nice . . .'

'. . . and biscuits and things. There's some in there for you. I sell them at the shop in Knockton.'

'So you've lived here always? And you, like, know the area? What's around here?'

'Pretty near always. And there's not much except for the odd farm. There's the old water mill, of course. And Menga's Tarn is just over that way –' she nodded her head to the north – 'but mind you don't go swimming there as it's terribly deep and there's steep banks all around. Death trap, really. Then there's Elonia's Vale too, just beyond the tarn. Gorgeous. Always warm and full of butterflies! Something about a particular flower that grows there. Other than that it's just the moors, but it's a fine place to run wild and get a lot of exercise.' She smiled at Fish, 'it'll do you good, get a bit of colour in your cheeks.'

Fish smiled back.

'Thank you,' said Alice. 'We'll make the most of it.'

❉

Twenty-something miles away, in a quiet room with pale green walls and worn blinds, a woman stirred. She made a sound that was half sigh, half groan and her eyelids fluttered open. She lay for a while, taking in the sunlight filtering through the blinds, the smell of disinfectant and clean sheets, the pain that washed through her whole body.

A door opened, letting in sounds of bustle.

'All right, Mrs Jones?' said a cheerful voice that didn't seem to expect a reply. The nurse leaned over the figure in the bed. 'The doctor will be along to see you shortly. You've had a nasty accident – do you remember?'

With difficulty, Susan nodded.

'We only know who you are because a lady found your handbag and gave it to the police. But don't worry, you're doing just fine. Here . . .'

The nurse pressed a button, and the top end of the bed rose so that Susan was half sitting. Pouring some water from a jug at the side of the bed into a glass, she held it to Susan's lips. Susan sipped gratefully. It tasted unbelievably sweet.

As soon as she could manage it she croaked, 'Fish?'

'Sorry? Did you say fish?' A puzzled frown creased the nurse's brow.

Susan made a huge effort. 'Son. With me.'

The nurse looked concerned. 'Your son? Do you have more than one?' She picked up something from the locker by the bed. 'This arrived this morning. It's from your son, isn't it?' She glanced at the postcard. 'Oh, I see. *He's* Fish! Here.' She tucked the card into Susan's unbandaged hand.

Eagerly, Susan read it.

Dear Mum

I hope you are doing OK and it doesn't hurt too bad. I can't come and see you yet because Crow's Cottage is too far away, but I'll write again soon. This is just to tell you that I am ALL RIGHT and not to worry about me. Just get better soon. When I do see you, I'll tell you everything. Remember the talk we had that Christmas Day? It's like that. Trust me.

Love,
Fish

Susan closed her eyes to stop the tears. She felt so weak, as if the accident had drained all her strength and will. But she remembered the look in Fish's eyes that Christmas Day, when he had told her to go to the doctor as soon as she could. And she remembered Dr Collins saying that if she had left it any later she could have been in serious trouble. Dying trouble. And she remembered the time a few months later when Fish had suddenly started smiling again. So whatever was happening now, whatever it was that she didn't fully understand but that must have something to do with the horrible curse they were all under, she trusted that Fish *did* understand and knew what he was doing. She knew that as his mother she spent all her time looking after him, and that was right. But she also knew that in ways she didn't always see he looked after her too, and whether that was right or not didn't matter. It's just how it was. And what the postcard really said, underneath the words, was that Fish was looking after her *right now*.

'He's not like other people,' she told the nurse.

'He sounds like a lovely boy and I'm sure he'll come and see you as soon as he can.' The nurse spoke absentmindedly, scribbling in the red folder at the bottom of the bed. Then she smiled at Susan again. 'In an hour or so, I think you might be ready to try a cup of tea,' she said. 'Would you like that?'

Susan nodded, feeling some strength leak back into her damaged limbs. The pain had lifted a little. She could make out bandages on her left arm and a cast on her

227

leg. Her ribs felt like red-hot pokers in her body, and her face hurt when she smiled or spoke or swallowed. But she was alive and still seemed to have all the same parts that she had when they had started out on their journey. And she still had Fish. Suddenly, she felt incredibly lucky.

In an hour and a half, after Susan had had another sleep, the nurse came back with some tea, and Susan found that sitting up and drinking was not as hard as it might have been.

❦

When they got back from Mrs Dunnet's they ventured into the downstairs toilet. Fish sorted out the spiders and Alice threw out the mouldy mat, dumping it in the shed along with the curtains that had spent the night on the front step. In there, the demons could play all they liked without bothering either of them. Getting the toilet working again was another matter, until Alice came up with the bright idea of dumping a bucket full of water from the pump into the cistern and flushing it that way. They tried it, using a paint-stained bucket Fish found in the outhouse. It worked.

'Great! Now, we've got all we need. If Penny helps us out with the shopping we can hole up here for as long as necessary.' She smiled at Fish. 'We don't have to look in any of the other rooms just yet, either.'

Fish was happy to agree. He didn't know what kind of life was behind the closed doors of the lounge, the upstairs bathroom and the other bedroom, and right now it could stay that way.

For lunch they drank some of Penny's milk and ate the cake and apples she had put into the bag with the other things. She had given them a bottle of lemonade too, which was brilliant because it was a hot day and they both felt thirsty.

Afterwards, as Fish's foot was still sore and they didn't want to go far, they tracked down to the nearby Menga's Tarn and spent the afternoon sitting under the trees on its steep banks. Then they went back to the cottage and sunbathed on the patio. There was no sign of the demon.

At six o'clock they finished off the bread that Alice had brought with her and some hard-boiled eggs, and at seven o'clock Alice's mother rang. Alice had charged up her mobile before she left, so it would last them a few days if they were careful and kept it for emergencies.

Fish looked at Alice. She was lying on the back step, ignoring everything. So he reached over, dug in the pocket of her jacket and pulled out the phone. He shoved it under Alice's nose. She mumbled and took it.

'Yeah? Oh, hi, Mum.'

Fish could hear a gabbled voice on the other end.

'M'at Fish's. Project for school.'

More gabbling.

'Dunno. Stay the night if Mrs Jones lets me.'

Listening carefully, Fish made out the words 'out' and 'late evening'.

'Right. Yeah. Will do. Have nice time.'

Alice pressed the end button and dropped the phone. 'She says, Hi, Fish, and to thank your mum.' She went back to dozing in the evening sun.

So did Fish.

27

WONDER

Grimshaw was so full of the idea of success it was like a fever in his brain. He wanted to get on and find the Mighty Curse as soon as possible, but he had one problem. Flute had told him that as a half-life he would be able to work out the whereabouts of the Mighty Curse by himself. The exact word she had used was 'divine'. But he didn't understand how. What was he supposed to do? Guess?

He went through what he knew of the Mighty Curse, which was very little. Basically it was somewhere in Real Space . . . No! Wait a minute!

Grimshaw screwed up his face, trying to remember. There was a clue tucked away in his head, something someone had said to him. His brow cleared as he heard again the voice of the Horseman . . . *that lies buried deep and sleeping . . .*

Buried! That wouldn't mean a graveyard of course, but somewhere deep underground. Maybe a cave. Grimshaw decided to start with the deepest cave he could find and straight away zapped to a Real Space library to look it up. Libraries in Real Space always seemed weird to Grimshaw as they were so harmless. Not at all like the ones in Grey Space, where all the fiercely hungry half-lives contained within the book covers made finding a book a real adventure.

While he was in the library he also looked up 'to divine' in a dictionary and found out that it meant gaining insight into the unknown by supernatural means, which didn't really help.

Dismissing the problem for now, he took a moment to read an article in the newspaper with the headline 'Doomsday Hits Town'. There were some details about his failed attempts to kill Fish Jones that he wanted to check – like the name of his Innocent Bystander.

While he was doing all that he realised that if he found the deepest cave in a book, it would mean that humans had been there, or they wouldn't have written about it. If they had been there, then they would have disturbed the Mighty Curse anyway, and it would have woken up and destroyed the world. Clearly this hadn't happened, so the right cave wasn't going to be in any book. In the end he set the geography hands of his chronometer for the deepest, biggest space it could find, pressed send and hoped for the best.

He had an anxious moment when he felt his substance sleeting through thick darkness. Normally, chronometer travel didn't come with much sensation, but travelling through miles of solid earth and rock clearly made a difference. It wasn't comfortable at all, and he was petrified at the thought that he might have got it wrong and would materialise mixed in with the rock, unable to move or even to reset his chronometer and escape. He would be trapped forever, like a fossil!

So his relief when he materialised in empty space was huge. But relief was almost instantly overtaken by wonder. He had expected a black hole, possibly containing the terrifying Avatar of the Mighty Curse. What he found instead was a vast cavern filled with beauty and magnificent design.

Perched on a huge pillar of rock in the middle of the cavern, Grimshaw gazed at the intricate upside-down spires that hung from the ceiling, and then looked down at the tier upon tier of pillars growing up to meet them. In many places spire and pillar had grown together to make columns of rock, decorated with random folds and ripples in the stone. It was like being in a fantastic Gothic cathedral. And everywhere was light. Actual light in the darkness! Not that he needed it to see things, because Grimshaw's vision didn't depend on light like human eyes did, but it was still very lovely.

Flicking his ears, Grimshaw peered at the rocks around him and discovered that they were shining all on their own. He had heard the word phosphorescent before and he knew what it meant, but he hadn't understood it until now. Looking closer, he saw that the rocks that weren't shining on their own were reflecting the ones that were. There were crystals embedded everywhere, multiplying the strange radiance. How many other places were there, he wondered, full of such glory? And it had never been seen by any eyes but his!

Taking his time, he studied the cathedral cavern. It was vast, and the air, trapped here miles below the surface, was warm, damp and still. Swapping his pillar for one on the other side of the cave, Grimshaw found a deep pool, its surface shining with reflected light. He could hear the soft plip of droplets falling into it. Each tiny bead of water must have seeped down through many layers of earth and cracks in the rock, past old fossils and buried civilisations, until finally its long journey ended up here in this deep, undiscovered place. He wondered how many years it had taken for the pool to fill up and if, one day, the cathedral cavern would become a drowned palace.

Still, this wasn't getting him anywhere, and one thing was certain: in all this glowing wonder, there was absolutely no sign of an Avatar, mighty or otherwise. Apart from Grimshaw, that was.

He sat for a while, waving his tail gently as he admired the soft, eerie glow of the phosphorescence, until it came to him that he was on the wrong track. The Mighty Curse, like all other curses, had been made by man. A man who was a great magician, true, but still a man. So it wasn't going to be buried at the bottom of a place no man had ever been. It would be near somewhere that people lived, or had lived once, at any rate.

Grimshaw liked books and had experienced a few in the Lock-Out Club. His favourites were adventure stories about things like long-forgotten cities in the heart of impenetrable jungles. Which right now seemed like an ideal place for hiding terrible demons. So he searched the Acts and Facts to find one.

An entry made centuries ago by a long-gone curse demon spoke of an ancient city, hidden deep in the heart of the Amazonian jungle. Pressing send, Grimshaw vanished from the cathedral cavern and felt again the sensation of being drawn through thick, dark earth. Suddenly this unpleasant feeling gave way to one of dappled brilliance and wet heat.

And there it was in front of him, a city so old and lost that no human eyes had looked upon it for hundreds of years. Grimshaw studied the city and the tropical forest that concealed it. The web was full of all sorts of information about jungles, for example . . .

Grimshaw flicked his ears. What was the point? They were only facts, and facts weren't the same as reality. Facts were just what was left when you took the reality out. He didn't need the web to see that the jungle was as different to the underground cathedral as he could imagine, but just as beautiful. Here the air felt like steam in a bathroom, only thicker and heavier. All around him, things buzzed, rustled and called. He knew that way up above him, above the trees that were tall enough to touch the sky, the sun was pouring its golden light down like a rain of fire. But he couldn't see it. The canopy of huge leaves and twisting vines cut out all but a few rays of sunlight, surrounding him in dappled greens and golds.

The city had become part of the jungle. Streets had been replaced by colonnades of immense trees, their roots ripping up the paving stones, and vines had torn down the ancient arches. Only the halls and palaces were still there, smothered in creepers and exotic plants. Now they were a playground for small monkeys, hunting territory for hungry leopards and (deep inside) sleeping quarters for legions of bats.

Grimshaw flicked from place to place, but nowhere did he see the slightest hint of a mighty Avatar. Clearly he was on the wrong track again. Even so, it was nice in the jungle.

Resting for a moment in the branches of a vast tree, Grimshaw watched the leopard cubs at play. Their glossy dark-spotted coats and their liquid eyes and graceful movements soothed him. One of them even climbed up and lay for a while with its soft side pressed against him as it yawned and dozed in the sultry air. He could feel it breathing, its life whooshing in and out of its velvet body in gentle sighs.

Sitting there, Grimshaw realised that however long he spent in Real Space, it would never be enough. He knew that the Earth wasn't paradise. It had terrible things in it. Death came in so many ways, often painful, and nature itself could wipe out whole civilisations with earthquakes, hurricanes and floods. But somehow the ruthlessness, the possibility of loss and suffering, made the beauty all the more beautiful.

The knowledge that sooner or later he would have

to leave the world and remain locked in the emptiness of Grey Space terrified him. True, there might be another Litany to work on, one created when they reburied Lampwick. And even when that was done, until Fish Jones completed the tasks he had to perform in the name of destiny, Grimshaw would be able to travel to Real Space. He flicked his ears thoughtfully, wondering if it was worth letting the boy live after all. But how long would he live for? A decade? Five? And after that? Centuries might pass with nothing happening. With Grimshaw being bottom of the curse-demon pile, scorned by everyone. Centuries before the last of Lampwick's bones crumbled to dust and ended both the curse and Grimshaw's miserable existence. By then oblivion would be welcome.

Closing his eyes against the thought, Grimshaw let himself relax, like the leopard, into the peace and warmth that surrounded him.

When he opened them again, he had an idea. The half-alive didn't dream, just like they didn't sleep, but as he lay there in a relaxed haze an image came to him. Water. Maybe the Mighty Curse was not buried in earth, but in water. Grimshaw flipped his ears thoughtfully, shaking off the lethargy that had overtaken him. Maybe this was what Flute had meant by 'divining' the answer? This kind of trance-like vision.

He thought about it. Not the sea, that wouldn't be right, because although humans travelled about on top of the sea, they didn't have a lot to do with it in the homemaking sense. A lake somewhere, perhaps? Grimshaw was about to set his chronometer to find the deepest water anywhere that wasn't the sea, when all of a sudden he remembered something else the Horseman had said, something he had overlooked. A feeling of excitement surged through him. Everyone knew that the Mighty Curse was created by Imenga, the most powerful wizard ever to have lived. But the Horseman had called him the great wizard of the Clouded Land!

The Clouded Land. Grimshaw had read and heard enough from some of the older demons to know that this could mean only one country. Britain.

So instead, he set his chronometer for the largest and (as an afterthought) *most mysterious* body of water in Britain and hit send. He materialised at the bottom of a lake somewhere in Scotland.

The shock as his body was catapulted from the hot, lazy air of the jungle to the icy-cold depths was immense. His un-material self swirled through the bitter, dark water as it closed around him, sucking him down and down and down. The weight of all the water was so great he could feel its resistance as he squeezed into full being, pushing its bulk aside as if it were solid rather than liquid. He opened his eyes on complete darkness – not even a glimmer of light filtered down to these black depths even though he knew it was the middle of the day. Fortunately, he didn't need light to see by, so he took a careful look around to see if the Mighty Curse was here.

He found a monster straight away. Unfortunately, it was a dead one.

Staring at the creature's whitened bones rising from the silt, Grimshaw sighed. It might have been a hell of a big monster when it was alive, but it had been a flesh and blood one, not an Avatar. He gazed at the length of its incredible neck that ran in wavy ridges along the lake bottom. In fact, most of it was neck; there didn't seem to be much body at all. Maybe it was some kind of serpent.

Grimshaw couldn't help a shiver. As well as dark and cold, it was so silent that it was like being in a world of eternal night. Then he slapped his head with his hand and groaned. He had just flipped here without thinking. His backpack would be soaked through, including Mrs Minchin and his notebook.

And then he had a moment of revelation. Divining! Flute had said that he did it all the time – and she was right. Divination was how he got clues on where to look for suitable accidents to finish off his Sufferers. All he had to do was look in Mrs Minchin and he would find directions to the Mighty Curse!

Before he could kick himself really hard for being so dense, the water swirled and eddied. He stiffened and peered around. He couldn't see anything, but it occurred to him that even if this monster was dead, it didn't mean there weren't others.

He gulped, swallowing a mouthful of ice-cold water. And then a great booming roar swept over him, a cry so huge and so lonely that his blood chilled in his veins and if he had had any hair it would have stood on end.

Grimshaw shook, crouching into the silt. Above him something vast and long and snake-like undulated through the dark lake. Its terrible cry echoed out again, sweeping through Grimshaw to rattle his bones like a grim warning.

With a trembling hand, he spun the dials on his watch and hit send just as the great serpent turned its monstrous head to see what it was that had come to disturb its empty world.

28

OLD BOOK, NEW BOOK

Standing on the back step of Crow's Cottage, Fish watched the sun go down. It had been a beautiful day and the problem of the curse demon had seemed a lifetime away, but now the last edge of the sun was disappearing in a bank of purple cloud and who knew what tomorrow would bring. With a sigh, he closed the door on the gathering night and went to find Alice.

She was upstairs, lounging on the quilt and preparing to spend the evening eating biscuits. The evening air was cool and she was wearing her jumper. Fish reached for Jed's jacket and pulled it on, then settled beside her and tried to get comfortable. There was something sticking into him, and reaching round to his back pocket he pulled out his old book. It must have been there since he had rescued it from the wreckage on the morning when his life had changed forever. Its cover, though battered, was a reminder of happy times in his lost home. It was also a reminder of his situation now.

'I'll read aloud from it if you like,' Alice said, pulling the lid off the container that Mrs Dunnet had put in with the milk, bread and eggs. 'We've got macaroons, ginger biscuits and cookies.' She began to fish around. Outside, the first drops of rain pattered on the window and the wind rattled the ancient frame.

While she rummaged, Fish absent-mindedly flicked the pages of the book, wondering if there was any way to break the curse and set himself and his mother free of the threat that hung over them. How could he find out? He flicked through the book a second time, then frowned and turned the light of the torch more firmly in his direction. The rain began to fall in earnest, drumming hard on the glass.

'Some of the cookies are chocolaty ones too.' Alice dug one out and began to eat. She glanced up at the rivers running down the window pane and then at Fish. 'What's up?'

Fish reached across her for the scrap of paper she had been writing a shopping list on and then looked for the pen. Silently, Alice retrieved it from behind the bottle of lemonade and handed it to him.

He flicked the pages of the book again, pausing every so often to scribble something down. Then he handed the paper to Alice. It said:

Toby
Green
Seven
Fortune
Hill

East
Knock
Tone

Alice read it out loud, then made a quick alteration to the last two words and read it again with the pauses in different places. 'Toby Green, 7 Fortune Hill, East Knockton. It's an address!'

Fish nodded.

'You telling me you got all these words, in this order, from seeing them in the book as you flipped the pages?'

They stared at each other.

'The same words each time?' she checked.

Fish nodded.

Alice put the paper down and shivered. 'That's creepy, Fish. Like some kind of message from . . . from . . . Destiny or something. Hang on.'

She rummaged in one of the bags to find the road map, which she spread out in front of them.

Fish put a finger on the spot where Knockton was, then ran it slowly eastwards, but it wasn't until the second go that Alice spotted it.

'Look, this street going off the main road here. Fortune Hill!'

They stared.

'Oh lor', ' mumbled Alice. She folded up the map around Fish's finger. 'OK, I guess tomorrow we could walk to Knockton. We can try and find this Toby Green bloke. Dunno why, but it's something to do, and maybe he'll know how to break a curse!' She put the map and the address carefully aside.

'Right. Now, I'm going to have some more biscuits. And then I'm going to sleep.'

❈

A second later, under a bush at the side of the house, a small figure popped into view.

Grimshaw scratched his ears and peered at the window high above, the one where a wavering light had just been switched off. Then he pulled the soaking pack from his back and dug inside, bringing out a sodden mass of paper, which he threw away, and a ruler. Then he pulled out another book, a brand new book picked up from a book shop on his way here, that was tucked into the back pocket of his drying trousers.

The new book was a story about a man who tore a world apart just to destroy his enemies. Grimshaw had chosen it because it seemed to fit perfectly, bearing in mind what he was going to use it for – finding the Mighty Curse to kill Fish Jones.

Carefully, he jotted down the words given by the new book, his brain on fire with the knowledge that he was nearly there, nearly at the point where he could win. And what a victory! He chuckled as it occurred to him that he would have the largest number of Innocent Bystanders *ever*. Then he looked at what he had written in his mostly dried-out notebook. It said:

World
Rings
Red
Hare
Mirage
Burnt
Offering

At first it didn't make sense, but he studied it patiently for a moment until he remembered that this time he was not looking for an event. This time he was looking for a *destination*. And since most calculations for destinations using the chronometer began with a reference to the equatorial and polar grid of the Earth, World rings was pretty clear after all! The next three were setting combinations and the last, well, the last was a reference to the end result.

He grinned, turned a page and wrote carefully: 'World Rings. Red Hare. Mirage. Burnt Offering.'

It was an address.

29

SOUL'S MIDNIGHT

Fish opened his eyes with a start, feeling as if his heart had missed a beat. It was pitch dark. Although the rain had stopped, clouds still swarmed across the sky, quenching the moonlight and driven by a chill wind. He lay still, his eyes open, trying to keep his breathing steady. He didn't know what time it was, but it felt like that point where night is at its most intense. Not actual midnight, which was too early, but between two and three in the morning, when life was at its lowest ebb. The midnight of the soul.

He went on lying still, letting his eyes adjust, raking them over the shadows that filled the room. The dark began to separate out into areas of lesser and deeper gloom. He could see the shapes of things and one of the shapes was that of something that shouldn't be there.

The demon was back!

In fact, it was not only back, it was sitting on the end of the quilt, watching him.

Fear sent shivers of ice along Fish's spine. Next to

him, Alice slept on, oblivious. He envied her. For a moment he wondered why he couldn't make out the gleam of its eyes. Then he remembered that its eyes were darker than any mere night. Of course he couldn't see them. Not even a reflection could live in those inky pools. Fish was ready to bet that those eyes didn't need light the way human eyes did. The horrible thing could probably see him as clearly as if it were day.

He squeezed his own eyes shut, pretending to be asleep, when every nerve in his body was alert for any sign of movement from the demon. Even with his ears straining to their utmost, he couldn't hear it breathe. He could make out Alice's soft and steady breaths, and his own more rapid lungfuls, but nothing else. No third creature. It probably didn't need oxygen.

There was also an absence of warmth. He could feel a weight on the blanket, but so slight it was barely there. The creature didn't have any real presence and maybe that was just right, because to the rest of the world the demon was something that didn't exist. Unable to hold in a shudder, Fish prayed that it wouldn't realise he was awake. If it did, it might attack him.

Alice moved, her shift in position ruffling the blanket. Her sighing breath filled the air before she settled back into a steady rhythm. She had flung an arm outside the cover and it lay there, the sleeve of her jumper rucked up and the bare skin exposed. Fish wished he could put it back in for her, out of the way. Just in case the thing reached out and touched her.

Tears pricked his eyes. He opened them and looked, hoping it had gone. It hadn't, of course. For all he knew, it would sit there all night. Terror crept through him on icy paws. Had it given up on accidents and come to kill him with its bare hands? How on God's Earth had he ever thought to escape it? There was nowhere that he could go where it would not find him. Nowhere. He had always known that, and yet somewhere in his heart he had foolishly hoped. And how stupid he had been to let Alice stay with him! Perhaps it would kill her too, just because she had dared to help him.

And when it had done with them, it would wait until Susan had heard the news of his death, until she was distraught and grieving, and then it would kill her too. Visit her in the night perhaps, like . . .

He tried to stop the thoughts going round in his head. Pictures of him and Alice lying in their makeshift bed as the sun rose. Unmoving, dead, murdered. Of nice Penny Dunnet stopping by to see if they were all right and finding their bodies all cold and still, with a look on their faces of such unending terror that it would haunt her dreams forever.

Closing his eyes again, Fish tried to relax his body, wondering if the demon knew that he was awake and was just waiting for him to doze off so that it could kill him while he was dreaming. Time ticked on and though he knew it could only be minutes, it felt as if he had lain there for a lifetime, died a dozen deaths in slow motion.

The pillow beneath his cheek was wet with tears and the sheet clammy with sweat. Every so often he looked, and always it was there.

Once he thought that it moved, shaking its head and twitching its ears as if bothered by something. Then it went still again.

And then at last he looked and it had gone and he could cry out loud, trying not to wake Alice.

✻

Crouched at the end of the quilt, Grimshaw knew that the power to end everything lay in his paws. The thought was exciting, but it scared him too, and he hated that he was weak enough to be scared. His head whirled with the yearning to be different, to be an Avatar to reckon with, to be tall and glowing-eyed and . . . and . . . just *different*.

Why must I be like *this*? he thought.

In the bed, the girl stirred, throwing her arm outside the blanket. For a moment Grimshaw had an absurd wish to lean over and pinch the soft flesh. To feel what a human felt like. He ignored it and then was angry with himself for ignoring it. Even now, he felt bound to the stupid Rules that wouldn't let him have physical contact with humankind.

Although Grimshaw could see in the dark perfectly well, it didn't mean that darkness was just like light. It wasn't at all. Light gave things colour and depth. Dark leeched all the colour away and just gave things a shape that was all shades of black and grey and that was oddly weak, as if it were part of the night and not a thing in its own right at all. He could see the boy and the girl lying there, night-time pooling in the sockets of their eyes and the creases of their skin. He could hear them breathing. The boy dragged air into his lungs like he was suffocating, and Grimshaw wondered if he was having bad dreams. If so, he hoped that he was in them. He would like to be the stuff of nightmares. He sniffed. There was a smell of salt tears in the air too.

It didn't make Grimshaw hate him any less. The boy might be brave, but he was also a menace. He and his destiny had brought Grimshaw to this, and when the Mighty Curse rose from its sleeping place and destroyed the world, it would be all the boy's fault.

He stared irritably at the pale shape of the girl's arm lying on the bedcover.

And Lampwick, useless trickster that he was. Third-rate conjuror with a scraping of magical talent and about as much integrity as a tin sovereign. Grimshaw clenched his fists, shaking his ears angrily. Even alive, the man had not been worth the flesh he stood up in. And if he had made an Avatar that was so powerless it couldn't even finish off its own Sufferers, then it was down to him if that Avatar had to take desperate measures.

Grimshaw grinned to himself. It was all clear in his head now. This was the only way that he could win. The Rules, the boy and his destiny, Lampwick, all the other Avatars, they were all driving him one way. Just one way.

And then Grimshaw felt a single moment of fear. Fear that ripped down his knobbly spine like a frozen claw. Because suddenly he knew that he was *actually going to do it*. He really was.

And he was going to do it now.

Fish lay awake for a while longer, tormented by the fears the demon had set loose in his heart. Then, exhausted, he fell into a sleep troubled by dreams in which a nameless thing chased him relentlessly through shadowy towns and over barren deserts where the only colour was grey and all the seas looked like glass.

When the first light of dawn crept through the window, he woke up. He lay for a moment, taking stock. Birds were singing and the world on the whole looked pretty normal. Not that it was, of course.

He rolled over and shook Alice.

'Uh? Wass time?' She rubbed the sleep out of her eyes and looked around blearily. 'Six o'clock! Fish!'

Fish was already sitting up, waiting for her to wake up properly. He didn't have to wait long.

'So what's up then? Is something up? Don't tell me that demon thing turned up in the night! Oh CREEPS! And what now? I s'pose you want to go and see this Green bloke as soon as possible? What? Like now? Can I at least have some breakfast?'

Fish laughed. One of the things he really liked about Alice was the way she always knew what he was thinking.

She sighed. 'OK. I s'pose we can just eat on the way, right?'

❀

It was a good thing that Fish's foot had improved a lot during the last day, because the walk to Knockton was a long one. As they trekked over the heathery moors they shared a breakfast of biscuits and chocolate washed down by what was left of the lemonade. The clouds had gone and it promised to be another fine day with a clear sky, a warm sun and a breeze smelling of heather and distant hills.

They went in silence for most of the way, which was normal for Fish, but not so normal for Alice. She was lost in her thoughts and Fish wasn't surprised. The day before yesterday her life had been normal, or at least as normal as it could be for anyone who knew Fish well. Now it was filled with a menace that she couldn't see, a threat of violent death, certainly to Fish and possibly to her too. She was far from home – her mother didn't even know where she was – living in a house with no gas or electricity and relying on the kindness of a stranger for food.

The town was just rising ahead of them when Alice's phone rang. Alice heaved a sigh and dug in her pocket.

'Hi.'

Mumbling from the other end.

'Fine. M'with Fish. Gonna have breakfast.'

More mumbling.

'I dunno. Might be, might not.'

Even more mumbling.

Alice sighed. 'Yeah, text you.'

Fish strained his ears but couldn't make out anything Alice's mum said.

'What? Oh.' Alice sounded surprised. 'You too, Mum, OK. Bye.'

She ended the call and gave the phone a puzzled look. 'She said be careful! That's not like her.' Alice was silent for a moment. 'You don't think she suspects anything, do you?'

Fish shrugged.

'Anyway, she's off to work now, so that's OK. Look, we're here.'

Ahead of them the fields ended in a shallow ditch and then a road. They joined it and went on past a row of cottages and a pub to end up in a street of shops and people that reminded Fish of the town that he had left behind as a burnt-out wreck only a couple of days before. He shuddered and glanced around.

Alice gave him a sharp glance. 'Is it there? No? Good thing too! Come on, let's find the Green bloke!'

A sign on the other side of the road told them that they were on Main Street. They wandered along until Alice said, 'Fortune Hill! There it is, eh!' She changed direction and led the way across the road and up the curve of the road. They didn't go far before they saw a pair of gates standing open on to a path. On the gates was a sign with one word on it: Seven.

Silently, Fish and Alice walked through the gates and down the path. There were trees and thickly growing shrubs all around them, and they had to walk a little way before they saw the house. It was a tall building in need of a coat of paint, but the garden around it, up to the trees, was neatly kept and full of flowers.

At the door, Fish stood for a moment, catching his breath, half not wanting to ring on the bell. He often got feelings about things, and right now he knew that inside this house was something so important that it could mean the difference between life and death. The knowledge terrified him and made his heart pump harder and harder, sending the life spinning frantically around his body as if it were trying to get away. But there was no getting away from fate.

Everything seemed very clear and sharp. He took a long look around at the world, almost as if it would be his last. It was nine o'clock in the morning and the day was still fresh. Overhead, and far in the distance, the silver dart of an aeroplane crossed the vivid blue sky. The air that washed around them was warm and soft as milk and gently rustled the trees.

Alice slipped her hand into his. Clutching it tight, Fish dismissed his terrors and stepped forward. It gave him a chill inside to think that he was really going to do this.

And he was going to do it now.

30

IN THE LIBRARY

There was no constellation reference, so the unknown place had to be in Limbo, which meant that it would only lead Grimshaw to a clue of some sort, not directly to the Mighty Curse, as that was sleeping in Real Space. But it would do.

Unfortunately, it also meant that Grimshaw would have to face Lampwick, as there was no other way back into Limbo other than through his Architect. But if Lampwick wanted to know what his demon was planning and commanded him to tell, then Grimshaw would be compelled to answer. And once he knew, Lampwick would most likely command Grimshaw to drop the idea and again Grimshaw would be forced to obey. He worried the problem around and around in his head, looking for a way past it, until finally he gave up, turned the dials to zero and hit send. There was nothing he could do but risk it.

'Oh, there you are! I've been wondering what you were up to, roaming around like a lost . . .'

'Can't stop.' Grimshaw held up a hand. 'Busy.'

'I'll give you busy!' Lampwick sat up straight with indignation.

Grimshaw was hurriedly rearranging dials. Ring settings Red Hare and then Mirage. And at the intersection he would find what he was looking for – information on how to turn the Earth into a Burnt Offering! And Fish Jones along with it.

'I Conjure Thee, Stay!' snarled Lampwick.

Grimshaw's finger froze over the send button.

'You can't stop me!' he snarled. 'I'm just getting there!'

'Getting where!'

'I don't know,' mumbled Grimshaw, 'but I had an idea about how to kill Fish Jones and I want to do it.'

Lampwick settled back on his coffin.

'Hmm, going to entertain me with another balls-up, eh?'

Seething, Grimshaw held his tongue.

'So, what is today's fantastic idea?'

'Not telling.' Grimshaw scrunched his eyes tight, wishing he had thought up another plan, an alternative plan convincing enough to put Lampwick off the trail.

Lampwick leaned forward, a slow grin tracing its way across his putty-coloured face. 'I Conjure Thee, Tell.'

Grimshaw screamed, his face twisting horribly with the effort to disobey. It was no use.

'I'm gonna blow up the World!' he yelled.

Lampwick paused for a moment, shocked. Then the grin got larger. It turned into a smirk and then a chuckle and then a laugh. The magician shook with mirth until tears began to trickle from the corners of his eyes. 'You? You couldn't blow up a rubber ring!' More screams of laughter, this time at his own wit, echoed around the crypt.

Grimshaw glared. Inside, behind the glare, he felt cautiously relieved. He had told Lampwick a shorthand version of the truth, but it had cost him every grain of his strength not to blurt out the whole plan. Happily, Lampwick had accepted it, which was a good thing, because Grimshaw didn't think he could hold back a second time.

Lampwick got control. 'So, how are you planning that, then?' It was a conversational question, not a command, but it still took Grimshaw biting his tongue hard to stop him answering honestly. Twitches shook him so hard he bounced around like a rubber ball.

'Um . . . I'm . . . gonna . . . OW . . . do something big . . . lots of fire and . . . death . . . like the biggest bomb ever only . . . OW . . . not a bomb . . .'

'What are you blethering about? Do you mean one of these modern nookiller things?' sneered Lampwick. 'I have heard of them, you know. And do keep still – you're making me dizzy.'

Grimshaw blinked. 'Nuclear,' he said sniffily. 'I think you'll find it's pronounced NEW-CLE-AR.' The twitches subsided a little.

Lampwick eyed his Avatar thoughtfully. 'Hmm. Interesting. Which power station are you going to

use? And how do you intend to get the boy there? No!'
He held up a hand. 'Don't tell me. Either it will be an
entertaining flop or it will work. And if it works it will
be big, I can see that. Think of the Innocent Bystanders
you could get with that one! It might even redeem you
for the lost chronometer fiasco. A bit.'

Grimshaw stared at Lampwick sullenly, but inside
he was laughing. He didn't know what fiasco meant, but
frankly he didn't give a fig. He had got away with lying
to his Architect.

'Personally I'm betting on the flop outcome,' went
on Lampwick, his usual sneer curling the corner of his
mouth. He waved a hand dismissively. 'Go on then, do
your worst.'

Without another word, Grimshaw went.

�֍

Earth rings reference Red Hare and Mirage turned out
to be a tall house at the end of a long drive. There was
a stretch of empty ground that might have trees in it in
Real Space, and then flower beds closer to the house.
Even though there were no flowers in them in the
Limbo version, Grimshaw could tell that they would be
flower beds in Real Space because the sections of bare
earth were neatly outlined with paving stones.

After the last update there had been a brief shower of
plane parts, forcing Grimshaw to take cover in a nearby
shed. Fortunately, most of the chunks had landed some
metres away, and the only thing he had to worry about

was getting round the portion of wing dumped in the middle of the drive.

Deciding that the clue must be somewhere inside the building, Grimshaw headed through the door and down a long hallway that would probably be painted a pleasant green in Real Space, but was a kind of sicky grey in Limbo. It led to a living room, a study, a kitchen and a dining room. And one other room, the one next to the living room.

Grimshaw blinked. It had to be a library – one full of old and powerful books too. Nothing in Limbo gave off that air of pulsating power like a library of old books. He sighed. Typical. The clue would be in there; it had to be.

Pushing open the door gingerly, Grimshaw peered in. The library was seething. Everywhere he looked, the half-lives contained in the pages were fighting to get out. He could feel the barely controlled power struggling beneath their dull surfaces, begging somebody to open them. Carefully, he edged around the door, leaving it open, then inched into the room, hoping the books wouldn't notice he was there. This side of the door, the air was thick with unheard sound and unseen life and it made his ears pop.

Because fiction was a creation of humankind, stories written in Real Space didn't translate well to Limbo. Or maybe it was that they translated a little too well! They took on an extra substance, becoming almost as real as their authors. Grimshaw had investigated plenty of fiction books in the Lock-Out Club in Limbo and knew how it went. They snagged the reader, dragged him in and went to work on him like a wraparound cinematic nightmare with a few stiff gins thrown in for good measure. Unlike Real Space TV adaptations and so on, Limbo books were never well balanced. They scooted through some parts of the story and exaggerated others, threw in a mix of ghostly background characters and larger-than-life personalities, changed viewpoint and setting at the drop of a hat and were coloured by the author's feelings at the time. It was like a vast roller-coaster ride with 3D pictures and no sick bag, and it usually left Grimshaw feeling woozy and gasping for breath. But sometimes it was fantastically wonderful too. It all depended on the book.

Non-fiction wasn't much better. All the knowledge and effort and desire to learn created a kind of hotbed of information just dying to shoehorn its way into the reader's head, often resulting in severe overload and (where encyclopaedias were concerned) brain explosion.

What's more, it was vital to go in concentrating on one book only. In a Limbo library, if you got dragged in unprepared, the books would take over, passing you from one to the next. It could be weeks before they let you out again – usually when you were comatose or brain damaged and so not paying proper attention.

Grimshaw studied the library thoughtfully. He didn't have a particular book in mind, but he did have a subject and he hoped that would be enough. Trouble was, where to look? One tall bookcase held only non-fiction, and here works on medicine, history, law and geography fought for attention. As he scanned over the shelves he caught flashes of content – blood-wet flesh and gleaming steel in *Dissection and Anatomy*, the screaming heat of battle in *A History of Britain*, a dangling noose in *Execution: The Facts*.

On the far wall he could see fiction, and here he glimpsed the velvet of romance and the rain-dark streets of a crime novel. The children's shelf was the most terrifying, chockfull of magical power practically reaching out to drag him in and swallow him whole.

And there, on the top shelf, was a section that didn't qualify as either fact or fiction. Myths and Legends.

Grimshaw flipped his tail thoughtfully. The Mighty Curse was a legend, all right, so maybe the clue was there. Perhaps, long ago, some human had told others the story of how the world nearly ended, and perhaps the tale had been passed from person to person down the generations until, finally, someone had called it a legend and written it down.

His inky eyes narrowed. Top shelf. Typical.

Looking around, he spotted one of those ladder things on wheels resting next to a large armchair. Ever so carefully, he stepped towards it. He was doing just fine until he began to pull it gently towards the shelf he wanted.

There was a tortured groan of metal and he realised

at once that the wretched thing had a squeaky wheel. Now there was no time to be careful – the books had spotted him! Yanking hard, Grimshaw dragged the ladder past *Dissection and Anatomy* as fast as he could, hurtled by the howling din of *A Lexicon of Demons* and skirted hurriedly around *Execution: The Facts*, but not before he had glimpsed a face with bulging eyeballs peering at him.

Crashing the ladder against the right bookcase he began to climb, praying that he would get past the children's fiction before *Gruesome Fairy Tales* nabbed him. He had just made it when his back paw slipped on a rung and before he regained his balance a bony, black-nailed hand shot out of *Gruesome Fairy Tales* and seized his tail. Hissing with fright, Grimshaw scrabbled to hold on. Already he could feel the stories pouring down his spine, burrowing their way towards his head. His vision grew cloudy as images of golden princesses, green-faced witches, rats and cats and saw-toothed ogres blocked out reality. He felt the ladder rock beneath him, the dodgy wheel locking as the other one spun, and suddenly the whole contraption tipped over, throwing him off. As he went, his flailing paws caught in the books, dragging them off the shelves. They sprang free, their pages flapping, their stories running riot on the air in cloudy shapes that grasped, trying to catch hold of the reader they knew was there somewhere. Catch hold of him and pull him in.

Grimshaw hit the library floor with a thud. He lay

on his back, gasping with shock and terror. Any minute now, all the escaped stories would sense his whereabouts and dive into his mind. If he didn't want his brain turned to mincemeat on the spot, he had to move fast.

Flipping from his back to his front, Grimshaw spotted a book that had fallen open practically under his nose. It was *Little-Known Folklore of Yorkshire and the Dales*. Reaching out, he slammed a paw into the middle of the book, flattened it down and stared in astonishment. The page he had hit upon was Chapter 32 and was called 'The Mighty Curse'.

Which was so what Grimshaw was looking for that he gasped and peered closely at the first line, only just remembering to ready himself for what was to follow. A moment later there was a hoarse scream as the story got hold of him, followed by a sizzle and a pop.

It wasn't a moment too soon. In the air over Grimshaw's now disappeared head, the stories – *Gruesome Fairy Tales* among them – had been gathering in a menacing cloud of colour and sound. With their potential reader gone, the cloud imploded, its contents howling with fury as they were sucked back into their books.

Gradually, a sort of calm returned to the library. Only the triumphant *Little-Known Folklore of Yorkshire and the Dales* seethed on.

31

POMP

As soon as they rang the bell, the door was opened by an elderly man. Fish took a step back and nearly trod on Alice.

'Hello?'

'Oh, um, are you Mr Toby Green?' asked Alice, giving Fish a frown.

'That's me. And you are?'

'Alice Craig. And he's Fish Jones. Can we talk to you a minute?'

Mr Green looked surprised. 'Oh, sure. Do you want to come in?'

'Yes, please,' Alice sang out cheerfully. She pushed past him, dragging Fish with her.

'The living room is . . . Oh you found it, good-o.' Toby Green closed the door and followed them in.

Alice was looking around the room. 'Hey, this is nice. Like your walls and that. Mum only ever has magnolia. It's dead dull.'

'I think colour is the stuff of life,' said Mr Green carefully. 'Would you like . . . um . . . lemonade? Not that I have any. Tea? The kettle is already on.' He waved down the hall towards the kitchen.

'We've come because we're looking for something. What's up, Fish?'

'I was about to ask the same thing,' said Mr Green. 'Your friend does look a little sick.'

They both stared at Fish. In fact, all three of them stared at Fish.

Who didn't know what to do. He looked at the third member of his audience. It looked at him.

'Oh lor',' said Alice. 'You can see something, can't you?' She smiled at Mr Green. 'Fish sees things, you know.'

'What kind of things?' asked Mr Green nervously.

Alice rolled her eyes. 'You name it. Dirt demons that hang around bins and stuff, dark lights around bad people, misty snakes around mad people, that kind of thing. And he hears stuff on dead telephone lines. And . . .'

'Deaths,' said Fish.

Mr Green focused on him, his eyes suddenly clear. So did Alice.

'I think you need to go to the doctor, Mr Green.'

'Right.' The old man nodded, his face suddenly pale. 'I should call it stuff and nonsense and throw you out, of course, but somehow . . .' he sat down heavily on a chair, 'I've not been feeling quite myself lately.'

The Death hung above and behind him, like a strange halo. Its tail rested on his shoulders, its bone-thin hands on his head and its wings, fanned out in a glowing arc, quivered in the still air. Its light-in-light eyes watched Fish patiently.

Down the hall, the kettle began to whistle, so Alice went to deal with it. Fish and Mr Green eyed one another cautiously, listening to the clink of china and the sound of pouring water.

'If you go soon,' said Fish at last, sitting on the sofa opposite Mr Green, 'they may be able to do something.'

'*Oh no, Fish Jones.*' The Death's voice was like a hint of cool air on a hot day. '*We let you keep your mother. You can't have this one too.*'

Fish felt ice between his shoulder blades. He shuddered violently, wondering why it was that only bad things made creatures, things like decay and neglect and cruelty. And death.

'Must be damned creepy,' said Mr Green, completely unable to hear a word the Death said. He managed a smile. 'What can I do for you, anyway? You didn't come here just to tell me I'm dying, did you?'

'Fish is cursed,' said Alice, reappearing in the doorway. 'And we got your name out of a book, like a clue, so we came to see if you can help us.' She was carrying a tray with three mugs and a packet of digestives. 'I made it in the mugs instead of the teapot, and I hope you don't mind about the biscuits. It's been ages since breakfast.'

Fish gave her a look. She plonked the tray on the table,

splashing some of the tea, and picked up a mug. Then she settled back and looked at Mr Green expectantly.

He watched them both for a moment. 'Curses?' he said. 'Well, it's interesting, but I haven't got much about curses. I'm a collector, you know.' The colour began to creep back into his face. 'Old books of any sort, some of them are quite rare. I've got an illustrated copy of *Gruesome Fairy Tales* that'd knock your socks off, and some excellent works on myths and legends . . .'

While he talked, Fish tried to ignore the Death. Which was difficult because the thing kept looking at him. Fish got the feeling it was curious, which bothered him, as he didn't like the idea that an Angel of Death found him interesting.

'*Our proper name is Avatar of Passing Over,*' it said. '*But you can call us Pomp.*'

Fish heard it, but thought he'd rather not know.

'*We carry the souls of the dead through to the other side and watch over those whose death is to be slow.*'

Like poor Mr Green, thought Fish, feeling horribly sorry for the old man.

'*Yes, like Mr Green.*'

Fish hunched his shoulders. He hadn't said anything out loud. The thing must be able to read his mind.

'*Your soul, actually,*' it said. '*We can see the questions in your soul's reflection.*'

By now, Alice was telling their host all about Fish's curse and how they had come to find Mr Green's name in a book by accident.

'*The Hand of Destiny,*' said the Pomp to Fish, '*is a curious thing. Even we know little about it. The lengths it will go to in order to save humankind. To save even one single soul.*'

'So that's it,' finished Alice.

Toby Green nodded. 'I must admit, it's a damned good story. But quite why it led you to me . . .' He frowned. Alice nudged Fish hard. 'Actually, there is one book you might be interested in. It's been a while since I read it, but if I remember rightly, there is something in there about a curse that was broken, or put off or something. It's a very old, little-known legend. But I believe it's true that many legends have their roots in real life.'

He got up and walked out of the room. Eagerly, Alice followed him, with Fish at her heels. Pushing open the next door along, Mr Green showed them a library, its walls lined with shelves all laden with old-looking books.

'Top shelf,' he said.

Fish pulled a ladder with a squeaky wheel into place alongside the bookshelves and climbed up.

'That's the one.' Mr Green moved to an armchair in the corner and sank heavily into it.

'You're tired,' said Alice sympathetically.

'Y'know, boy –' Mr Green looked at Fish – 'I might just take your advice about the doctor. Though,' he sighed, 'perhaps I should think about getting my affairs in order. Go see my daughter in Australia, maybe. I always wanted to do that, but kept putting it off. Work and all that.'

'Now's the time,' said Fish firmly. 'I'm sorry.'

Mr Green smiled. 'Never mind, dear boy. Look on the bright side. It's not everyone gets advance notice! Now, if you don't mind, I'd like you to leave. You can take the book. Consider it a gift.'

As they turned to go, Fish sent a last look at the Pomp.

'*Because,*' it said, answering the question he had thought of ages ago, the question about why only bad things made creatures, '*good things all come from, and go back to, the same source. And there is only one Avatar of Love.*'

And then they were outside again, clutching the book that Mr Green had given them and blinking in the brightness of the sun.

Sitting on a bench on the village green, Fish held the book quietly for a moment, hoping against hope that somewhere inside it would be the information that they needed to know. How to break a curse.

He opened it at random. A face swam out of the page at him, its inky eyes wide with gleeful amazement, its needle teeth bared in a horrible grimace. Fish gasped, the book fluttering in his hands as he nearly dropped it. The curse demon was in the story! Not in a real way, but somehow *behind* the words that curled across the page.

With a catch of his breath, Fish recovered just enough

to slam the book shut. He looked up to see Alice staring at him.

'Let me guess,' she said, 'whatever is in there, it's something we need to know?'

Fish nodded. Carefully he opened it again, flicking through to the same place as before. This time he saw only words. Chapter 32.

They bowed their heads and together they read the story of the curse of Imenga the Mighty.

32

THE MIGHTY CURSE

Right back at the very beginning, when most of the world was covered in forest, and bears walked in the woods of the Clouded Land, there lived a magician of immense power. He was called Imenga the Mighty, and no one dared to challenge him. He took everything that he wanted, and all those who displeased him were turned into ashes and spread on his vegetable garden. He had many sons and daughters, but they were given no land or name or even a house, for the magician wanted everything for himself and would give up nothing.

One day the eldest of his sons said to the other sons, 'Our father is a great magician who owns the world, and yet he keeps all the land and the power and gives nothing even to his own children. We will die as poor as the people in the village.'

And the second son said, 'It is true. Indeed, we are as poor as the bears in the woods. Poorer, for we know that we are owned and they do not.'

And the first son said, 'I shall ask him for land on which to build a house. For I have a wife and I need a home to put her in.'

So the first son went to his father and said to him, 'Dear father, you have all the wealth of the world at your feet. All I ask of you is some land on which to build a house for my beloved wife.'

But his father said, 'No. If I gave you land on which to build a house then I would not own the world. You must stay here in my palace and you will live in comfort and want for nothing, but I will own you and your wife too.'

Three months later his wife came to him and told him that she was pregnant with their child, and so the first son went back to his father and he asked again.

'Dear father, who owns the world, all I ask of you is some land on which to build a house for my beloved wife and for my child who is yet to be born. Give me this and I will work hard for you and keep the land rich and beautiful.'

Again his father said, 'No. You must stay here in my palace where you will want for nothing, but I will own you and your wife and your child who is yet to be born.'

So the first son went away. But his heart was filled with rage and so, as soon as the child was born, Imenga's son took a dagger which he concealed in his cloak and went to his father again and said, 'Dear father, who owns the world, all I ask of you is some land on which to build a home for my beloved wife and my child who is just born. Give me this and you will have my sworn loyalty forever.'

And again his father said, 'No. I will own the world and you and your wife and your child who is just born along with it.'

So the first son said, 'Then I will take what I want, as you

272

have taken everything that you wanted,' and struck his father down with a blow through the heart.

And as Imenga died he spoke these words:

'If I am to die and become ashes then all that I owned in life will die in terror and howling darkness and will become nought but ashes also.'

And then he died.

As everyone knows, a curse made with a dying breath is always kept, and this one was made of the dying breath of the greatest of all magicians. Even as Imenga spoke, the Mighty Curse was born from his mouth, and it was terrible. The body of Imenga was turned to ashes and a great pit was carved in the face of the Clouded Land and from it the Mighty Curse rose against the sky. It was so vast that it blotted out the sun, and as it spread its great wings of death a howling wind tore across the Earth, ripping up the forests and destroying all in its path. And yet it had only just begun.

And everyone ran before it in terror. But the first son's wife, whose name was Elonia, did not want her newborn child to die before it had even begun with its life. And so Elonia ran to the great pit where the Mighty Curse was rising in all its dreadfulness against the sky, preparing to turn the world and everyone in it to ashes, and she said:

'Only great love can stop great evil, and you are evil. And my love for my newborn child and for my husband who is its father is far greater than my love for my life. So I will give you my life as proof of this, and I will have command over you and you will stop.'

And the Mighty Curse replied to her, 'No curse can be

broken before it is complete, unless at the behest of the Greatest Love of all Great Loves. But to love something more than you love your life is great enough to stop me for a time. Give me your life as proof, and I will sleep and the world will be safe until I am awoken again.'

So Elonia threw herself into the pit and the Mighty Curse sank back down into the depths and slept.

And so, because he had freed the world from a tyrant, the first son got land on which to build a home for his child who had just been born. But because he had committed murder he lost his beloved wife. And every day for the rest of his life he went to the pit where Elonia had given her life for him and for her newborn child and cried. And he cried so greatly that his tears filled the pit and the deepest of all waters covered the Mighty Curse where it lay.

But nothing would bring Elonia back.

33

TRUMPS

'I don't know where *that* gets us,' said Alice, laying the book between them on the wooden slats of the bench. 'I mean, all it says is that curses can't be broken, they can only be put off, and *that's* no help.'

She frowned. 'Do you think it's all true? That this really happened all those years ago and the Mighty Curse is sleeping deep in the ground, waiting to be woken up? I suppose the thing that's sleeping is the Mighty Curse's demon, like your curse's demon only . . . well . . . *bigger?*'

Fish tilted his head and looked up at the sky, only half listening as Alice spoke. A train of thought was forming in his mind and he wanted to follow it.

He knew that he was next on the demon's list. He knew that it was having trouble killing him – after all, it had had a fair few cracks at it and yet he was still here. He knew that it wouldn't move on and kill Susan until it had dealt with him. So what was it up to now?

'I s'pect,' murmured Alice, 'that *your* beastly demon is off plotting something really big. I mean, it's not gonna just keep on with the falling junk and car accidents, is it? It'll want something you *can't escape* . . .'

Fish found himself thinking about Imenga, who owned the world and would rather destroy it all than give away even a tiny part.

'. . . I mean, something *nuclear*. Even if it means taking out other people . . .'

But, thought Fish, surely it would be crazy to wipe out everything just to get one insignificant little person. Bonkers.

'Because let's face it, the thing must be barking by now. Mad as a hatter. You've cheated it at every turn . . .'

Only, went on Fish's head, to the demon, killing Fish Jones isn't insignificant. To the demon, killing Fish Jones is everything.

'. . . so all it can do is play its trump card. And from where I'm sitting, that looks like . . .'

Fish swallowed hard, because if his thoughts followed their natural course back to the story they had just been reading, there was only one conclusion.

'. . . the Mighty Curse.'

There was a moment of complete stillness. Fish and Alice locked gazes. All around them the world paused and even the birds stopped singing for one eerie moment. And then it all went on as before.

'Oh bum,' said Alice quietly. '*Your* demon's going to wake *its* demon up!'

As one, they scrambled off the seat and began to

move. By the time they reached the edge of the village, they were running.

�֎

'I would have thought,' snapped Tun, gazing down at Grimshaw with his piercing eyes switched full on and his arms folded, 'that you would be searching Real Space for the Mighty Curse, not playing in the books, as usual.'

'Like I care what *you* think,' muttered Grimshaw dizzily. He was sitting on the ground outside the house trying to get his breath back. Having chewed him up, the story had spat him out on the library floor. After the whirling cacophony of the Mighty Curse Grimshaw's head was spinning, but he had had the presence of mind to reset his chronometer before the other books worked out that he was free. He was glad to be outside again, taking in deep breaths of old socks and waiting for his brain to calm down.

Tun went on glaring. 'Really, I thought you had more backbone!'

Grimshaw glared back. It was clear that Tun didn't yet know what Grimshaw had found out. But the Acts and Facts operated like a grapevine. Any significant deed done or word spoken soaked through the dead air like ink through blotting paper, alerting demons everywhere. Although there was always a delay, any moment now Limbo would know exactly what Grimshaw had been up to.

Because he had been inside the story, Grimshaw had

seen the place where the Avatar of the Mighty Curse had risen like a dark cloud against the sky. He knew where it had fallen to sleep and where the waters had closed over its head. All he had to do was get there fast, before anyone worked out where he was going. Quickly, he fiddled with his chronometer.

'Off now, are you?' said Tun. 'About time. But then it is a big task for such a minor demon and I suppose a little cowardice can be forgiven.'

'Thanks,' sneered Grimshaw. The dials were all aligned correctly.

Tun turned to survey the Limbo landscape, his eyes raking over its grey greyness. He waved an arm expansively. 'Remember, small one,' he boomed, 'all this will be gone if you succeed.'

Grimshaw's finger paused over the send button. Was that a touch of fear in Tun's voice?

'You're chickening out, aren't you?' he said scornfully.

Tun ignored him. 'But can such a miserable creature as you find the strength and determination to wake the most fearsome curse demon in history from its sleep? Hmm?'

'You bet,' snapped Grimshaw, and hit send.

Tun spun around, his black cloak sending ripples of darkness into the grey light. He gaped. And then the grapevine reached him.

Limbo was normally silent anyway, but for one eerie moment even the silence was silent.

'Satan's rump!' murmured Tun as he gazed at the space where Grimshaw had been. 'He knows where it is!'

✣

In the room with the sunlight on the walls and the smell of antiseptic, Susan opened her eyes. She had been asleep and dreaming of the old days, before she had disturbed the remains of Lampwick the Robber. She woke suddenly, feeling as if someone had called her name.

For a second everything was still. It was an eerie stillness and it seemed to Susan that even the birds outside her window fell quiet. And then everything was normal again.

She lay for a while, thinking about it. She was not a superstitious person, but there were things in her life that took more explanation than logic could provide. Fish was one of them. He had always been different, and although Susan loved him with all her heart, there were times that she didn't like to think about when she found him a little frightening. So, even while she told herself that the moment of eerie stillness was merely a lull in the birdsong and the sounds of the ward that coincided with a gap in the traffic, the part of her that knew better than to trust mere logic was going into overdrive. She thought that maybe, when . . . *if* . . . she got to Crow's Cottage, she should have a long talk with Fish and find out the truth. Even if it terrified her, it was time she knew about her own son. She was ashamed that she hadn't had the courage to do it before.

She drew in a slow breath and tried sitting up. It hurt in places she didn't know she had, but it didn't kill her.

'Oh my rear,' she groaned quietly, and reached for her clothes.

'Mrs Jones,' said the doctor, appearing in the doorway with a disapproving frown, 'you have a broken rib and leg, extensive bruising and some bad lacerations. I really wouldn't recommend—'

'Question,' said Susan patiently, 'if I walk out of here now, am I going to drop dead?'

The doctor looked bewildered. 'Well . . . no.'

'There you are, then!' She smiled. 'You see, there is somewhere else I have to be, and provided I can get there alive, then that is where I'm going.'

He opened his mouth and then shut it again. He knew determination when he saw it. He cleared his throat.

'Well, Mrs Jones, you'll need antibiotics and some painkillers. I'll make you up a prescription now, if you'll give me a moment.'

'You've got as long as it takes me to get dressed and ring for a taxi,' she said, and gave him a smile that made his day.

❀

Grimshaw sat for a moment on the edge of the deep lake called Menga's Tarn, peering at the water that dazzled his eyes with its reflected glare.

He knew he was safe now. Even though everyone in Limbo would know what he was up to, nobody could stop him. Lampwick couldn't travel to Real Space and neither could the Sisters or the Horsemen. The only ones who could were those few curse demons who had an active list and they were probably already in Real Space and busy. They wouldn't catch up with the Acts and Facts until they got back to Limbo, by which time it would be too late.

Picking up a stone, he tossed it into Menga's Tarn, wondering how deep it was, how far down the Avatar of the Mighty Curse was sleeping. The ripples spread out, disturbing the glassy surface of the water. Below them lay the answer to the problem of Fish Jones. The only thing Grimshaw hadn't figured out yet was what to do when he found the Mighty Curse. He would have to wake it up somehow, start the demon once again on its task of world destruction.

Still, time for that later.

He set the dials for the bottom of the tarn and hit send.

❆

Fish and Alice ran on in silence, Alice with Mr Green's book clutched in her hand. It didn't take much brain to work out where they had to go. The book was about local legends. This legend included a Mighty Curse, a sorcerer called Imenga and a deep lake. It had to be Menga's Tarn, the deep, steep-sided pool where they had spent yesterday afternoon.

It felt like they had been going for ages when at last they spotted its dark waters glinting in the sunlight away to the left of the road. They changed direction, diving off across the fields. Leaping through the long grass they hurried on, sweat cooling on their spines and necks, stalks tickling their legs and grass seeds dusting their arms. Somewhere along the way, Fish's foot had begun to hurt again and he was limping, but it didn't slow him down.

And so they reached the edge of Menga's Tarn, where the banks fell down to a stretch of water that looked like wet silver and smelt like hot tin or the air just before lightning strikes.

'There's a way down,' said Alice, pointing to a cut in the steep sides.

She led the way through the trees and shrubs, stumbling down the earthy slope to a stone ledge just above the water. There was barely room for the two of them and side by side they stood and looked out over the surface of the tarn. This close the water looked like glass. Beneath it was midnight.

Alice shivered. 'It's deep,' she said nervously. 'Deep and dark, but mostly deep. What are you going to do? Find the Mighty Curse's demon? Will you be able to guard it? Make sure your demon doesn't get to it! We'll camp out here if we have to. But be careful! Don't get too close – you don't want to do its job for it.'

Fish took off his shoes and Jed's jacket and gave them to Alice.

'Well,' she said with a rueful smile, 'they don't call you Fish for nothing.'

Fish leaned over and kissed her cheek. Then he breathed deeply and dived in.

'I'll wait for you,' she called, as the waters closed behind him.

34

MENGA'S TARN

The water should have been cold, but it wasn't. Fish swam deeper and deeper, through water that felt like blood-warm silk, but he couldn't see the bottom of Menga's Tarn. Above him, the light began to recede and a blue as dark as the shadows of night enclosed him. If anything, the deeper he went, the warmer it got.

He paused, floating upright, suspended in this strangely silent world of green-blue light and inky shadows. Turning his head this way and that, he tried to see into the dimness around him. There was no break in the stony walls and still no sight of the bottom. So he jack-knifed and pushed on down, swimming into the dark. The sides of the tarn were drawing in, narrowing down to a funnel at its heart, so he headed for that. Because of his natural ease underwater, Fish had had a lot of practice at holding his breath, but by now even *his* lungs were feeling the effort.

Nearing the bottom, he became aware of movement below him, as if part of the darkness that gathered at the base of the tarn was alive. There was something there, something that had purpose. His heart turned over with fear as he realised what it was. The demon of Lampwick the Robber's curse had already arrived.

�֍

Grimshaw was digging, scrabbling around in the mud as he tried to find a way through to whatever was beneath. Seeing him, Fish didn't pause to think, because what he needed to do was too frightening to think about. He had to stop the creature now. At once, with a flick of his legs, he propelled himself down, right on top of the demon. Reaching out, he grabbed it.

Feeling the boy's touch, Grimshaw froze with shock. In his entire existence he had never had contact with human flesh before, not even the slightest brush of a finger. And now here were two very human arms, wrapped around him, trying to pull him away! He went rigid, his eyes wide with a mixture of fear and astonishment. Unknown sensations battered at his brain, and for a moment he was nearly overwhelmed by the feel of delicate bones clad in warm, wet skin, full of blood that pounded as it pushed energy into every corner. How could something so small hold so much life! The boy's muscles flexed as he turned his face to the light above them and begin to swim.

Fish hung on to the demon, pulling him back towards the surface. He swam as fast as he could, trying to ignore the way the creature felt – like an armful of dense, slithery mist. And then Grimshaw snapped into action, struggling and squirming in the boy's grip. Fish hung on desperately, trying to gain height, to get the demon up into the air where he could trap it, stop it from doing what it wanted to do. By now his lungs were on fire and flashes of light sparked inside his eyes like mini-fireworks. Water swirled, filling his head with a bubbling roar.

Twisting, Grimshaw slashed with his paws and felt skin under his claw tips. Fish thrashed wildly and then fell suddenly still. Grimshaw was free! Paddling hard, he headed back to the bottom of the tarn.

Fish was in trouble. Pain like cold fire burned on his arms and chest where the demon's claws had raked him.

I can't swim! He thought. I can't breathe!

Blood roared in his ears and the flashes in his eyes were dazzling. The precious oxygen in his lungs was finally running out. He was going to die here, he knew it, drowned in Menga's Tarn while Alice waited above, unable to help.

Alice. His mother. Jed. He had to stop the demon!

Jerkily, he willed his arms into life and thrust his body down, looking for the demon again. This was his last chance, he must catch it now! He had seconds left before he could hold on no longer. Already, darkness was creeping over the edge of his vision and he felt strangely cold and numb.

But the creature had gone and silt had oozed back into place where it had been digging. Fish dived at the spot, pushing in hands first and forcing his body after them. Suddenly, everything gave way and he was sliding through the mud until he shot out the other side, like a bar of soap through wet hands. He fell, rolling into a ball as he went and landing with a thud on the rock below.

The shock made him gasp. Fortunately, there was something to gasp in other than water. He dragged the air into his lungs in great ragged breaths. Silver suns exploded in front of his eyes and the roaring in his ears became thunder. Water splattered on his head, washing some of the mud from his face and ears. After a few moments he recovered a little, the spinning in his head calmed and the silver suns faded.

Gingerly, Fish sat up and looked around. The air was warm and felt like a steamy bathroom. Water trickled somewhere. A dull reddish glow, coming from a point down and to his left, gave him enough light to see that he was in a narrow split in the rock, quite tall but barely wider at the bottom than he was. He had been lucky not to have cracked his skull on the sides as he fell. Peering up the funnel of rock, Fish wondered why the contents of the tarn weren't falling on his head. But although water ran down the walls and dripped in places on to the ground, either the silt plug was very efficient or some other force kept the tarn at bay. The other thing he saw was that the demon had gone.

Grimshaw was in a great cave, a layer below the narrow crack where Fish gasped for breath. He was perched on the edge of a shelf of rock, peering into the depths of the vast fissure that lay beneath Menga's Tarn. Far, far below him, something glowed. It was a glow that pulsed slowly, but steadily. He had found the Mighty Curse.

He glanced behind him, but there was no sign of the boy just yet. He wasn't drowned, Grimshaw knew that, and soon he would be here to try and stop what was about to happen. Which meant that if he was going to do it, Grimshaw had better hurry up. And he *was* going to do it, because killing Fish Jones and defeating Destiny was everything he had worked for, everything he wanted.

Now he had found the Mighty Curse, he wasn't sure how to wake it. He wondered about using Imenga's own words, the words that had created it, but that didn't seem right. After all, Grimshaw wasn't about to die and he certainly didn't own the world! So instead he leaned over the pit and prepared to shout out the thing that had brought him here, all this way to the edge of the abyss. But before he could speak, he heard movement behind him. It was coming from the tunnel that led to the cave above and it had to be the boy.

The gap was so narrow that Fish had to lie on his tummy and half crawl, half slither down it, grazing his arms and elbows and scraping his toes as he went. The bathroom mugginess made the air feel as thick as soup in his lungs. Sweat prickled in his hair and down his back, and his injured foot had begun to bleed again, but carried by his own momentum, he scrabbled out on to a broad expanse of rock. Yards away he could see the edge of the pit and the shape of the demon crouching over it, outlined against the red glow that came from the depths.

Grimshaw turned to look at the boy, flattening his ears against his head and snarling, 'Don't think you can stop me now, Fish Jones!'

Fish scrambled to his feet. The softness of the demon's voice made the creature seem less like an evil persecutor and more like a being.

'Please,' he said, putting everything he could into his voice, 'please don't do it. It can't be worth this, just to kill me!'

He looked into Grimshaw's corner-to-corner black eyes, willing him to understand. Grimshaw snarled again, looking more cat-like than ever. Then he reared up as tall as he could stand.

'Doing this,' he said, almost dreamily, 'will make me GREAT!' He spat out the last word, flinging his arms wide. 'It will make me *terrifying*!'

As he spoke, Grimshaw looked into the boy's eyes and saw fear there. Fish was shaking like a leaf, his whole body one great heartbeat about to be stopped forever. Grimshaw could see how much courage it took for the boy to face him like this, but he dismissed the thought because he didn't want it right now.

'You *are* terrifying!' cried Fish.

It was too late and Grimshaw had turned away. He leaned forward and called into the depths.

'O Mighty Demon of a Mighty Curse, wake up and kill Fish Jones, even if it takes the world to do it!'

For a moment there was silence, absolute silence, and then, far in the depths, something stirred. The rocks shook and a deep rumbling began, like thunder that wouldn't stop but kept growing. The red glow began to pulse faster, speeding up until it was one long fiery glare. Light climbed the walls of the cavern, rising up from the pit like vines of blood. But in the pit, as deep as the eye could see, was not light. The red glow had a heart of darkness and it was moving steadily up. The Mighty Curse had woken up and now it was coming to finish its task and turn the world to ashes.

✤

Up on the banks of Menga's Tarn, Alice looked at the sky. Wedges of dark cloud had begun to form on the horizon. A wind was gathering too. It lifted her hair and made the trees toss restlessly. It was a warm wind and brought with it a smell of bonfires. She shivered, feeling lost and afraid.

Sounding strangely lonely, her phone rang. She answered it.

'H'lo?'

'Alice?' Her mother's voice seemed a long way away. Further than just half the country.

Alice shivered again. 'Mum?'

'Where are you?'

'Um, I'm at Menga's Tarn,' said Alice. 'Half way

between Crow's Cottage and a place called Knockton.' She couldn't think of any lies that would do. Besides, it was way past time to lie. There was a long silence before anyone spoke again.

'Can you come home now? It's . . .' Her mother paused, struggling to find words for the strange feeling that crackled in the air like thunder. 'The clouds are turning dark and I think you should come home.'

Alice wished she could. 'Sorry, Mum, I'd really like to, but I've got to wait for Fish. I can't let him down, see.'

Her mother was silent for a moment. 'I'll come and find you,' she said. 'Shouldn't be too difficult.'

Alice drew in a wobbly breath. 'But what about your work?'

'To hell with work,' said her mother, and hung up.

Alice listened to the empty phone for a moment and then put it back in her pocket, feeling a little braver.

Before she could turn her attention back to the tarn, there was an ear-spitting crack, like a vast whiplash snapping across the countryside. Beneath her feet the ground shook and she screamed as rocks, trees and bushes trembled and slid, ripping away from the steep sides of the tarn and crashing heavily into the water. Steam rose into the air in serpent coils and Alice fell to the ground, wrapping her arms around her head. Soil and stones rattled around her, and a huge groaning filled the air, rolling out over the meadows and woods. Now the tarn was boiling like a cauldron, filled with wreckage from the land. Above, the sky was full of birds that wheeled and dived in great black swathes against the dark clouds. Shivering with terror, Alice dug her nails into the mossy ground as the land shook, falling apart around her. But her heart was filled with dread because she knew what had happened. Fish had failed, and beneath the earth something terrible was rising.

Even though the Mighty Curse was not yet free, the world knew what was coming and trembled. Angry clouds gathered fast and the seas that lapped Britain's shores grew restless. A hot wind blew, and with it spread a feeling of alarm, a premonition of what lay ahead. Everywhere, people stopped what they were doing and ran to watch the skies, calling to their loved ones.

❦

Some miles away from Menga's Tarn, but only a few, Susan stared out of a taxi window at the clouds that coiled and twisted like serpents. Suddenly, as if every feathered creature for miles had all risen at once, birds filled the sky. They swirled in great dark swathes against the clouds, dipping and circling restlessly.

'Oh Fish!' Susan murmured.

'Don't worry,' said the cabby, the one who had delivered Fish and Alice to Crow's Cottage just two days ago. 'I'll get you there.'

He drove on into a landscape that would be comfortable in anyone's nightmares. The end of the world was on its way.

35

THE DARKEST OF NIGHTS

The ground was shaking and chunks of rock broke loose from the ceiling and walls of the cave, crashing down around Fish and Grimshaw. The angry light that swarmed around the Mighty Curse was so fierce that it filled the pit, seeping out into the cavern above, far ahead of its source. Fish was still on the ledge, but further in, closer to the pit. All he could see was the black edge where the rock ended and the depths began, and the outline of Grimshaw crouched low and peering down. Although Fish wasn't near enough to look into the depths and see the Mighty Curse as it tore upwards, he knew in his heart that the beast was as vast as a mountain, with wings like storm clouds, eyes that spat lightning and breath like sheets of flame. He also realised that it must be coming from so far down that it took time for it to break free of the pit.

Quickly, Grimshaw spun the dials on his chronometer and zapped a little further away, reappearing behind Fish, just where the tunnel opened into the cave. He wanted to watch until the end of Fish's life, to see his own triumph as it happened.

Fish stood, staring at the light as it grew, tears pricking his eyes as he realised what he had to do. He knew that he loved his life and didn't want to lose it. But he also knew that he loved his mother and Alice and Jed *more* than he loved his life. And if that was true then maybe it wasn't too late after all. He could send the Mighty Curse back to sleep again, just as Elonia had done! She had offered up her life – couldn't he do the same?

The knowledge that to save the ones he loved most in the world would mean giving up his own life tore into his heart like a red-hot knife. He trembled so much he could barely move, but he didn't stop to think about it. If he hesitated for just a second, his courage might fail and then they would all die. Everyone. And he would still die anyway, so what was the good of that?

His breath coming in ragged gasps, Fish began the long crawl towards the edge of the pit. He had to go on his hands and knees because he couldn't stand. There were no pauses between the earth tremors now, and the ceaseless shuddering grew steadily more violent, throwing him face down to the ground again and again. But still he crawled on, going as fast as he could, grazing his hands and knees and leaving a trail of blood from his wounds. The red light burned his skin as it grew stronger and he drew closer. He could feel the demon's eyes on him, watching from behind. He only hoped that he would be able to fight it off if it worked out what he was doing and tried to stop him.

Grimshaw was watching all right, hanging on as the world ripped itself apart around them. A grin of satisfaction curled across his face.

The grin vanished. Something terrible dawned on him. This might be the boy's destiny! To save the world from Grimshaw! He'd been trying so hard to beat Destiny that he'd brought about the very event that allowed it to be fulfilled. The realisation shook Grimshaw to the core. His heart went cold and hard with anger. If the boy sacrificed himself to save the world, then he'd be dead and Grimshaw would have killed his Sufferer, but it wouldn't be the same. Grimshaw wouldn't have beaten Destiny; he'd have just given it a helping hand. He would be cheated of his greatness.

Grimshaw snarled, his clawed paws clenching into fists and his corner-to-corner black eyes filling with even darker darkness. He had to stop the boy somehow.

An ear-shattering, grinding rumble, greater than the constant shaking of the earth, threw him to the ground. When things had subsided enough to let him scramble unsteadily upright again, he saw at once what had happened. The tremor had split the rocky floor in two and a rift had opened up between Fish Jones and the pit he was struggling to reach. A rift too wide and too deep for the boy to cross. He would not reach the Mighty Curse before it broke free and set about its task of devastation.

Now, Grimshaw screeched his victory aloud. He had done it after all! He might be only a small third-rate demon, but Grimshaw had done what no demon had done before. He had beaten Destiny!

The boy turned his head, and Grimshaw saw in his eyes that he knew he had failed. But the look Fish Jones gave the demon made him stop jumping for joy. It was a look full pain and desperation that sliced right through Grimshaw and set a storm of doubt raging in his head. What was the boy going to do? Surely there was no way he could stop this now? Instinctively, Grimshaw closed his outer eyes and opened the inner one, the one that could look a little way into the future, to make sure that the doom he had set in motion was really going to happen.

Fish looked around wildly, trying to see a way past the crevice that lay in his path, but there was no way across, nothing he could do to reach the Mighty Curse before it broke free. Light poured out from the pit in a blaze, and as he gazed in horror something began to appear. A dark shape, its horned head rising into the cavern, its vast wings furled behind it.

He began to lurch towards it with no plan and no hope, only desperation to spur him on.

❦

Standing on the top of a skyscraper in London, Limbo, Tun watched the city change as everything Blinked.

It was not any of the usual three-hourly update points. This was different. Things were happening so fast that Limbo was synchronising with Real Space at the rate of a Blink every five minutes. Back in Real Space, worried people were trying to get home, and cars in Grey Space flicked into and out of being, moving in jumps as the traffic built up. Some of them had been deserted as their owners gave up and went on foot, leaving their vehicles in the middle of the road, or even parked on the pavements. Aeroplanes fell out of the sky with every Blink, strewing their wreckage over the city streets as they plummeted to the ground, the metal carcasses vanishing with the next update as Limbo recreated itself again and again.

With every Blink, the detail got less until the buildings were just concrete shapes. The London Eye was a skeleton of fused metal etched against the sky, and the Houses of Parliament had become a vast slab covered in random scribbles of stone. Big Ben was a faceless column staring out over a meaningless jumble of concrete. Even the air no longer smelt of old socks, but of distant bonfires instead.

Tun hunched his skeletal shoulders, tucking his clawed hands into the folds of his dark robe. Deep inside his cowl, the terrible eyes glowed with a feverish excitement that was half-fear, half-exultation.

Far away to the east, the Sisters paused. Lady dropped the Wanderer she was holding. Trembling, Flute took Rage's hand.

'What have I done?' she cried. 'I should have left well alone. I didn't think he would do it! I was so sure he would choose to let the humans live!'

In the crypt, Lampwick the Robber yawned. There was nothing for Limbo to update in his stone cell, and he couldn't smell the strangeness in the air. He knew via the Acts and Facts what Grimshaw was planning to do, but nothing more than that. He had worked out a few choice phrases to offer when the Avatar came back with yet another miserable failure.

For something to do, he sat up straight, cleared his throat and began to rehearse them out loud.

❋

His inner, future-seeing eye wide open, Grimshaw cried out with horror. It was so terrible that his heart stopped with shock. It was a good thing he didn't need it.

It was really going to happen! Laid out before his future vision was the end of the world. The empty Tarn filled with tumbled rock, the land stripped bare with its green coat of trees withered and burnt, the sky a turmoil of shrieking birds, storm clouds and lightning. He saw the Mighty Curse stretch its wings, sending hurricanes to rip up the meadows and the woods and the houses. Thunderbolts arced from its eyes and a single roar shook cities to the ground and turned the air to an inferno. He saw Fish and Susan Jones and all the noble humans devoured in a moment of white-hot flame as humankind was swept away, its flaws and goodness become nothing but whirling ash in the firestorm.

Beyond that he saw the sea, its restless waves boiled to vapour, and the mountains torn down from their heights, the clouds gone and the deep blue sky turned to fire. He saw the underground cathedral as it crumbled, its columns and shining rocks shaken into dust. And he saw the jungle, its hidden cities torn apart, the monkeys burned to cinders. The tree that he had rested in flaming against the dark sky, and the leopards . . . the beautiful leopards . . . cowering as fire found them and stripped their lovely coats from their bones. And last he saw the monster in the lake, no longer vast and dark and powerful, no longer even bone and flesh, just so much ash in a world of ashes.

Watching the destruction, the pain of loss filled Grimshaw up so completely he felt something break inside him. All that incredible beauty, all that fierce and savage grace swept away in a torrent of fire. Beside that pain, the disgrace of the lost chronometer, of having Survivors, all that was nothing. Not worth a tear, let alone the world. And what was the admiration of other demons when he could have the delight of visiting Real Space? Even the memories, the knowledge that the world was there, was worth an eternity of respect from the likes of Hanhut and Tun.

Tears pouring down his face, Grimshaw stared in horror as he saw what the Mighty Curse would do to the Earth he had unknowingly come to love. He saw it as it would soon become. The sky filled with boiling clouds, the sun shrouded from a world without even the smallest, tiniest living thing to stir in its grey dust. He saw the darkest of nights and he was its creator.

Grimshaw opened his eyes again.

'NO!' he howled. And began to run towards the Mighty Curse.

�֍

Alice screamed as the earth shook, the banks of the tarn splitting apart as the force of the Mighty Curse rose beneath them. Stones and earth and the shreds of trees fell like hail around her. There was one last ear-shattering roar and then, suddenly, she felt the shaking grow less violent. She lay for a moment, gasping for breath, her heart hammering and her face smeared with dirt and tears.

But the cracking of wood and the tumble of soil was definitely slowing, and when she was brave enough to peer up at the sky she could see the clouds already growing lighter.

Pulling herself to her feet, Alice didn't try to stop the tears running down her face. She was trembling with fear and misery as she gazed around. The wreckage of trees, shrubs and fallen earth clogged the tarn. Most of the water had boiled away and its banks were no longer steep. Above, the wheeling flocks had broken up and the heavy clouds were dissolving as quickly as they had come. Even as she turned her head to look, the sun appeared, bathing the ruined heath in warmth and light. It made her cry all the harder.

Fish was dead. He had to be. The Mighty Curse had been woken and now it was asleep again, and it would take a life to bring that about. Fish's life.

Alice drew in a shuddering breath and wiped her face on her sleeve. Although she knew he must be gone, somehow she couldn't give up just yet. Going to the very edge of Menga's Tarn, she threw back her head and called his name, putting every ounce of breath she had into the shout.

'FISH! *FISH!*'

Her voice echoed on the air, and it seemed to her that everything was suddenly still and silent, listening. Overhead, the sun grew stronger and the sky began to turn that particular blue that is the colour of infinity.

'Fish?' said Alice again, her attention caught by a small sound. 'FISH!'

She began the scramble down through the rubble of split trunks and torn branches, catching her clothes and hair on their twisted fingers as she went.

36

AFTERMATH

All around Fish was absolute darkness. Trembling, he lay in the suffocating heat and dust, unable to see and hearing nothing but the uneven thud of his heart.

The last thing he had seen before the Mighty Curse had stopped its destruction and had sunk back into the pit, dragging its fire and death with it, had been the demon, bounding towards him. He had felt the softness of light paws on his head as it used him for a springboard to leap the fissure, soaring through the air as gracefully as a cat and landing on the edge of the pit. The creature's soft voice echoed around the cavern, cutting through the sounds of destruction, as it cried out, 'Take me, and let the world live!'

It took one more bound, its twisted shape silhouetted for a second against the fiery light, and then it was gone, plunging into the heart of the abyss.

The demon had done what Fish couldn't do – it had sacrificed itself to the Mighty Curse as Elonia had done all those years ago. It had sent the Mighty Curse back to sleep again.

All Fish remembered after that was a sound like immense stones grinding deep in the heart of the Earth and a roaring wind that howled through the cavern as the Mighty Curse retreated. The gale had nearly taken him too, but he had clung on to anything he could, grazing his fingers to the bone. And then it was over and silence and darkness had swarmed back into the cavern, encasing Fish in a rocky tomb.

He gasped, trying to calm the panic rising inside him. The Mighty Curse was gone and the world was safe, for now at least, but Fish wasn't. He could still die here in the caves under Menga's Tarn. Exhausted and shaken to his core, Fish was too terrified to move in the darkness in case he fell into the torn rock around him. Suddenly, he raised his head and listened, straining every nerve to hear. There had definitely been something. A shout, maybe. It was faint, very faint and muffled, filtering down from the outside world, but it was a shout all right. It was Alice!

Her voice gave him the strength he needed to move and, slowly, Fish began to inch towards the sound, or at least to where he thought the sound was coming from. He hadn't inched far when he felt a soft touch on his skin, cooling his scraped and battered limbs. Air. Now he began to move in earnest, ignoring the pain that gripped every muscle. Eagerly, he started the long crawl up the slope to freedom.

❧

In Limbo, the news was already spreading.

Tun raised his hot-coal eyes to the grey sky. There was madness in them. He breathed in the air, smelling once again the stale aroma of old socks. Below him, the city of London lay spread out like a grey plaster model that nobody could be bothered to paint. The details (such as they were in Limbo) had come back, and the fiddly bits on the Houses of Parliament were all in their proper places. Parts of the last plane remained scattered across the streets, and the traffic was still oddly placed, but otherwise everything looked as dull and useless as normal.

'This is it, then,' he murmured softly, although there was nobody there to hear. 'All that is left to me. Forever.' If anyone had been there they would have seen his night-black form tremble.

He stood for a while, thinking about Grimshaw, the Avatar who had done what no Avatar had ever done before and whose name would go down in the long halls of curse-demon history as the One Who Died.

'Death,' Tun shook his head. 'How can an Avatar die?!' He gave a deep-throated laugh full of crazy pain, then drew in a long, shuddering breath and pulled himself firmly together.

'Still, fantastic things do happen. Reminds me of the time I faced Ugrith Ombre, the most terrible of all the House . . .'

He fell silent and looked around at the emptiness. He frowned. After a long pause, he considered his options.

They were very few. Then, with a huge sigh, he pulled out his chronometer, aligned the carvings for the Lock-Out Club and pressed send.

Far above him and away to the east, so high in the sky that the land below was just a pattern, Lady grabbed Flute by the hands and spun her around in the air, both shrieking with joyful laughter. Rage watched them for a moment, her arms folded and a look of satisfaction on her face. The Sisters' job was to teach the Wanderers to die properly, and that was fine, but a curse demon? That was better than fine, that was a miracle! Right now, the Sisters of Gladness were very glad indeed.

Unlike Lampwick. In the shadowy depths of the crypt, he cleared his throat nervously. Being Grimshaw's Architect, Lampwick had been one of the first to get the news of his Avatar's death. He was still trying to get a grip on it.

'Dead!' he muttered, filling his voice with scorn. 'I'll show him dead!'

Nothing said anything by way of reply. The silence went on for a while.

'Hrmph.' Lampwick drew himself up and projected his voice. 'I Conjure Thee, Come!' Suddenly, for the first time ever in saying those words, he felt a little silly.

There was silence. Nothing came.

'Curses don't get broken just like that, you know,' he grumbled.

Again, nothing said anything by way of reply. The silence went on for a while longer.

'Ahem.' Lampwick looked around into the shadows, noticing for the first time how very shadowy they were. 'Grimshaw?'

He clambered off his coffin and lurched around the crypt. Then he lurched round again. Then he cocked an ear towards the doorway.

'Hello? Is . . . is anybody there? Grimshaw, is that you?' Lampwick's voice wavered.

There was no reply. Lampwick felt a coldness gather in his heart. The silence went on for a long time.

A very long time.

※

At the bottom of the dip, Alice saw a wide crack in the rocky earth and a hand. The hand groped towards the sound of her voice and she grabbed it, scrabbling in the mud to find more of him. She heaved and pulled Fish through the gap until he slid out, covered in mud and blood and popping from the gluey silt like a cork out of a bottle. Then she hauled him up the slope to a dry bank of earth and let him sit and gasp in the fresh air.

While Fish got his breath back, Alice tried to wipe some of the mud from his face with her sleeve. It wasn't a great success. As well as dirty, he was torn and ragged, and through the rags she could see five pale marks running across his chest and arm, like the trace of scars from a clawed paw. She shivered, knowing that he must have fought the demon hand to hand. It hadn't cut the skin, but it had left its mark just the same.

'I thought you were dead! How did you stop the Mighty Curse? I mean, you were the only one down there to stop it. Apart from the demon, that is . . .' She peered at him. 'Was it the demon? Why? Why would it do that? Why would it go to all those lengths to kill you and then give its life to stop what it had done?'

Fish shook his head.

'I get it – we'll never know!' Alice scanned his face for a long time, then settled next to him, pulling him over so that he could lean against her and rest. She smiled.

'We'll sit a while and then go back to the cottage. We can sort you out and you can rest. Then, by tonight, my mum'll be here, and she can get us home tomorrow.'

Fish glanced at her. There was a look on Alice's face that he hadn't seen before, or at least that he had seen shadows of and thought was the real thing, but now knew better. Alice was happy.

'Mum'll find us, she's good at stuff like that. She can find her way round anything. And she'll bring food and things with her too. She's good at planning.'

Fish was worn out and he ached to the bone, but the sun on his back was warm and the air was clear and sweet. When they finally got going he felt light-headed with relief and a sense of freedom. They walked slowly, Fish leaning on Alice. As they reached the crest of the hill, the moor was laid before them, bright in the sun. In the distance they could see Crow's Cottage and the long strip of road winding past it. On the road was a taxi. It slowed down as it drew closer to the house, and then it stopped.

'It's too early for it to be my mum,' said Alice. 'She'll still be on the way.'

The taxi stood for a long moment before the door opened and the driver got out. He pulled open the passenger door and helped someone climb down. Then he got back in, slammed the door and drove away. The person left standing on the road turned to study the cottage. Fish gasped. Then he began to move in a limping run, his weariness and pains forgotten. Alice let him go on. She stayed where she was, watching the new arrival organise her crutches and begin to hobble up the pathway. The limping figure of Fish made it to the foot of the hill and began to run in earnest, calling out so that Susan heard him, stopped at the cottage door and turned to wait.

Alice lingered until Fish reached his mother. Then she took in a deep breath of heather-scented air, felt the sun on her face once more and set off down the hill to join them.

37

THE BRIGHTEST OF DAYS

Grimshaw squinted into the light. He was flying. Or at least something was carrying him through the air. It was strange because a moment ago he had been falling into a pit of fire and darkness, feeling the skin burn away from his bones.

'Is that you, Flute? Or one of your sisters?'

'Not the Sisters,' answered a voice calmly.

The world spun for a moment and he landed on his paws on soft grass. He looked up to see what had been carrying him and stared into the eyes of one of the Pomp. He frowned, puzzled.

'I'm only an Avatar. I can't be dead like a human is dead, right?'

'Right.'

Grimshaw flicked his ears anxiously.

The Pomp sighed. 'Unless . . .'

'Yes, what is it?'

'Every half-life carries a seed. And sometimes, though rarely, that seed grows. And if it does, then the half-life gets to be a proper life. And if it is a real life, then it can have a real death.'

Grimshaw screwed up his forehead. 'Sorry? I don't think I understand. I'm only a very small curse.'

'No half-life is too small,' said the Pomp. Its light-in-light eyes watched him thoughtfully from its shining face.

'That can't be right. I mean . . .'

'But if you gave up your half-life and yet you are still here, then it must be right.'

Grimshaw thought about it for a moment. He couldn't deny that this was true and yet . . .

But he was still here. There was no denying it. He gave up the fight and looked around instead. The Pomp had dropped him on a mountainside where small flowers bobbed in a warm breeze. On his left, the mountain fell away in a steep cliff that plummeted down to a sea as blue as a sapphire. Beyond the sea and stretching to the far horizon he could see the green, gold and purple sweep of the land as it rose and fell in forests and heaths and heather-clad hills. The cliff was so high that between the land and the top of the mountain hung a single ribbon of white cloud.

'It's beautiful.' Grimshaw felt pride swell in his heart. 'Are the monkeys all right? And the leopards? And is the cathedral cavern still there? And what about the monster?' He paused for a second, then went on. 'And the people? All the noble humans? Like the boy and Susan Jones. Are they all right?'

'They are all just fine.'

With a sigh, Grimshaw went back to the view. Until it struck him that there was something wrong. Something was missing. He couldn't see a single town or city.

'If they are all right, where are they then?'

'They are where they are meant to be. The world is still going on, it's just doing it somewhere else. You are dead, remember.'

Grimshaw rubbed a paw over his ears. 'So . . . where am I?'

'Limbo,' replied the Pomp.

Grimshaw's ugly face wrinkled up in his effort to understand.

The Pomp took pity on him. 'Limbo is not just the place where the half-alive and half-dead live. It's also a gateway, see? Or we should say *gateways*, since there are two of them.' The Pomp laughed softly. 'We have to say, though, for a while there we weren't sure which one you would choose. Up or down.' She smiled at him and then went on, 'But the real thing you have to understand about Limbo is that what you see around you depends on how you look at it. And now you are seeing what is really there, not just what you think you see.'

Grimshaw gazed up at her. 'It might not be the Earth, but it's still *wonderful*! Do you see it like this all the time?'

'Oh yes. And the Sisters too. And probably the Horsemen, though we don't think anyone has ever asked them.'

Grimshaw flipped his ears thoughtfully, trying to work it all out.

'It's funny, really. If I hadn't wanted to be a great and terrifying demon, then I wouldn't have wanted so much to kill the boy. And if I hadn't wanted to kill the boy, I would never have woken up the Mighty Curse. But, if I hadn't tried to find the Curse in order to kill the world, in order to kill the boy too, then I wouldn't have *seen* the world and everything in it. And then I wouldn't have understood right at the final moment exactly how . . . how . . . *wonderful* it was and I wouldn't have saved it.' He thought for a moment longer. 'It does my head in, actually.'

'We can see why.'

'And you know what? The dumb thing is that I had what I was trying to get all along. To Fish Jones, I *was* terrifying!' Grimshaw sighed and shook his ears. 'But what I don't get is the boy. I thought that he had a destiny – more than one, in fact. And if so, then surely one would be saving the world from me trying to kill him! But he could *never* have got there in time. I'm glad he's not dead though. He . . .' Grimshaw fell silent.

'Yes?'

'He was the only one who ever took me seriously.' Grimshaw flipped his ears again. 'I thought I hated him, but you know I kind of liked him too.'

His eyes roamed over the landscape again, completely missing the darkness that lay deep beneath the surface of the blue sea. 'Gateways?' he asked a moment later, catching up with the Pomp's earlier explanation. Then he looked upwards. He gasped. The top of the mountain was not the top. The usual layer of misty cloud that lay over Limbo like a ceiling had gone and at last he could see what was there. The mountain went on rising into the brilliant sky, much higher and further than he had thought. His corner-to-corner black eyes went large.

'The way won't be easy,' said the Pomp. 'There are . . . mitigating circumstances for most of the things you did. After all, you were simply your Architect's tool for all those lives that were forfeit under the curse. It is not you who will be judged for that. But for one particular thing there is no excuse at all.'

'Steve Moore,' said Grimshaw, almost without thinking. 'The man in the truck. He was an Innocent Bystander.'

The Pomp smiled. 'You found out his name? That's a good start. But now you are growing a soul you will be expected to atone for his death.'

'How?'

'Oh, we don't know that, we're just a Pomp. I expect there will be a task for you to do, and don't think it will be easy. Still, you'll find out, all in good time.'

Grimshaw was busy staring up the slope towards the light. The light that now had nothing in between him and it at all. He swallowed.

'Can I . . . um . . . ?'

'If you can see the way, then you can go there.'

'Thank you.' Grimshaw shook his head. 'It's all

beyond me really, but it must be all right if you say so.' He began to struggle out of his backpack. 'And I don't understand about the boy and his destiny at all. I mean, if I saved the world, then what did he save?' He dumped the backpack on the rocks and laid his notebook and pencil tidily on top.

'You,' said the Pomp, and disappeared.

But Grimshaw didn't hear her. He had already turned his face to the brightest of days and set off on the long climb ahead.